The Shattered King

The Gareth and Gwen Medieval Mysteries

The Bard's Daughter (prequel)
The Good Knight
The Uninvited Guest
The Fourth Horseman
The Fallen Princess
The Unlikely Spy
The Lost Brother
The Renegade Merchant
The Unexpected Ally
The Worthy Soldier
The Favored Son
The Viking Prince
The Irish Bride
The Prince's Man
The Faithless Fool
The Honorable Traitor
The Admirable Physician
The Shattered King

The Welsh Guard Mysteries
Crouchback
Chevalier
Paladin
Herald
Bardd

A Gareth and Gwen Medieval Mystery

THE SHATTERED KING

by

SARAH WOODBURY

The Shattered King
Copyright © 2025 by Sarah Woodbury

This is a work of fiction.

www.sarahwoodbury.com

To my Gareth & Gwen

CAST OF CHARACTERS

Gwen – Prince Hywel's spy, Gareth's wife
Gareth – Prince Hywel's steward, Gwen's husband
Llelo – Gareth and Gwen's son, investigator
Dai – Gareth and Gwen's son, Dragon member
Meilyr – Bard, Gwen's father
Saran – Healer, Gwen's stepmother
Tangwen – Gareth and Gwen's daughter
Taran – Gareth and Gwen's son
Angharad – Gareth and Gwen's daughter

Owain Gwynedd – King of Gwynedd
Hywel – Prince of Gwynedd
Cadwaladr – King Owain's brother
Gruffydd – King of Deheubarth (deceased)
Gwenllian – Queen of Deheubarth, Owain's sister (deceased)
Anarawd – King of Deheubarth, Cadell's brother (deceased)
Cadell – King of Deheubarth (current)
Maredudd – Prince of Deheubarth, Cadell's half-brother
Rhys – Prince of Deheubarth, Cadell's half-brother

Huw – Cadell's steward
Iestyn ap Meurig – brother to Ifor Bach, the Lord of Senghenydd
Maurice Fitzgerald – Norman lord, cousin to Cadell, Maredudd, and Rhys
William de Carew – Norman lord, Maurice's brother, castellan of Pembroke Castle
Gilbert de Clare – Earl of Hertford
Roger de Clare – Gilbert's brother
Richard de Clare – Earl of Pembroke, Gilbert's nephew

Dragon members
Evan, Aron, Iago, Steffan, Cadoc, Gruffydd
Dai (see above)

How we arrived here ...

The Shattered King is the seventeenth *Gareth & Gwen Medieval Mystery*. By now, the series has covered eight years and includes a large cast, the specific details of which might not come instantly to mind. So here's a quick refresher!

A true historical event opens *The Good Knight*, the first book in the series: in 1143, Cadwaladr, the brother of Owain, the King of Gwynedd, hired a band of Danish mercenaries from Dublin to ambush and murder Anarawd, the King of Deheubarth, who was traveling to his wedding to Owain's daughter.

Yes, this really happened.

Once his treachery was uncovered, Cadwaladr fled to Dublin, where he hired more Danes to invade Gwynedd. The Danes just wanted to get paid, however, and they were ultimately bought off with gold and cattle. Owain allowed Cadwaladr back into his court, but stripped him of his lands.

Wales during this period was divided into multiple small kingdoms. In the north was Gwynedd, led by King Owain. In the south was Deheubarth, ruled in 1151 by King Cadell, Anarawd's younger brother. At times, Deheubarth allied itself with other Welsh kingdoms (including Gwynedd) against the Normans. This most notably occurred in 1136, after the Normans executed King Owain's sister, Gwenllian. At the time, she was married to Gruffydd (Anarawd and Cadell's father) and was the mother of Cadell's two much younger half-brothers, Maredudd and Rhys.

After the war, King Owain appropriated for Gwynedd a northern region of Deheubarth, known as Ceredigion, which he gave to his brother, Cadwaladr. In 1143, after Cadwaladr's treachery, he gave these lands instead to his son, Hywel. It was only after Anarawd's death that Cadell, Anarawd's younger brother, who had assumed the throne of Deheubarth, began claiming that Owain had stolen the lands rather than acquired them through an agreement with Gruffydd, as recompense for helping him defeat the Normans.

Since then, although Gwynedd and Deheubarth have at times been allies, the resentment at the loss of Ceredigion runs deep amongst the southerners. In 1150, Cadell, who is not related to Owain by blood, invades Ceredigion, hoping to take back some of the lands lost to Gwynedd.

By January of 1151, he has failed to recapture even a portion of his lost territory. That doesn't mean he isn't continuing to try …

1

"We need to go." Gareth burst into the common room of the guest house. "The men of Deheubarth have reached the northern crossroads!"

"Is this from Dai?" Gwen looked up from where she'd been nursing little Angharad, their daughter born five months ago in August. "Has he returned?"

"He's readying our wagons even now."

"The crossroads are hardly more than a mile from here." Meilyr had been teaching Tangwen to play his flute, and now he gently set his granddaughter on her feet and stood up. "I thought Cadell's men were retreating south?"

"Some of them have apparently decided the best way to get

south is to go east first."

Yesterday, Gareth and Dai had arrived at the commandery, cold and hungry but relieved to report that Cadell's men had abandoned their siege of Hywel's castle at Aberystwyth. While they'd watched the bulk of the army depart by the quickest avenue south, Gareth had been worried about the direction of a few of the stragglers. For that reason, he had sent Dai north to the crossroads at first light to make sure the road remained clear.

From the crossroads, Cadell's forces could effectively block all routes north, west, and east out of Ysbyty Cynfyn.

"How long do we have?" Gwen asked.

"I don't know exactly. Dai says Cadell's men took the watchtower at Goginan and sacked the church. I can't imagine it will be long before they look for riches, or at least provisions, at Ysbyty Cynfyn."

"And here we thought things were going so well." Meilyr seemed entirely calm about something that was setting Gwen's own heart racing.

"Do you really think they will harm us here?" His white hair mussed, Commander Reginald came through the doorway, wringing his hands. Even before the siege, it had become a habit for him.

Reginald had survived the inquiry that had followed the events of last spring. The hospital and commandery at Ysbyty Cynfyn had not closed, but its commander appeared to Gwen to be a broken man. The subsequent months had not improved his ability to handle a crisis. He was no longer addicted to poppy juice, but he was still suffering from its after-effects—and might for the rest of his life.

For the whole of this past summer and autumn, Prince Hywel had been in the ascendancy in the unwanted war against Cadell, King of Deheubarth. In every skirmish, Hywel's forces had emerged victorious. By November, they had been breathing more easily, sure their prince had Ceredigion well in hand. They'd been right about that—up until Cadell had moved an entire army north in a matter of three days over the Christmas feast in order to lay siege to Hywel's castle at Aberystwyth.

Throughout these same months, Gareth and Dai had assumed the role of spy for Hywel, together and separately—though mostly together. It had been they, in fact, who had ridden into the castle on Christmas Eve to warn Hywel that Cadell's men were coming. Then, to Gwen's never-ending gratitude, Hywel had sent them out again, to the commandery, to warn her and the monks of what they faced.

Meanwhile, rather than fleeing or burning his own castle to the ground to prevent it from being captured and held against him, Hywel had used the brief window of opportunity Gareth and Dai's warning had given him to lay in provisions and fortify his defenses further. Gareth and Dai had watched Cadell's army come on and then retreated, knowing there was nothing they could do to aid Hywel or their friends as long as Cadell's army surrounded the fortress.

In this, for all the agony of looking on helplessly as their friends suffered, they were lucky. The last thing any soldier wanted was to be stuck on the wrong side of a siege, with no option but to wait until the enemy gave up or he himself died of starvation. Gwen had been on her knees in the church every day since then, praying for the people in the castle, while simultaneously thanking God for

Gareth's and Dai's deliverance from that fate. It was bad enough knowing Hywel was trapped.

That said, from the start, he had been wiser than Gwen and Gareth in that, months ago, he had sent Mari and their boys home to Gwynedd. Gwen had been prevented from following the same road, first by her pregnancy, then by Angharad's infancy, and then by the onset of winter. At least, with the siege lifted, Hywel and their friends were safe—unlike Gwen and her family.

"If Cadell discovered churchmen were supporting Hywel, he didn't hesitate to order the sacking of their churches and monasteries in the borderlands." Gwen started putting Angharad into her carry sling, doing her best to copy her father and remain matter-of-fact about something she saw as a true disaster. "Not usually the best way to win over a populace."

"Cadell has never cared overmuch about his people, as long as he maintains his power," Meilyr said. "Though, to be fair, he has had his hands full with the Normans more than we have in Gwynedd."

"He will believe us to be harboring men loyal to Hywel." Reginald's hand-wringing continued. "Who will stay and defend us?"

"You *are* harboring men loyal to Hywel as long as we are here." Gareth swung their young son, Taran, onto his hip. At three and a half, the little boy wasn't all that little anymore, and thus was rarely carried. At the unexpected change in elevation, he squealed with delight, having no notion of the terror filling his parents. "That is why we are leaving. Once we are gone, you won't need a defense. You are Hospitallers. You run a hospital and a monastery. Even

Cadell's men will see the inherent foolishness of harming you, your people, or this commandery in any way."

They had planned for this. Maybe some part of them had expected it. With all other routes closed to them, their choice in this moment was two-fold. They could either use the footbridge across the gorge to the west of the commandery (leaving most of their possessions behind), or flee in their wagons by the main road that ran from that same northern crossroads, past the commandery, to points south. They would hope to stay ahead of Cadell's army long enough to find another avenue east that would loop them through Powys and back to Gwynedd. Either way, their intent was to pass as itinerant bards, which wasn't even a deception, given that Meilyr was the greatest bard of his generation. Gwen had sung with him many times before her marriage, even in Deheubarth itself.

Gareth and Dai were going to be harder to hide. They weren't going to leave their horses and swords behind, not while in enemy territory. In addition, if someone asked Gareth his name, he wasn't going to lie. The best plan was to keep to themselves and not to have to answer at all.

With Angharad snuggled on her chest, Gwen took Tangwen's hand. Having just celebrated her sixth birthday, the little girl's eyes were perceptively wide. Taran might be oblivious to the anxieties of his elders, but Tangwen had heard everything they'd said and knew all was not well.

Thus, Gwen endeavored to inject a bit of fun into the day. "We're going on a journey!"

Playing along, Gareth chucked Tangwen under the chin. "It will be just like in the old days before you were born. Except then, we didn't have the lovely wagons we have now, just an old cart." As he met Gwen's eyes over the top of their children's heads, she saw a measure of resolve within him she knew from experience to flow from a deep well. She hoped he saw the same in her. As always, they were in this life together, whatever it gave them.

"It has been a long while since we took out the wagons," Gwen added. "What are you looking forward to most?"

"The horses!" Tangwen gave a little skip out the door and then took off running towards Dai, who, with the help of two monks, was hitching the horses to the wagons parked in the center of the monastery courtyard. He'd already saddled his and Gareth's mounts.

Gwen paused on the threshold, her hand reaching for Gareth's arm. "We're going to be all right."

"I know." He kissed the top of her head. "Come what may."

"Don't worry about Llelo either. If he needs protecting, Rhys will see to it."

Gareth managed a laugh. "Just think, he could have been with Cadell's army this whole time. Maybe he's on his way to Ysbyty Cynfyn even now."

"Which means we really need to get going," Gwen said. "We want Commander Reginald to be able to say he just missed us."

2

Day One

Llelo

Llelo was not on his way to Ysbyty Cynfyn. In fact, he was about as far from his parents as it was possible to be without sailing to France. He wasn't even in Deheubarth, not really, a fact which he pointed out once again to Prince Rhys, as a warning about the ill-advised nature of the current proceedings.

As the youngest brother of the King of Deheubarth, at not quite nineteen (the same as Llelo), Rhys had little say in the missions on which he was sent. For the last few weeks, instead of participating in the battles in the north, which had been ongoing since Christmas, he had been kept at home. It was Maredudd, Rhys's brother, two years older than he, who was leading the charge against Hywel's fortress in Ceredigion. Meanwhile, Rhys crouched with Llelo behind a bramble-covered log in the Coed Rath, a forest a few miles north of Tenby. In his words, he was *doing nothing of note.*

"Cadell said my job was to hide right here in order to *watch and learn.*" Disgust dripped from Rhys's voice. "Learn what? Why this particular spot? I'd rather be up a tree than huddled in the bracken on my belly behind a log, barely able to see what is happening below me. Why couldn't we at least be hiding with the rest of his *teulu*?"

Llelo couldn't answer that. They'd left their encampment in the hills at dawn in order to arrive here well before the meeting time of midday. He didn't know why he and Rhys had been made to hide in this particular spot any more than Rhys did. They were well concelaed, however, which appeared to be Cadell's goal.

The king himself was standing with two men of his *teulu*, or personal guard, in a large bowl-shaped clearing, doing as much of nothing as Llelo and Rhys. Back in Dinefwr, Cadell had told everyone they were going hunting. But even if the forest was renowned for its deer, it wasn't a safe or sensible place for Cadell to have chosen to hunt, not so near the Norman castles of Tenby, Begelly, and Sentence. And that wasn't even to mention Carew! They were surrounded by Norman strongholds here. Any Norman who came upon them would see through the ruse and assume they were here to spy out the land for an upcoming attack.

That assumption would have been incorrect, too.

Rhys was still grumbling. "I don't like hiding. It's no stance for a knight. My brother is ashamed to have me at his side, otherwise I would be out there with him. He can't even put on a good face for propriety's sake. Worse, he doesn't see the point."

Llelo didn't actually think that was what this was about and said so. Nobody in his right mind would ever be ashamed of Rhys. "Maybe, for once, he's trying to protect you."

"We know that is unlikely to be true." Rhys scoffed. "And if it were, and my brother really thought this meeting was as ill-advised as you do, he shouldn't have agreed to it."

"Sometimes, you just have to take a chance. Earl Clare's offer was too good to pass up."

Last night in their encampment, the king had explained to his men that they were not, in fact, going hunting today, but rather meeting with Roger de Clare, a younger brother of Gilbert de Clare, the Earl of Hertford. He and Cadell had been in negotiations for weeks about a truce between Deheubarth and the Norman forces occupying south Wales. Cadell was eager to conclude the treaty so he could turn his full attention to evicting Hywel from Ceredigion. He even hoped to enlist these Normans in the endeavor.

When Rhys had made his objections to this meeting known to Cadell—in private, not in front of his men, since he knew better than to do that—Cadell had set him down with a few choice comments along the lines of *you will do as you are told and you will like it.*

Cadell cared not at all that Hywel was Rhys's first cousin. Hywel was no blood relation to Cadell. Of course, being cousins had never meant very much to Cadell. Before he'd taken Wiston Castle with the help of Gwynedd four years ago, he'd taken Llansteffan from another cousin, Maurice Fitzgerald, a child of Cadell's aunt Nest, who'd married the Norman Gerald of Windsor. Maurice's elder brother, William de Carew, was the castellan of Pembroke Castle. Both men served Richard de Clare, Earl of Pembroke, who happened to be a nephew of Earl Gilbert. Llelo supposed that if lords didn't ever fight against family members, there'd never be any warfare at all!

As far as Llelo knew, Earl Richard had played no role in the treaty Cadell was making with his uncle. If there was going to be a compact with him, it was going to be negotiated separately.

"We know the real reason my brother put me here," Rhys said darkly. "He is going to betray me to Clare."

"You don't know that. We have no proof your brother is plotting against you," Llelo said. "And if he really was going to turn you over to them, it would be better to have you where he can see you."

"Something isn't right about all this, though." Rhys's tone was no less foreboding than before. "Just the fact that he lied to everyone in Dinefwr about why he was coming here shows us that. You feel it too."

"I can't demur. I do feel it too."

This *feeling,* in fact, was why Llelo had spent these last months beside Rhys. Rhys had called, and Llelo had answered. Nothing that had transpired since then had given Llelo cause to regret his choice to come.

"You know as well as I that it is not unusual for the son of one mother to fear the children of his father's second wife," Rhys said, "even if those children have given him no cause to feel that way."

"It is not unusual at all. What's more, hostage-taking—and giving—is a tried and true method of ensuring one's enemy sticks to his bargain. The higher the value of the hostage, the more confidence the hostage-taker can feel about the treaty." One of Llelo's jobs these last months had been to speak difficult truths to Rhys. At the same time, as soon as he spoke, he wished he could take it back. Feeding Rhys's fears was not going to help today.

"If I survive these next hours, I must redouble my efforts to be accommodating." Rhys let out a breath they could see in the frigid morning air. "What Earl Clare wouldn't know is that if he accepts me as a hostage, Cadell will feel free to break the treaty at any time because he doesn't care if I live or die." His voice rose a bit in his ire, but not so much it carried as far as the clearing.

Or, at least, neither Cadell nor his men looked their way.

Llelo shot Rhys a quelling look. "You have concocted this entire scenario out of whole cloth, my lord. My father says speculation has its place, but not without better evidence than we have so far gathered. You could lose all sorts of time following your suspicions to a nefarious end before you discover you are entirely astray."

Rhys took in a deep breath. "Thank you for being here, Llelo. This is exactly why I asked you to come."

3

Day One

Rhys

Rhys clenched his hands into fists, feeling more unsettled by the moment. His conversation with Llelo had not made him feel better about any of what was happening. He tried always to remain in control of himself and his emotions. Of late, that had become harder to do.

"The possible threat to me aside, this treaty is going to have ramifications for *years*." Being kept away from the negotiations was angering him more than it should have. As the youngest son, even though he was only two years younger than Maredudd, he was used to being an afterthought. "On top of everything else, I can't believe Cadell is going to ally himself with a *Clare*. He's selling me to a *Clare*."

"Not all Clares are bad. My family has had dealings with the Earl of Pembroke, most recently last spring. Lord Richard seems like an honorable man." Llelo had told Rhys this before. He was trying to keep Rhys calm, which Rhys appreciated, even though it didn't work.

"Maybe so. Since his father's death, he has ruled Pembroke with a steady hand. But you must never forget, even for a moment, that he, too, is a Norman. They are as fickle in their loyalties as the wind. You can't trust them."

"In comparison to the Welsh, of course, who are so steadfast."

It was a fine bit of sarcasm. "I do admit our people tend to have a narrow view of our own interests most of the time." Rhys outranked Llelo by a wide margin, but in the time Llelo had been in the south, they had learned to speak to each other like brothers. When Rhys had sent for Llelo, begged for him to come, really, he had known his request was unreasonable. Dangerous, even. He'd asked anyway.

Llelo had not only answered his call, he'd done it, to all appearances, without question.

There had been barriers to him coming, not the least of which was that he would have to travel alone through a war zone to reach Rhys. Of far greater issue had been how Rhys was to present him in his brother's court. Cadell had met Llelo before. Or, at the very least, he'd seen him. They'd all been together in the same hall four years ago at Dinefwr, during their victory at Wiston Castle, a time when Gwynedd and Deheubarth had been working together. Llelo had been fifteen, same as Rhys, and thus unworthy of notice in Cadell's eyes. That's when Llelo's family had met Richard de Clare for the first time, too. The three of them—Rhys, Llelo, and Richard—were similar in age, and they'd been thrown together a bit because of it.

Acting in Rhys's favor was the fact that Cadell had been poisoned at the celebratory dinner, and thus hadn't cared one way or another about his brother's friends after that. In addition, four years on, Llelo was virtually unrecognizable, being larger in every way, with a credible mustache and beard. Rhys didn't think he himself had changed all that much. He was the same tall and slender shape he'd been his whole life, even if he'd finally started filling out his mail.

None of that mattered as long as Llelo remained the son of Gareth, the steward to Prince Hywel of Gwynedd, with whom Cadell was currently at war. But while it was impossible for Llelo to come to Deheubarth entirely as himself, he could leave bits behind. Rhys personally didn't struggle overly with the sin of lying, but Llelo found it harder—not surprising, given the father who'd raised him.

Thus, they'd compromised. Firstly, Llelo had grown that nascent mustache and beard. And secondly, in a much more momentous act, he'd taken the initial step towards joining the holy Order of the Knights of the Hospital of St. John of Jerusalem, known as the Hospitallers. The mission of the order was to succor pilgrims, initially on the road to Jerusalem, and then more broadly across Europe—including in Wales. Llelo's family had stayed most of this last year at the commandery of Ysbyty Cynfyn—*ysbyty* meaning *hospital* in Welsh—in Ceredigion, established on the north-south road to the great monastery of Mynachlog Fawr.

Ysbyty Cynfyn's commander, Reginald, had been delighted to incorporate Llelo into the Order as a novice knight, knowing full well Llelo could change his mind freely at any time in the first year. Reginald didn't want him to join the Order and then regret it any more than Llelo did.

If, after a year, he still wanted to take his vows, he could then do so. And if, instead, he wanted to leave, he could do so, without punishment or penalties, either in this world or the next.

Rhys honestly didn't know if joining the Hospitallers was the best path for Llelo. For now, it provided excellent cover, and Llelo was determined both to stick out his service to the Order for the year, as a commitment to God, and to maintain his position in Rhys's retinue. Rhys had introduced him to Cadell as Sir Llywelyn, which was entirely correct. *Llelo* had only ever been a pet name, one that was commonly utilized throughout Wales, since so many men were christened with the same name. It also meant that if Rhys slipped up at any point and called his new companion *Llelo* instead of *Llywelyn*, nobody would be puzzled by it.

Thus, for the last three months, Llelo had dressed as a Hospitaller knight should. Mostly, that was similarly to Rhys and everyone else in Cadell's retinue, in mail armor and sword. But Llelo additionally wore the black tunic with a white cross on his chest as a symbol of his order. He had a matching cloak, too, with a white cross on his left shoulder. The women of the court had been admiring, to say the least, which was a little ironic given that becoming a Hospitaller would ensure Llelo could never be with any of them.

And when asked about his parentage, Rhys simply gave Llelo's birth father's name instead of attributing him to Gareth. It felt to both Rhys and Llelo a bit like a betrayal, but since it was no less than the truth, it had been an eminently practical solution. Gareth (naturally) had been the one to suggest it in the first place, in the process of giving his blessing to the entire endeavor.

Llelo had begun his sojourn in Rhys's company simply by watching his back, along with learning the lay of the land, so to speak, and the ins and outs of Cadell's court. It was only in the last month, since Maredudd's departure for the north, that he had begun to step out on his own. He wasn't a natural spy, a fact which he'd warned Rhys about from the start, not with the father he had. He had a spy for a mother, though. Before he left, Gwen had impressed upon him the merits of waiting and watching and taking his time.

"All jesting aside, fear of treachery is my guess as to why your brother has hidden us here," Llelo said. "That's why the rest of his men are hidden on the other side of the clearing. It isn't because he doesn't want you to know what he's doing or because he's betraying you to Clare. It's because he fears Clare's motives and wants to protect you."

"I suppose that could be true." Rhys couldn't help feeling dubious.

Suddenly, Llelo grinned. "Maybe your brother isn't intending to sell you as a hostage. Maybe he's meaning to offer you up as a husband, to seal the deal he and Earl Clare are making. The earl has never married, but I hear he still has managed to produce several daughters, some of whom must be of eligible age by now."

Rhys couldn't keep the look of horror from his face. "I'm already promised to King Madog's daughter, Gwenllian!"

"You aren't married yet, though, are you? Your brother has never had any trouble making multiple, contradictory deals, playing all sides against each other until he finds the one that suits him best.

You are just as much a pawn in the field of matrimony as you may be on the battlefield."

Rhys almost put his face into the dirt at the thought. He'd met Gwenllian last year and liked her. They weren't married yet because she was only fifteen years old. She was also a child of Madog's liaison with another woman, rather than with his wife Susanna. That wouldn't have been acceptable at all, since it would have made Gwenllian and Rhys first cousins, since their mothers would have been sisters.

"I hear hooves." Llelo was suddenly poking at him. "They're here!"

4

Day One

Rhys

Upon hearing Llelo's warning, Rhys's head came up, at the same moment the Norman riders entered the clearing. To start, it was just three men.

At the sight of Cadell and two of his retainers waiting, the leader reined in and dismounted. He removed his helmet too, out of respect, since he was greeting a king. With three men each, neither group was viewing the other as a threat.

Rhys, however, sucked in a breath to see the Norman leader's face. "That isn't Roger de Clare."

Almost in the same instant, Cadell said, speaking in French, which would be the only language the Normans knew, "Where is Lord Roger?"

The man ducked his head in apology. "His horse threw a shoe a mile back. He sent me on ahead to greet you, so you would not be concerned at our lateness."

It was Llelo's turn to frown. "That's hardly a reason. Clare could simply have borrowed another man's horse. It isn't as if he is going to walk—"

But Rhys waved a hand to silence him, wanting to hear his brother's reply.

"And you are?" Cadell said.

"Gerald de Grosmont, commander of the Tenby garrison."

Cadell nodded, as if these origins were only to be expected. The Normans had built a castle at Tenby and then imported settlers from England to live in its adjacent walled town. The Welsh, as had been the case across so much of south Wales, had been evicted to make room for them.

While it might make sense that Clare was riding with men from Tenby, Rhys thought as little of Gerald's answer as Llelo had of his previous one. Rhys had fought Normans in the past; he'd been involved in negotiations too. He understood, as he knew Cadell must, even if he was keeping his manner impassive, the irregularity of Gerald's presence.

"I'm getting a sick feeling in my belly," Llelo said from beside him, very under his breath and only stating out loud what Rhys himself had been thinking. "All may be well, and I'm worrying for nothing, but your brother needs Gerald to tell him what's going on *right now.*"

If he'd been allowed in the clearing, Rhys would have been able to let his brother know something wasn't right. Thinking of it, and feeling more urgent with every heartbeat, he made to push up.

"Cadell is sure to listen to me now, and since no man from Tenby would speak Welsh, I'll just—"

But Llelo's arm came across his back, forcing him to stay down. "No. You won't."

Fury roared through Rhys like oil poured on a fire. He hated that he had been told to hide; he hated being contained; and, in that moment, he hated Llelo. "Let me go! What do you think you're do—"

He cut himself off abruptly at the sight of Llelo holding up one finger, silently asking him to stop.

All of Rhys's princely instincts were telling him to override his friend, to throw off his encompassing arm and step over this infernal log they were hiding behind. But Llelo's quiet certainty brought him up short. He was self-aware enough to understand where his anger had come from. As was so often the case, it was a product of frustration and fear.

So he reassessed, thankfully before he had risen high enough to draw the attention of Gerald or the other men in the clearing. Llelo was trying to tell him something. Rhys wasn't sure what it was yet, but he reminded himself that this was why he'd sent for Llelo in the first place. Settling back onto his belly, he turned one hand palm up, asking without speaking for Llelo to explain.

Llelo put his mouth close to Rhys's ear, still with his arm across his back, in case he decided to try to rise again. "Do you trust me?"

Rhys felt a flash of impatience. "With my life, as you know."

"Then come." Llelo released Rhys and backed away, still on his belly. With a curl of a few fingers, he indicated Rhys should retreat with him deeper into the woods. Cadell was still standing with Gerald and the two other Normans in the center of the wide, bowl-shaped clearing, apparently waiting for Roger de Clare to walk a mile. Their position was somewhat downhill from Rhys and Llelo's current location.

Finding a spot farther away would limit Rhys's ability to hear what they were saying, but he should still be able to see what was happening.

So Rhys came, like Llelo, nearly on his belly, moving as a stalking cat might, though oddly in reverse. He crawled backwards as carefully and quietly as he could, even if he didn't yet have a full understanding of why. Most of the trees were bare in this area, providing little overall cover, but there were mounds of fallen leaves, bracken, brambles, and downed trees all around, along with a few pines and yew, all of which were available to hide behind.

Llelo eventually found them a new spot from which to watch, sixty feet or more from where they'd been. They were back on their bellies as before, but this time behind a half-fallen-down stone wall. They were also set up at a slightly different angle to the clearing than before, their heads peering just over the crest of the rise, or the lip of the bowl, depending on how one perceived the clearing.

At that point, Rhys finally felt able to prod his friend. "Why did we move?"

Also as before, Llelo put his head close to Rhys's, not wanting his voice to carry. "I fought with King Owain's forces when we ambushed Ranulf of Chester's men on the road to Holywell. I will never forget the way my father studied the terrain. Before the assault, he positioned us as best he could. Something about how Cadell is situated down there reminded me of it, and not in a good way. We aren't playing the part of King Owain's forces in this scenario, but Ranulf's. If I am wrong, I will beg your forgiveness, and that of your brother, but if I'm right—"

Llelo broke off speaking as the captain of Cadell's *teulu* rose up from the place where he'd been hiding with the rest of Cadell's men on the opposite side of the clearing from Rhys and Llelo, their horses hidden from view on the reverse slope. He walked quickly, not to say hurried, down the hill and across the grassy space in order to speak low in Cadell's ear. Even if Rhys and Llelo had stayed in their previous spot they wouldn't have been able to hear.

Cadell's posture stiffened at what his captain had to say and then both men turned to Gerald.

Cadell's back was to Rhys now, so he couldn't see his brother's expression. Gerald, however, was looking directly towards them. Even from this greater distance, Rhys could see the sudden predatory smile that transformed his face.

5

Day One

Llelo

The men from Tenby arrived from the south in a thunder of hooves, fifty men on horseback with swords and axes and even a crossbow or two.

Llelo had feared betrayal, and it had come.

This time, before Rhys could try again to push to his feet, Llelo threw himself on top of him and held him down. This was different from earlier, when he'd acted merely as a gentle restraint on Rhys's instincts. Although Rhys was taller, Llelo was heavier, and he mentally willed his body to become a dead weight. "No. You can't. It would be suicide." He put all the fear and urgency he was feeling into his voice, no longer needing to whisper since the men in the clearing were past hearing.

"My brother—"

"—is outnumbered two to one. Three to one! He will live or die by his own skill with a blade and that of his men. We cannot be among them." Llelo tried to swallow but his throat was a solid lump.

"Cadell went down in that first foray." The grief in Rhys's voice threatened to overwhelm Llelo too.

Before the Norman force was fully in the clearing, Cadell had the foresight and skill to vault himself onto Gerald's horse, which had been standing nearby, its reins trailing. Sword in hand, he then met the initial blows brought against him with equal force. But even if he could have fought off the number of cavalry coming against him, the horse was not his own, and it did not respond to him as it would have to its master. Just as Cadell was trying to counter two men at once, the horse reared and tossed him to the ground.

By then, the rest of Cadell's *teulu* had mounted their horses and stormed down the hill from where they'd been hidden, roaring as one in anger. Even now, Cadell's captain and the other two men of his *teulu* stood over Cadell's prone body, but they were hard-pressed, encircled as they were by enemy riders.

So Llelo nodded from above Rhys. "You can't help him by dying yourself. You have to think of Maredudd now, and Deheubarth."

"We can't just—" Rhys began to rock his hips back and forth, begging Llelo to release him so he could get up and fight.

"Yes, we can." Llelo kept pressing down.

"Honor demands we avenge my brother."

"And we will. But there is no honor in dying in an ambush. We stay here because we must, so we can live to fight another day."

At last, Llelo's words penetrated Rhys's anguish. It was what he knew to be true in his heart, even as that same heart railed against the reality before them. Finally, Rhys put his head down. His face would have been in the dirt if he hadn't pillowed his forehead on the back of his hand. Under normal circumstances, Rhys was not impulsive and was rarely overcome with anger. He could see death in that clearing as easily as Llelo.

He sobbed into the grass and fallen leaves beneath him, and despaired.

Rhys couldn't bear to look, but Llelo couldn't look away, transfixed and horrified by what he was seeing. By instinct, he was sorting the men in the clearing according to the colors they wore. Cadell's personal guard didn't all wear exactly the same gear, but their colors were primarily yellow and red. The Tenby garrison, by contrast, wore shades of green.

Llelo had no doubt the battle before him would haunt his dreams lifelong. That didn't mean he could stop watching, nor cover his ears, like a child refusing to hear that it was time to go to bed. It suddenly came to him that if Rhys couldn't watch, Llelo needed to watch for him. To do otherwise would have been cowardly.

He wished now he had thought to further protect them by covering their prone forms with branches or brambles. His black cloak somewhat resembled the moist earth beneath him, but he and Rhys were not otherwise hidden all that well. If one of these men from Tenby decided to explore the surrounding woods, looking for strays or stragglers, he was bound to see them.

Slowly, Llelo pulled his hood over his head and then spread his cloak wider to cover them both. Then he grabbed a handful of leaves and strewed them across his back, taking special care to cover the white cross on his left shoulder. It was the contrast that would catch a watcher's eye. And any movement.

As Rhys lifted his head again, Llelo whispered to him to stay still. He obeyed, breathing shallowly, like Llelo was. With a fear that made Llelo want to vomit, he watched as a few men did start to circle around the clearing on horseback, one even coming deeper into the woods for a last circuit. In so doing, he passed directly over the spot where Llelo and Rhys had been secreted not even a quarter of an hour earlier. Llelo had never prayed so hard in his life as he did then for the man to decide he had looked hard enough and not turn towards them.

By contrast, Rhys's entire body was tensed, preparing to spring up if they were spotted. If his impulse remained to attack, he might even be wishing for the man to find them. "Have they seen us?" His voice came low but clearly to Llelo's ears.

"Not yet." Llelo carefully turned his head, tracing a route through the woods with his eyes that would allow them to escape if it came to that. He wasn't afraid to fight. He had fought before, most recently beside his father and Dai in a skirmish against Cadell's men. At that time, Rhys thankfully had not been among them. Llelo had seen enough of war to admit he wanted to live. He also believed he should feel no shame in doing so.

That wasn't the reason he had held Rhys down, nor why he was seeking a further route by which to escape. Llelo wanted to live, it was true. Even more, he saw it as his job to ensure that Rhys lived. Someday, Rhys would understand that Llelo had saved his life today, even if he hated him for it now.

It was almost a blessing to see, after another two dozen heartbeats, the fight end. Cadell's men had given a good accounting of themselves, despite being surprised and outnumbered. Three Normans were dead and another six wounded. Of Cadell's forces, only four out of the sixteen or so who'd come to the rendezvous remained alive. Two of these were Llelo and Rhys themselves. The last two had managed to survive the battle in the clearing but now surrendered by letting go of their swords and falling to their knees before the men of Tenby who surrounded them.

One of Gerald's soldiers toed a corpse, which Llelo took to be Cadell's, near his feet. "Are we bringing the head back to Tenby as proof he's dead?" He spoke in French, which meant these two surviving Welshmen likely couldn't understand him.

Llelo almost wished he couldn't either. But he spoke French, and, with the conclusion of the battle, the wind had died, allowing the Normans' voices to carry through the still air. Even the birds had quieted out of respect for the death of a king.

"Proof?" Gerald scoffed. "Earl Clare doesn't want this attached to him. He wants it to be as if we were never here."

The soldier let out a puff of air that was like laughter, as he made a broad gesture to encompass the clearing. "How?"

Gerald smiled, not taking offense. "Take everything of value." He himself reached down and collected Cadell's sword from where it had fallen near the body. "We will arrange the scene so that anyone who comes upon it will believe Danes are responsible, as they were with Anarawd."

"That prince of Gwyneth, Cadwalader, might even be blamed again!" This came from a different soldier. His tone was gleeful, even as he butchered the Welsh pronunciations. "Gwyneth and Deehay-barth are at war, after all."

Llelo understood why the Norman soldier was feeling so jubilant. He had survived the battle to live another day. He was walking on clouds right now, with no thought of the men he'd killed. As a Norman, perhaps he would never feel the pain of it. Maybe Normans didn't feel things the same way Llelo did. Though, even as that notion passed through his head, he thought of his Norman friend, Hamelin, alongside whom Llelo had been knighted. Llelo liked to think Hamelin would not have stooped so low as to ambush a king and be joyful about it afterwards. In truth, Llelo couldn't be sure.

Gerald nodded. "We leave him where he lies. All of them. Soon, someone will come looking, by which point we'll be back in Tenby. Make doubly sure we have left no trace of ourselves for anyone to find. We will throw everything we collect from them in the sea on the way home, so this can never be traced to us."

Not all of the soldiers were happy about that. This was a king's company; the gear on the bodies was the finest in Wales. To get rid of it was smarter, though. Gerald was right about that.

Then the rider who'd made a circuit of the clearing spoke up. "What about his brother? He was supposed to have been here, too, but I don't see him."

"Cadell lied to us," Gerald said the name as if it were English, with only one *l* instead of two, "and we lied to him. I'd call it a fair trade."

6

Day One

Llelo

Llelo clapped a hand over Rhys's mouth a heartbeat before Gerald used Cadell's sword to slash the throat of one of the surrendering Welshmen. A different soldier skewered the second, and these last two men of Cadell's *teulu* flopped dead to the ground.

Rhys's face was back in his arms, beyond agony at what he'd just seen, his shoulders shaking in silent sobs. Llelo, for his part, was unable to turn away. He understood now how important it was that he memorize every detail of these events. He wasn't watching just for Rhys or Maredudd anymore. Without his testimony, and Rhys's, if he could stomach it, the Norman tale could easily become the one the world believed. Thus, the profound concern amongst the soldiers below him that none be left alive in that clearing to report how the King of Deheubarth had died. They wanted the Danes blamed, or Gwynedd. Cadell's people would need a full accounting, once Llelo and Rhys escaped this place. If they escaped it.

Rhys had spoken of his own honor, but for a knight to be implicated in an ambush like the one these Normans had just perpetrated was the height of dishonor. It tainted every man still living in that clearing. Except—and this new thought left such a sour taste in Llelo's mouth he wanted to vomit—if they didn't see the Welshmen they'd murdered as included in the very concept of honor (or dishonor). They'd been able to slaughter Cadell and his men because, to them, they were no better than livestock. Of less value, even. A good milking cow could feed an entire village through a hard winter.

While some of Gerald's men loaded the Norman dead and wounded onto horses, some of which belonged to Cadell's men, others began stripping the Welsh dead of everything easily portable—swords, knives, rings, if men wore them—as a Dane would. It would take too much time to remove their mail, which was very valuable but hard enough to get off a living man without his help. Gerald, meanwhile, went to his saddlebags and retrieved a length of fur, as might adorn the collar of a cloak. He draped it artfully over a bush near the scene and then dropped several coins near where Cadell was lying. Also left behind were the strap from a saddle and a scabbard, each in a different part of the clearing.

By the time he'd finished, all of his men but his own second-in-command had left the clearing. They gave the scene a last look around, glanced with satisfaction at each other, and rode away.

At that point, Rhys didn't have to throw Llelo off, because Llelo pushed to his feet on his own accord. He entered the clearing two paces ahead of Rhys, going first to the body of Cadell, even if that was the last place he wanted to look. Cadell was lying half on his side, pressed up against another of his fallen companions, while his captain sprawled across his legs.

All around were torn bodies, and underneath that, grass and mud and blood. Llelo's right boot slipped in it, and he barely caught himself from going down on one knee. Only because he'd been trained by his father to check once, and then check again, to make sure someone was really dead, even when it was obvious, did he bend to touch two fingers to the side of Cadell's neck. It was bloody from a head wound that had poured blood down the side of his face.

And, come to think on it, was bleeding still.

With the back of his hand now to Cadell's lips, at first he didn't believe what he was sensing, telling himself it was his imagination. Then he placed his ear fully to Cadell's chest.

He wasn't mistaken. "He's alive, Rhys! He's alive!"

Cadell's chest rose and fell, and his heart was still beating, strong and steady despite his obvious wounds. He'd hit the ground with such force Llelo had almost felt it in his own body. That head wound seemed to have come from the fall, maybe the result of a rock or a sharp stick. The reason Cadell was half-rolled over was because Gerald had wanted a good look at him. Too bad for him he hadn't done his due diligence to ensure Cadell really was dead. In truth, Gerald should have thrust a sword through his midsection to ensure it. Somehow, despite how casual he'd been about the slaughter of more than a dozen men, the mutilation of the body of a king was a bridge too far.

Admittedly, Cadell looked dead. He was white as a linen sheet, except for the blood in his hair and on his face and neck. Head wounds bled like the devil himself. Thankfully, Gerald had been in a hurry and hadn't stopped to wonder why the wound still seeped.

Unlike Llelo, Rhys had given in to instinct and avoided his brother's body, so now he scrambled across the clearing towards him, almost tripping over the dead in his haste. When he reached Cadell's side, he fell to his knees beside Llelo.

And then, defying all expectations, Cadell opened his eyes. "Good. You obeyed me."

Rhys grabbed hold of Cadell's hand and started rubbing it between both of his. "I stayed hidden like you told me to. I didn't want to. Llelo made me."

"You saw what they did?" At Rhys's nod, Cadell closed his eyes again. "I heard the Tenby captain say Clare wants to make sure there is no chance of this falling back on him. Sloppy work on their part, not making sure I was really dead. Though, to be fair, I wish I were."

Llelo was glad Cadell was talking. At the same time, he had been around enough sick and wounded people to know he could soon get his wish, depending on how his head wound progressed and what other parts of him might be injured.

With a couple of heaves, Llelo shifted the body lying across Cadell's legs and then, heedless of the king's dignity, began patting him down, looking for additional wounds. Again, that was as his father had taught him. "My lord, if you could tell me what hurts—"

"It's what doesn't." Cadell's voice cut through Llelo's uncertainty. "I can't feel my legs."

Llelo froze, his hands hovering around Cadell's knees. "I shifted your captain off of you. Could it be they became numb and are taking a moment to recover?"

"My feet won't move."

Llelo glanced towards the toes of Cadell's boots, which were pointed at the sky.

Rhys still hadn't let go of his brother's hand. "We'll get you home. The healers will see to you."

"No." Cadell used his other hand to push at Rhys. "Leave me here. Stand up and walk away right now."

"What? Don't be absurd." In his entire life, Rhys probably hadn't so forthrightly refused an order his brother had given him. The idea that Cadell had ever wanted him dead now seemed ludicrous, a fantasy rooted in fear rather than what was really happening.

"I'm not being absurd. I'm done for, and all three of us know it. I'm saying out loud what you need to admit."

"We'll get help. All we need is a bier and—"

"A bier is for carrying the dead!"

Rhys was stuttering through his reply when a shout came from the top of the rise, within the trees and not far from where Llelo and Rhys had been hidden.

The pair of them swung around, fearing, of course, that it was Gerald and his men returning. Instead, Iestyn ap Meurig, brother to Ifor Bach, the Lord of Senghenydd, rode towards them with ten men.

Above his head rippled the golden lion banner of the House of Dinefwr.

Help, however unlooked for and unexpected, had come.

7

Day One

Gareth

Gareth hadn't meant to take on more people, but once the wagons set off down the road from the commandery's gatehouse, he couldn't deny anyone in need. The first to arrive was a family from the village adjacent to the commandery, consisting of a husband, wife, and their three young children. They were followed by a widow and her two nearly grown daughters.

Gareth had been driving his family's cart. With the arrival of the father of three, a man named Meicol, he handed over the reins. Meicol took them without comment and sat himself in the driver's seat in Gareth's place. Now on the ground, Gareth walked to the back of the cart to confer on these events with Gwen, who had been sitting on one of the beds. Angharad was asleep beside her, while Taran and Tangwen played with blocks on the floor.

Although Gwen welcomed the mother and children without hesitation, Taran made a face as if he was going to protest at the in-clusion of others into his game. At a stern look from his father, he handed one of the blocks to a boy about his age. Three breaths later, the two were fast friends. Gareth then helped the widow and her two daughters into the back of Meilyr's wagon. Having come to terms himself, in the intervening moments, with having so many more people in his entourage—mouths to feed and (more importantly) people to protect—Gareth mounted his horse. Dai had been on horseback already, and now they took up positions at the front and back of the wagon train.

It seemed to Gareth they were not so much a company of bards now as a caravan of refugees. As he thought about it, with so many children among them, maybe he could be less fearful of being mistreated if his identity were discovered. Even Cadell's men, who seemed to think little of churches, might balk at harming children.

Two miles south of Ysbyty Cynfyn, they'd navigated the bridge across the Afon Mynach. At that point, they all breathed a sigh of relief. It would be at least as slow a traverse for an army as it had been for them. The rain that had fallen most of the morning began to abate too, which made the roads less likely to mire the wagon wheels in mud. That said, if they did encounter an army, better weather might make them more inclined to look seriously at Gareth's little band. Wet soldiers made for negligent soldiers. It was just a fact.

By the time they'd come another four miles, they were within a half hour of a different commandery, that of Ysbyty Ystwyth. At that point, the last two of their number arrived: a young man who appeared out of the west, bow and quiver on his back. He swung himself over a stone wall and started loping beside Gareth's wagon as if he had always been there. When asked, after a ducking of the head, he gave his name as Ieuan and his age as seventeen. The second was a man of about forty-five who introduced himself as Bran. They'd stopped beside the road to water the horses. Bran had come up to them with a pronounced limp and an accent that had a tinge of the north about it. That wouldn't serve him well in the direction they were going. Gwen gave him water and a bite of food, too, and then, with a shrug of consent at Gareth, Meicol let him take a turn at the reins.

Bran seated himself with a practiced air that said he knew all about driving wagons. Gareth hadn't pressed Meicol or the widow for much in the way of information about who they were and why they had feared staying in their village more than being on the road with him. He hadn't concerned himself much with Ieuan, either. But they were approaching the end of the day now. A lone man of Bran's age was a different prospect than a man with a family. If Gareth was going to be able to sleep in his company tonight, he needed to know more about him.

And then, before Gareth could even ask where home was for him, Bran began talking: "It was a hard day on my leg—" he slapped his thigh, "—let me tell you, but I have been following you since the river. Never could catch up until now."

"We are almost to the commandery," Gareth said. "They—"

"—can't help me any more than they'll be a help to you. I have been a soldier. Oh, the monks there might do their best to protect me, but what can they do against the army that is coming? I fought for Hywel last year. Anyone could tell them." Now, he rubbed the spot on his leg which seemed to be giving him trouble. "I was wounded, which is why I wasn't in Aberystwyth. I have been to the commandery before. Some might remember me. They might mention my past in a vulnerable moment or in hopes of saving themselves. I'll be in for it then, just like you and your son."

Gareth's eyes narrowed. "Why would you say that?"

"You're Lord Gareth, aren't you? And your son, Dai. Everybody knows who you are."

Gareth had no memory of ever meeting Bran, but he and Dai had ranged all over Ceredigion for nearly a year. Many more people had seen him than he had met. It didn't bode well for keeping himself anonymous going forward. "Do you have family somewhere?"

"None living." Bran made a qualifying motion with his head. "None who'd remember me, leastwise."

Gareth wasn't sure what Bran meant by that, but he let it go for now. Since the other man was a decade older than Gareth, likely at one time he'd had a wife and children. But some men never married, and some were struck by tragedy. Gareth had lost his parents at a young age. Gwen's mother had died at Gwen's younger brother's birth, and by then all of her grandparents were dead. Nobody could predict the future. Gareth had decided long ago to live as well and as fully as he could up until he couldn't.

The canvas sides of the wagon were partially rolled up, and he glanced to where Gwen was sitting with the children inside the wagon. There was a new game now, involving chasing a bead around on the floor, trying to be the first to get it into a cup.

Turning back to Bran, he said, "If we are stopped, you may be in more danger with us than you would be on your own."

"You have your wife and children with you, as does Meicol. You can't think they would come to harm?"

"I hope not, but I couldn't leave them at Ysbyty Cynfyn to find out."

"I would feel the same. I do feel the same. I'll take my chances." Bran gave Gareth a sardonic smile. "Same as you." He sounded like an old soldier who, as Gareth had just been ruminating, had also learned to take the world as it came.

Gareth gave him a nod of acknowledgment and then slowed his horse so he could resume his position at the rear of the wagon. This time, Gwen came to the back to talk to him. With all the rain they'd had, the wagons weren't kicking up dust, which could make being at the end of the line unpleasant. "Having made it safely this far, am I wrong to think things are slightly less precarious?"

"I don't know, *cariad.*" Gareth wanted to reassure her, but he also knew that he shouldn't, because he didn't know.

"How far behind us do you think they are?" She meant Cadell's army.

"It depends on whether Hywel's men are in pursuit. If not, they are free to take their time. They sacked a village church. I can't help but worry about the innkeeper I talked to last spring, or the owner of that tavern at the crossroads who helped Llelo and Dai."

"If you were Hywel, would you have pursued them?"

Gareth was forced to give her another shake of his head. "I don't know that I would have, but I wasn't in the castle either. This isn't a war like any other we've fought. There are few pitched battles here. It's all about wearing the other side down. Hywel won this one, but Cadell is determined, and I fear he will be back for more before long."

"Meanwhile, the common folk suffer the most. Even if Ysbyty Cynfyn isn't destroyed, it could be a lean rest of the winter for the monks there." Typically, Gwen was thinking of others before herself. "I just wish I knew *why*?"

"We do know why, Gwen. Cadell wants Deheubarth whole again and doesn't care that it's at the expense of Hywel or violates the compact his father made with King Owain. To Cadell, that was years ago, before he was king. He gets to make the decisions now, and he has no loyalty to the past. Certainly, he has none to his stepmother's family. They aren't his relatives. He doesn't have to care about them. If he can't get the better of the Normans to the south, he'll take what he can from the Welsh to the north."

"He has no honor."

"I imagine he thinks honor is either for fools or for those who can afford it. Or, he looks honorable to himself, regardless of what those of us who oppose him think." Gareth was walking his horse, and he had to pause to navigate a particularly deep hole in the road. "Really, that doesn't make him all that different from our lord. While Prince Hywel has matured over the years as his responsibilities have grown, he doesn't have as finely honed a sense of honor as I, preferring at times expedience or practicality over doing what is demonstrably *right*."

"Mostly, he appreciates that in you," Gwen said. "We have accepted long since this difference between the two of you. He made you his steward because of it!"

"Of greater concern to me right now is what happened when Cadell's men arrived at Ysbyty Cynfyn."

"You fear they attacked the commandery too?"

"Less that, than what Cadell's men learned when they got there. Will they be told we had been there for months and where we went?"

Gwen's chin hardened. "I have not been impressed of late with Commander Reginald's resolve."

"Commander Reginald will tell the truth and would not see it as a crime if it meant saving his commandery."

"But the children—"

"Not only am I Hywel's steward, but Dai and I have been everywhere these last months, as Bran just reminded me." Gareth interrupted her, not to silence her, but because her voice had gone high for a moment in her anxiety, and he didn't want to worry the children behind her. "We are among those Hywel trusts most. Either of us could give Cadell a detailed report on Hywel's forces, his resources, and what he might do next."

Gwen took in a breath and let it out slowly. "They would also want to prevent you from reporting to Hywel what you know about Cadell's situation, now that the siege is lifted."

Gareth grimaced. "If Cadell made any threat to you or the children, I would tell him everything."

"I would like to think that would be petty, even for Cadell," Gwen laughed without amusement, "but I have come to see that it wouldn't."

8

Day One

Llelo

"You should have let me die, I tell you!" Cadell was utterly furious with Rhys, Iestyn, himself, God, and probably the entire world by this point. He sounded shockingly sincere in his wish for death.

Because of it, Llelo had warned Rhys to remove the belt knife at his waist, lest Cadell try to grab it in order to do himself an injury. He had seen the king eyeing it earlier. The idea of Cadell slitting his own throat would have been preposterous yesterday. Today, it was terrifyingly real, on top of all the horror that Llelo and Rhys had already witnessed.

"Cadell—" His brother's accusing words left Rhys unable to articulate a thought, a rare situation for him.

Iestyn, however, was implacable. "You are being unfair, my lord. Your brother could no more leave you to die than he could cut off his own sword arm. If dying is God's plan for you, you can die on the road as easily as in that clearing."

"Then *you* should have killed me, old friend. A quick upthrust under the ribs, and I would have been rid of all this. My head feels like someone has taken a pickaxe to it."

"Regicide? You suggest my name be shamed across the centuries? Would you have it be said that I murdered my closest friend in life?" Iestyn could talk to the king this way because they were friends, as he'd said, and also because Iestyn's brother, Ifor, was married to Rhys's sister, Nest. That made Iestyn and Cadell brothers-in-law by marriage.

Cadell's mouth worked. Even in his fury, he had to recognize the futility of his recriminations. Cadell had spent most of the day in unbearable pain, alleviated only by the juice of the poppy. That put him to sleep, however, which was why, only now as the sun was heading towards the horizon, he was coherent enough to make accusations. But if he was well enough to shout at his brother and his friend, then he wasn't, in point of fact, on the verge of dying. To have killed him, even in a misplaced sense of mercy, would truly have been regicide.

Llelo had been an unwilling witness to this conversation because he was one of the men currently enlisted to carry the bier upon which Cadell was lying. They had been taking it in turns carrying him, four men at a time, since they'd left the clearing. At first, the bier had been truly makeshift, consisting of a hemp tarp from someone's saddlebag, slung between two fairly straight branches. That had been functional, but extremely difficult to maneuver, and they'd struggled to keep the tarp from shifting. Twice, they'd dropped Cadell to the ground.

Then, one of Iestyn's men, who was from the area originally, had noted they were within a mile of a local church, St. Issell's. Like every church in Wales, it would have an actual bier, for the purpose of carrying a coffin from the church or laying out room to a grave. And the community was one of the few that still remained Welsh. If their Norman masters weren't about, they might be willing to help.

Iestyn sent the local man and three others to find out. They'd run all the way there and all the way back, even while carrying the bier. Having something sturdy upon which Cadell could lie had made their task far more manageable. Admittedly, the fact that the bier was normally used for carrying the dead, as Cadell had pointed out to Rhys back in the clearing, had done nothing to improve the king's mood.

Early on, someone had suggested they make for either Amroth or Llansteffan, both formerly Norman castles but now controlled by Cadell. Amroth, unfortunately, was a bit of a ruin at the moment, since much of it had burned in the taking of it, and it had been only partially rebuilt. Llansteffan was surrounded by other Norman strongholds. It might be reachable if they could steal a boat and sail Cadell to safety. But as Rhys was quick to point out, even if they managed to acquire a sufficiently large and seaworthy ship, none of them were sailors. Even more, once out to sea, they would have to contend with the very basic reality that the Normans controlled every other castle, village, and town on the south coast of Wales between Pembroke and Chepstow.

In other words, they were walking Cadell out of the Coed Rath or not leaving at all.

They'd traveled maybe three miles since then. Even with the improved bier, it was heavy work marching through the forest. By now, everyone had come to see that no matter how many men rotated through the task, it was going to be a long walk to get themselves out of Norman territory.

With a grateful smile, Llelo allowed another man to take his place, not even breaking stride to do it. Relieved of his burden, he let the bearers get ahead of him, shaking out his arms in relief.

"He's right, you know." Rhys, who had also been replaced at the bier, set off beside Llelo.

"Who? Cadell or Iestyn?" Llelo slowed his pace to allow the two of them to fall more towards the rear of the company. It wasn't entirely so they couldn't be overheard. If they were back here, others would set the pace. When either were in the front, with their long legs and youth, their tendency was to walk too quickly and outpace everyone else.

Their small force was also taking turns riding the available horses, with anyone on horseback tasked with scouting around their position. The entire company, which was really only a dozen men anyway, plus Cadell, couldn't progress any faster than the men who carried Cadell could walk. The job had become, more than anything, and maybe more than ever, to protect the king, dying or not, paralyzed or not.

"Cadell is right that I could have spared him what looks to be a painful and ignominious future. I could see how injured he was. I could have slipped my knife under his ribs into his heart, and nobody would have been the wiser. Except you." Rhys made a motion with his head. "It honestly never occurred to me."

"I suppose you could have done all that, but for the rest of your life you would have had to live with the fact that you'd killed your brother. An hour ago, he was incapable of speaking, thanks to the pain in his head. In the same way, the numbness in his legs could be temporary. He wouldn't thank you for killing him prematurely, if he's back to walking and riding a month from now."

"Well, he'd be dead, then, wouldn't he? We wouldn't know one way or another until I met him again in heaven. Or hell, I suppose, if killing him took the both of us there." Rhys's tone was matter-of-fact, which made Llelo feel a little better about his frame of mind. He was starting to recover. Both of them had seen death and carnage before, but neither had ever witnessed anything like the ambush in the clearing. "I also should have been the one to ride to Maredudd."

"No, Rhys. Iestyn made the right decision there, too. We don't know for certain where Maredudd is. We can't have you riding off into the wilderness."

During the interlude in which Iestyn's men had run for the bier, Iestyn had singled out two more for further duty: one to ride to Maredudd to tell him he must return to the south at once; and the second to Caerfyrddin, a castle the Normans called Carmarthen, which was situated on the very edge of Welsh territory. Once exclusively a Welsh stronghold, the Normans had built it into a motte and bailey castle, which itself had been rebuilt many times over the decades, as the region had gone back and forth between Norman and

Welsh control. Currently, the castle was Cadell's, captured during the same period he'd taken Wiston. It was the first Welsh castle they would come to, but also the most precariously positioned, right on the border between Welsh and Norman-held territory.

They would have liked to make Dinefwr, Cadell's primary seat in Deheubarth, but that was another twenty miles farther on. An impossibility. From Caerfyrddin, a different rider could take the high road to Dinefwr. All would be shocked to hear what had happened to Cadell, not to mention to his entire *teulu*. That was an additional grief Llelo didn't think the men here had yet encompassed, focused as they were on the task at hand.

"Maredudd is at Aberystwyth," Rhys said.

"Maybe."

Rhys gave Llelo a dark look. "What do you mean *maybe*? We know he is besieging Hywel's castle there."

"We know he *was* besieging it." From the start, both men had accepted that they would have to agree to disagree on the merits of the attack on Prince Hywel's holdings in Ceredigion. Rhys didn't want to fight his cousin, but he also resented the way King Owain had appropriated (or, to speak as Cadell did, *stolen)* that entire region of Deheubarth after the 1136 war. Never mind that it was part of the treaty the two kings had made as a condition of Gwynedd's participation. "What we don't know is the outcome. Even if Maredudd is where we think he is, between the mucky roads and the weather, who knows how long it will take for the messenger to get to him? If Cadell does die, God forbid, you will be needed here."

Rhys's chin was still sticking out in a posture of stubbornness. His heart wanted to believe the best of people while his mind was capable of seeing the worst. "I don't understand what you're saying. Why would I be needed?"

Llelo turned his head to look directly at his friend, who must be more shocked than he'd thought to be seeing the future so unclearly. "One brother may be on his deathbed. The next is in enemy territory leading a siege. Tomorrow you could be the only member of the House of Dinefwr left standing. You would then be king."

"I don't—" Rhys broke off at the intense look Llelo sent him.

It had been Llelo's job from the very beginning of their relationship to speak the truth. He wasn't going to stop now, just because that truth was difficult for Rhys to encompass. "You may not be the heir to the throne of Deheubarth yet, but if Cadell dies, or is no longer capable of leading, you will be."

9

Day One

Gwen

"Help me down. I'd like to walk for this last bit." Gwen had placed Angharad in the sling again. At intervals, everyone in the wagon had walked beside it. Now that they were within striking distance of the commandery of Ysbyty Ystwyth, Gwen was finding her legs restless. "I can only hope the commander can provide us with shelter for the night—and isn't interested in spending very much time on questions."

Ysbyty Ystwyth, like Ysbyty Cynfyn, was a Hospitaller commandery. And like Ysbyty Cynfyn, it was located on the pilgrim road to the great monastery of Mynachlog Fawr, which had been founded sixty years earlier by the then King of Deheubarth, Rhys ap Tudur. At the time, he'd been in the ascendancy against the first wave of Norman invaders to this region.

King Cadell had paid for the rebuilding of the abbey after the ruinous wars in which Prince Rhys's mother, brothers, and father had lost their lives. When Hywel had taken over the area, he hadn't touched the monastery except to assure the monks he had no intention of harming them in any way. He'd said the same to the Hospitallers at both Ystwyth and Cynfyn, even though their foundations were Norman instead of Welsh.

The abbey was even more remote than the Hospitaller commanderies, since it lay in the hills to the east, a few miles off the road they were on now. Its existence was the reason the two commanderies had been established in the first place. Most of the larger settlements in Ceredigion were on the coast, like Aberystwyth. The deeper into the countryside pilgrims traveled, the more in need they could become.

Like many Welsh holy sites, there had been a religious community of some kind at Mynachlog Fawr before Rhys ap Tudur had established the current abbey. Perhaps eventually it would be superseded by yet another foundation, especially if control of the region went back to the Normans. Christian armies were supposed to protect churches and monasteries, but if an invading commander learned that monks were harboring or abetting his enemy, he might raze their abbey to the ground. Such an eventuality didn't bear thinking about. Hywel was having enough trouble with Cadell and his brothers.

"If not, we might be able to skirt it and make for Mynachlog Fawr tonight. It is only another five miles farther on." Gareth dismounted and, hand-in-hand, he and Gwen set out beside the wagon, Gareth leading his horse by its reins. "I don't want you to be fearful, Gwen. While very little of what we've seen out of Cadell's camp of late has made sense to me, I do honestly believe our lives are not in danger."

Part of Gwen wished she hadn't said anything because his words had the opposite effect he'd intended. She'd kept half an eye all day on the road behind them, and now fear roiled her belly again as she considered the road ahead. Still, there was very little in this life she didn't share with Gareth, including her worst fears. The same was true of Gareth in regards to her, which was why he'd answered her honestly. They shouldn't start hiding things from each other now. "What went wrong in Aberystwyth, do you think? I was so relieved to hear the siege had failed, I never asked."

"Disease. Within an army, it's never just a few men. As more fail, more start to despair. Men desert. The battle is lost before it's begun."

"In only three weeks? They had five hundred men!"

"A few sickened within a day or two of starting north. Two becomes ten becomes a hundred very quickly in close conditions. The storms added insult to injury. Marching north to besiege Hywel's castle in the middle of winter was clever. If Dai and I hadn't spotted them early on and ridden hard to stay ahead of them, Hywel would have been completely surprised. But there's a reason armies don't fight in winter, and what happened to Cadell's force at Aberystwyth is one of them."

"I do remember," Gwen said. "That first storm continued nigh unceasing for three days."

"I've lived through similar conditions. Soaked day and night, unable to light a fire because there's no dry wood—or anything dry at all. The men would have suffered through cold or undercooked food. Dai and I were watching from afar, so we were able to speak to the local people who were conscripted to help with fodder for the horses or physicking Cadell's men. A plan that had started in surety and enthusiasm turned very quickly to misery. They endured three successive storms and were no closer to taking the castle than when they'd started. The churchyard at St Hychan's saw fifty new burials in a matter of a fortnight."

Gwen had been wet at times, too, this last month, but she'd been able to retreat inside the commandery buildings. "And Cadell's commander couldn't order the burning of the castle, like Hywel did at Llanrhystud last spring, because everything was soaking wet."

Gareth made a qualifying motion with his head. "In truth, Hywel was lucky in the weather and Cadell's men unlucky. More than anything, I think that's why they retreated. God was not on their side, and they knew it. The inclement weather and the spreading sickness told them so as loudly and clearly as if it had been shouted from the top of Hywel's keep."

Gwen glanced over her shoulder at the road behind them. "I wish I knew what was happening with them." She met her husband's eyes. "Laying waste to the countryside in Ceredigion is not the best way to subdue people Cadell wants to rule. It's what Normans do. But then, they spend the rest of their lives barricaded inside their high walls."

"Maybe Cadell has spent so much time with Normans he has come to see their way as the correct one."

"Either that or he—" Gwen broke off as, up ahead, Dai raised a hand, calling for the caravan to halt.

Meilyr and Meicol reined in the horses pulling the wagons, allowing Gareth and Gwen to catch up to where Dai was standing. He was off the road, having dismounted, talking to a man perhaps ten years older than Gareth.

At their arrival, Dai motioned his parents closer. "Cadell's people have taken the commandery at Ystwyth too." Like Meilyr at the start of the day, he was admirably matter-of-fact about something that was, in fact, a disaster.

"How many?" Gareth asked.

"A hundred. No more than that."

"A hundred against the few of us is still impossible."

Dai gazed back down the still empty road behind them. "Can we—"

"We can't go back." Gareth was as sure with Dai as he'd been with Gwen.

Dai dropped his voice to a whisper. "I could stay with Mam and the children, while you—"

Gareth cut him off. "While I what? Flee? Ride back to Ysbyty Cynfyn or Aberystwyth?" He gave his son a long look. "Do you truly think I could ever abandon my family?"

"To save your life, I would want you to."

"Would you be the one to leave, if I asked?"

"Only if you ordered me to, and then under protest." He bit his lip. "I would do it if it meant saving a life other than my own."

Gwen bent her head, more proud of her son than she could express.

Gareth put his arm around Dai's shoulders and squeezed. "Neither of us will go. As your mother and I concluded before all this started, we will face whatever comes … together."

10

Day One

Rhys

“**M**aredudd doesn’t know about me, does he? I mean, about who I really am.” Llelo and Rhys had been talking about Cadell, but now Llelo switched to talking about Rhys’s other brother.

Rhys shook his head. “I didn’t tell him.”

“I have never asked before because I felt it wasn’t my business, but can you tell me why you kept him in the dark? I know you trust him more than anyone.”

“It isn’t that I don’t trust him—” Rhys broke off before he admitted he trusted Llelo and his parents more than his own brother. It was strange to have such faith in people he, in many ways, barely knew. At the same time, their fidelity was an absolute in his life. Llelo had come to Dinefwr when Rhys had called, with his parents’ approval. He’d joined the Hospitallers for him. He’d saved his life. It wasn’t really possible to imagine a better friend.

So, he sighed. "I love my brother, and I *would* trust him with my life, but—" He stopped, unable to carry on with this last truth either, now that it came to it.

"He feels the need to impress his elders more than you do."

That drew Rhys's gaze. "You do go straight to the heart of every issue, don't you? How did you figure that out so quickly, despite never having spoken with him?"

"Because I feel the same as he does."

"I would not have said you were much like Maredudd."

"I am an older brother, who feels the pressure of a younger, more capable brother pushing up at him."

Rhys had to wrinkle his nose at the comparison to Dai.

Llelo gave a little tsk to see it. "You know as well as I that Maredudd is far more reckless and pig-headed than he should be. He could get himself killed quicker than Cadell. While Cadell made a mistake today, he is a strategic thinker. Maredudd is a fine fighter and a leader of men, too, but he's also full of bravado and rage. If nothing else, if he becomes king, you are going to have to do the strategizing for him. I respect that you won't usurp your brother's throne, but you need to start thinking like a king."

Rhys's jaw clenched. "You have never described either of my brothers that way to me. I could be angry."

"But you aren't, because this is what I'm here for."

Rhys shook that off like a fly buzzing around his head. Since Maredudd hadn't been at Dinefwr four years ago, he'd never met Llelo or Gareth. Maredudd and Rhys had encountered each other so infrequently of late, Maredudd hadn't questioned the arrival of this strange Hospitaller knight in Rhys's midst. It was a sad fact that the two of them hadn't been as close in recent years as they had been as children. Cadell had kept them apart with different adult roles, and Rhys had come to wonder if that was on purpose. Certainly because of it, he had trusted Llelo more than his own blood brother.

And really, Llelo *had* been speaking truths to Rhys all along, albeit not so bluntly as today. Maybe Llelo's newfound assertiveness arose from witnessing the ambush. The vision of it was constantly before Rhys's eyes, like he was seeing the world through a veil of light and dust.

They would share that for the rest of their lives, no matter what became of them. "I can only repeat: Cadell is the king; he is in pain and he's injured, but his mind still works as well as ever."

"That may be, but already these men are looking at you differently. You hadn't noticed?" Llelo was still speaking quietly, which only served to make his words more forceful rather than less.

"I guess I had. I didn't understand why." Rhys shook himself. "They shouldn't be thinking about me in that way. Cadell is alive."

"For now." Llelo was relentless. "But how long will men follow a king who can't walk? Whose head aches so much he is out of his mind with pain when he isn't insensate with poppy? There will be defections within his court, sooner rather than later. Men will jostle for power. What will you do then?"

"Not have this conversation, that's what."

"You're being stubborn. You have to know it."

Rhys was being stubborn, and he did know it. He couldn't admit it yet, though, not even to Llelo, who studied him for a long moment without speaking.

And then for longer. The silence dragged on for so long that Rhys had to succumb with a bit more of the truth. He could have cursed Gareth for teaching Llelo the technique if he hadn't also made Llelo the man who'd saved Rhys's life today. "If I am being honest, which I always try to be, at least to myself, I am feeling guilty for ever suspecting Cadell of treachery. Whatever my former fears, I can see no path forward but to revert once again to loyal brother and subject."

"As you should. I never meant to imply otherwise. It is my job to continue to be suspicious and to advise you accordingly."

"You don't think Cadell is speaking the truth, even now?"

Llelo pressed his lips together as he thought. "Let's just say I am not convinced of Cadell's beneficence. Regardless of his current predicament, he conspired with Cadwaladr to assassinate his older brother *and* King Owain Gwynedd. That Owain isn't dead, too, appears to be a result of circumstance and luck, not for a lack of trying. Cadell sent an assassin to Gwynedd. My guess is the man lost his nerve or was simply incompetent."

"Or maybe he took his payment and ran."

"Regardless, he has not completed his task ... as far as we know," Llelo added darkly.

As they continued to plod along, side-by-side, Rhys thought about the fear that had prompted him to summon Llelo months ago. It had felt like a last resort, as if whatever treachery Cadell was plotting was coming to fruition. "Just now, when Cadell wasn't asking me to put him out of his misery, he was wanting more *dwale*. It is the only thing that relieves his pain."

Llelo skittered a glance in Rhys's direction. "I hope everyone knows to be careful about his dosages. If the pain doesn't subside soon, he is going to have to learn to live with it—so he doesn't go the way of the monks at Ysbyty Cynfyn." He had long since related to Rhys the full story of the events of last spring. Rhys had visited Llelo and his family there, on a mission of his own, not knowing how serious their own investigation would turn out to be.

But even having been told the story, Rhys hadn't fully comprehended the reason *dwale* was made with vinegar: patients had a need for it, but they would never develop a taste for it. Rhys himself had been injured last year—healed now to a long scar down his thigh—and at the time had choked down the potion for the relief it brought. He did not long to taste it again, no matter how much pain he might experience. Toughing it out was better than that unique, bitter vileness.

Rhys had been expected to heal well and hadn't been in as much prolonged pain as Cadell. While the king's pain might not, in the end, be as continuous as it was in this moment, Rhys could see the pessimism in the faces of everyone around him.

So he said now, "It is time for me to thank you. Not just for saving my life but for everything you have done for me and for Deheubarth up until this point. And for everything I know you will continue to do. If I seem ungrateful, it is because of a flaw in me, rather than in you. Do not allow me to chastise you, even for a heartbeat. You saved my life today. By saving mine, you saved Cadell's too, since it was you who discovered he still lived. Don't ever stop speaking as you have been. I might whine and wail at you when what you say isn't what I want to hear. But that is my problem, not yours."

"Thank you," Llelo said softly. "Please know I could never mean to hurt you."

Rhys gave a little scoff. "The truth I need to admit is that I don't want to be king, at least not yet. If I ever thought about the possibility, I envisioned becoming king in my old age, simply because I am the youngest son."

"Youngest sons have become kings before. And sooner."

"I suppose so, though I never saw it as more than a remote possibility, not worth thinking about, and certainly not worth dwelling on or planning for. I once had three older brothers—five, if you count Morgan and Maelgwn, who died with my mother when I was four years old. All of them should have married and had children of their own, putting me farther and farther from the throne with every year that passed. Maredudd and I surely should have been surplus to requirements."

"Except six is now three, and soon could be only two. Two is a very different number from six. Two makes you the *edling* and the only representative of the House of Dinefwr currently in Deheubarth. Even if Cadell lives, he will need help over the next days, weeks, or months running his kingdom."

"Maredudd—"

Llelo overrode him, even more forcefully than before. "Maredudd can lead the army, but the person who should actually be running things? That needs to be *you*."

Rhys drew in a breath. Over the course of their conversation, the more Llelo had persisted in forcing Rhys to think about the rule of Deheubarth, the more he had resisted the idea. But this last comment, for whatever reason, gave him pause. If Cadell were to die and Maredudd to become king, how would Rhys feel? Could he follow orders from yet another brother, when he knew them to be foolish or wrong?

All of a sudden, Rhys squared his shoulders. It wasn't his intent to influence the men around him, but the few who were closest, acting as the rear guard with Rhys and Llelo, straightened a bit as well.

They also picked up their pace, such that in a matter of a hundred feet, they'd caught up to the bier again. As Rhys came abreast of his brother's form, Cadell put out a hand to him, and Rhys took it. To do so felt like the most natural thing in the world, despite the fact that he had never done it before today. Neither man had been disposed towards affectionate gestures. They'd come a long way in a few hours.

"You are going to survive this, Cadell," Rhys said. "Believe it. More than that, *want* it. We're not going to be able to do anything for you, if you aren't also looking out for yourself."

Cadell had turned to look when Rhys spoke his initial words, but now he closed his eyes. He still held Rhys's hand, however, perhaps more tightly than before. "There has to be retribution. You know it."

Iestyn was walking on Cadell's other side. "We don't need to worry about that yet, my lord. Our first task is to get you safe. We are hanging on by our fingernails here, surrounded by the *Saeson*." That was the Welsh word for the invaders, originally Saxons, but applied equally to English and Normans.

"Safe? I don't want to be *safe*."

In a flash of clarity, Rhys realized *this* was the moment Llelo had been talking about. With Cadell incapacitated, even Iestyn, who had decades of life on Rhys, was looking to Rhys for answers.

He had to provide them. He had no choice, never mind how inadequate he'd felt ever since he had lain impotently on his belly in the leaves and grass of the forest, Llelo sprawled on top of him, holding him down.

"Maredudd and I will hunt down every man who did this if we have to spend the rest of our days doing it. Anyone associated with this treachery is living on borrowed time. We will raze Tenby Castle to the ground. I swear it." Rhys had spoken loudly enough for not only Iestyn and Cadell to hear, but for the men carrying the bier.

As before, there was a subtle straightening of shoulders, emblematic of the men's shared purpose. They didn't have to wonder anymore about what was happening. They'd needed a direction, and Rhys had given them one. What's more, they knew now that when they needed Rhys to take charge, they could count on him to do it. From long experience, they respected men who were able to speak aloud what had to be done.

As Iestyn moved more towards the front of the troop, talking to one man or another, as a means to further raise their confidence, Cadell tugged on Rhys's hand, getting him to lean closer. "Well done, brother." He spoke in French this time, a language none of the men around them would understand. "Now the hard part begins. I am sure you've realized by now that the men of Tenby are not the only traitors. We have another in our midst. If I don't survive this journey, don't repeat my mistakes. You can't trust *anyone.*"

11

Day One

Gwen

Their party came to a halt at the front gate of the commandery. It was still standing, even if the monks, whom the soldiers had gathered in the central square, were looking uniquely miserable. As the day had worn on, the air had turned colder, rather than warmer, with the weak sun that had graced them with its presence this afternoon no longer peeking through the cloud cover. Given the drop in temperature, it might even be preparing to snow. More likely, the weather would do what it usually did this time of year, which would be to remain just too warm to snow and give them more rain.

Cadell's army was even now swarming all through the commandery. What they were not doing, Gwen was pleased to see, was robbing the place, harming the monks, or burning the buildings to the ground. If she had to guess, the burning of the church to the north had not been part of a larger strategy to intimidate the populace. It showed instead that the captain of those men had less control over them than did the commander here. He couldn't be the same man, since a giant canyon separated the two places. Gwen's family's caravan had crossed on the only bridge.

With their arrival, an older man, judging by the lines on his face, of average height and with thick shoulders, detached himself from a group of soldiers milling near the gatehouse and came onto the road to speak to Gareth. He was trailed by a second man, who looked to be a younger version of himself in height and weight, though with brown hair instead of gray and finer features. Both were dressed well, in sturdy boots and thick cloaks, the better to keep out the weather, whatever it decided to do. Both also wore mail, indicating their relative wealth and possible nobility. Gwen didn't recognize either one.

The older man stopped a pace outside the gatehouse. "Who are you?"

This came out as a question, but Gwen knew it for the command it was. The man also spoke in Welsh, as he would. Probably Cadell's entire retinue and every single one of the men in this army were Welsh and spoke it natively. There was no reason to question this truth. That didn't mean Gwen, who'd spent most of her life regretting the Normans' very existence, didn't feel it was wrong, somehow. Normans were the enemy. Or should be.

Gwen knew how Gareth was going to reply before he did. He appeared to spend a few heartbeats examining his reasoning and resolve for the hundredth time since they'd left Ysbyty Cynfyn. But, as always, he came down on the side of telling the truth. The wagons full of women and children could have allowed them to travel unmolested to some safe haven within Wales. If they'd managed to evade the soldiers entirely, Gareth could have carried on as merely the son-in-law of a bard. He hadn't wanted to put away his mail and sword, however, not while still in a war zone, fearing he might need both at a moment's notice. And now, a commander within Cadell's forces had just asked him a direct question.

He couldn't lie any more than he could turn his skin to green. "I am Gareth ap Rhys."

Gwen was standing a few paces away, with Angharad in her sling. She didn't even sigh. She knew her husband; she knew the man he had chosen to be. That he would tell the truth, even under these circumstances, was, of course, where honor was lost or found—when it was hard, not when it was easy. Maybe some part of Gwen wished Gareth wasn't quite as rigid in his interpretation of right and wrong at times, but she couldn't have all that was remarkable about him without that part too.

The man blinked once. "You are steward to Hywel, son of King Owain Gwynedd?"

"Yes."

"We have been looking for you." The man smiled, not like a cat who'd licked a bowl of cream, but genuinely, up into his eyes.

Gwen found herself blinking back her own surprise, less that they would have been looking for Gareth, because they had to have known about his activities after all these months, but that this commander would admit to it.

"Have you?" Gareth managed to keep his voice steady.

"For some time, actually." The smile was still there, turning more into one of satisfaction, as for a job well done.

Belatedly, Gwen realized Gareth should not be engaging with this man. Probably he should have sent one of the other men to the front to speak to the soldier instead. It was too late now for that regret, and Gareth wouldn't have countenanced it anyway. But, as a consequence, Gareth gave up his weapons, once the older soldier told one of his men to disarm him, even going so far as to remove his bracers and depriving them all of the tiny knives secreted within the leather.

Meicol and Bran, the two older men in their party, received the same treatment, neither of them happy about it but not protesting. Rather than coming closer as Gwen had, Dai stayed a bit to the back of the caravan, but he couldn't escape either. Nor could Ieuan, in the end. Although encumbered by the least gear and provisions, he was revealed to be surprisingly well-armed, not only with the bow and quiver on his back, but with two knives at his waist and a third in his boot. None of the blades was of high quality, but he could be given credit for coming prepared. Soon all four were made to stand in a row a pace behind Gareth.

After that, even Gwen's father, who had been sitting resolutely on his wagon seat this whole time, was forced to get down. He had only his belt knife to give up. The women and children, Gwen among them, were gathered in the road by now too. None of them had been hurt or abused, and while the older soldier asked each for the knives they wore at their waists, he made sure to keep a step back and not to touch them. Gwen deliberated about giving up the knife she carried strapped to her calf under her long skirt, but in the end left it where it was. It was a matter of practicality and protecting her family. It wasn't as if Gareth had offered up his bracers. They'd just taken them. She took his reticence in this as a sign there was a difference between answering a direct question honestly and submitting oneself willingly to the slaughter.

The soldiers then began a search of the wagons, which was accomplished in near silence by all parties. None of Gwen's people said anything at all, beyond some grumbling on the part of Meilyr, who told the soldiers looking through his possessions not to damage his instruments.

It was the twang of a harp that prompted the older soldier, who'd spoken to Gareth first and had been walking up and down on the edge of the road while his men went through the wagons, to swing back. "Who is this, then? Who travels with you?"

He'd come to rest right in front of Gwen, so she chose to answer. "You are looking at my father, the esteemed bard, Meilyr ap Mabon. You see also my son, Dai—"

"I am Bran, and this is my son, Ieuan." Bran instantly made the young man a part of his own family.

Gwen had been about to do the same, not because she genuinely intended to adopt another youth but because Ieuan's parentage did not matter in this moment. Besides, Bran was right that a man and boy traveling together were less immediately suspicious than either traveling alone. "Among us also are Meicol's wife, Mari, and their small children; Nest, a widow with two daughters; and my father's wife, Saran, who is a healer. I am Gwen, Gareth's wife, and these are our three youngest children."

The older soldier absorbed all this with a glance at each person as Gwen listed them off. "What was your destination?"

"We were heading to the abbey at Mynachlog Fawr." By naming the abbey, and really by answering instead of Gareth, Gwen had been trying to make clear they were not a threat. They had no idea what lay in store for them. There was no chance these men were going to release them on their own recognizance. But they might consent to confinement at a large and well-established abbey.

"Thank you, Tomos. I have heard enough. I'll take it from here." The second man, who'd watched the proceedings this whole time with an unreadable expression, moved to the fore. "As Tomos said, we have heard of you. Have you heard of me? I am Maredudd ap Gruffydd, brother to King Cadell."

12

Day One

Gareth

Relief overtook Gareth's surprise. "My lord, it is an honor to meet you."

"Pretty words, but you serve my cousin. Leave him with me." The latter comment was not directed at Gareth, but at his men, including Tomos. With a flick of his fingers, Maredudd sent them all away.

Tomos didn't want to go. "My lord, are you sure?"

"Do not worry, Tomos. He will not harm me."

"But—"

Maredudd turned on the older man more fully. That Maredudd was two years older than Rhys meant he was two years older than Llelo too, since those young men were born within a few months of each other. In other words, Maredudd was young, barely twenty. "I appreciate your concern, but it is misplaced. This is the great Gareth ap Rhys, as you have already discovered. I am safe with him, regardless of his ultimate allegiance."

Tomos bent his head. "Yes, my lord." The pair were obviously very familiar with each other, beyond the older man's station as second-in-command, for him to question Maredudd that way in front of his captives.

"Leave their weapons and gear with me. I need you to ready the men to continue the journey. Like our friend here, I want to reach Mynachlog Fawr by this evening." Maredudd shot Gareth a wry look. "As it so happens, we were headed there, too."

This time, Tomos didn't protest. Once he'd gone, Maredudd began to pace. For the first time, Gareth could see the family resemblance. Otherwise, except for his coloring, which was dark like Rhys's, the two looked nothing alike.

That was helpful to Gareth because, despite his initial relief in knowing he was being captured by Rhys's brother, Maredudd was *not* Rhys. Rhys, were he here instead, might have made the observation that his underlings hadn't yet learned not to question his judgment. Gareth would have then commiserated with him and told him he was doing well, like a kindly uncle might.

Gareth didn't know Maredudd at all, and now was not the time for forced confidences, not until he had a better sense of the man. Maredudd also needed time to take the measure of Gareth. It was delightful—nay, beyond important—that Maredudd not only knew who Gareth was but, to all appearances, respected him. A moment ago, as his family was being searched, Gareth had been cursing his inability to lie. He had thought that, by giving his name, he had condemned his whole family. It was his job to protect them, and he had failed because of this ridiculous notion of honor. And here, the reason Maredudd was able to stand before Gareth unprotected was because of that very honor.

It was a good reminder of who he was and why he did what he did. Trying to change that, regretting how he'd lived these last fifteen years, would be a betrayal all on its own.

"I cannot release you." Maredudd looked at him from under bushy eyebrows. "You know this?"

"I suspected that might be the case."

Again, if this were Rhys, Gareth would have spoken freely about this oddly shared circumstance. He didn't want to be a captive, and Rhys wouldn't have wanted to capture him, but they both had obligations that required it. For now, Gareth didn't trust Maredudd enough, and maybe not even at all, to do anything more than assent.

"Since I am loath to imprison babies or have it appear so to my men, who know who you are too, I have a question for you. Don't answer immediately if your first response isn't *yes*. Please think about it seriously first." Maredudd took in a breath and let it out. "Would you be willing to work for me, in exchange for freedom of movement for yourself and your family?"

Gareth's first impulse was not, in fact, to say *no*, but to glance towards Gwen, who had moved close enough to hear. He very much wanted to know what she thought about Maredudd's query. To look at her would indicate uncertainty, however, which he couldn't afford. So, instead, he hedged. "I suppose it depends on what you mean by *work*."

"Ah, a diplomat, not ready to commit. I suppose I knew you would be, given my brother's description of you. And, as I said, I would rather you ask questions than say *no* outright." Maredudd gave him a thoughtful smile. To be totally honest, Gareth would have preferred not to see it. He didn't like being predictable, even though it seemed he was. Entirely. "In short, my captain is dead. I need you to discover who murdered him." And then he picked up Gareth's sword from the pile of weapons his men had left at his feet and held it out. The sword was still in its sheath with the belt wrapped around it. "Temporary service, I assure you. Determine who murdered my man; travel with me while you do. That's all I ask."

All, Gareth felt like saying. "Where is it you travel?"

"South."

And if I don't? was foremost on his lips. He didn't speak those words. He already knew the threat: *do this, and your family will remain unmolested.* Maredudd hadn't needed to say it.

"Even were I to agree, what makes you think I could be of help?"

"You are renowned for investigating murders, are you not? I can't help but think more than good fortune has brought you to me. I have a murderer to find, and here you are, the very man capable of finding him."

"Who have you had investigating the death so far? Won't he mind me coming in and stepping on his toes?"

Maredudd didn't have an easy answer to that. Or, at least, he didn't want to give one, because he studied Gareth's face for a long moment. "Only a few of us know how Rhodri died. It was the first night out from Aberystwyth, and I saw no reason to unsettle the men more than they already were."

"So, if I am understanding you correctly, you want me to in-vestigate a murder that nobody but a few of you, plus the murderer, even knows was committed?"

"That's it exactly."

If faced with anyone else, or any other circumstance but this one, Gareth might have laughed. Instead, he took his sword from Maredudd's hand. They both knew he had no choice but to help. He could tell himself no murder should go uninvestigated, but he knew he was doing this to protect his family. And maybe that was another saving grace for him, in that Maredudd was asking him to do the one thing that was already within Gareth's purview. There was no betray-al of Hywel here.

Still, Gareth felt diminished to hear himself agreeing. "I will swear no allegiance."

"I do not ask for it. Only your skill and your honesty."

Gareth genuinely wasn't sure what Hywel would make of this change of direction. He wasn't entirely sure himself! Nonetheless, as he unwound the belt from the sword, he nodded his acquiescence. "Both of those, in this instance, I can give you."

13

Day One

Llelo

Rhys was walking beside Llelo again. Though, really, they were both trudging by now. The day had, in a word, waned, not because it was that late but because this time of year allowed them barely eight hours of daylight. They'd met the men from Tenby shortly before midday. They'd walked many miles since then. And now the sun had set.

The two of them had once again fallen farther back from the end of the line of marching men, having both just finished a turn carrying Cadell. The king appeared to be asleep. Or maybe he was unconscious. It was hard to tell. Regardless, his silence was a relief. For the last hour, he'd been out of his mind with pain. He wanted to rise from the bier, to walk, to run. Everyone feared he would never do any of those things again.

In the hours since they'd put Cadell on the bier, they'd come about halfway to Caerfyrddin, on the whole making excellent time for walking men, especially carrying the dead weight of their king.

They'd just concluded a rough hour avoiding the Norman stronghold at St. Clears. The castle had a grand view of the river valley it protected because it sat at the confluence of the River Taf and the Dewi Fawr. Thus, if they were to avoid being seen, they had to skirt it to the north. That meant walking through higher ground and rougher terrain. A short while ago, they'd arrived back on the main road again, with the promise of making straight for Caerfyrddin now that it was dark.

Mile after mile today, Llelo had been unable to stop his mind's review of the ambush. As soon as he reached the end, he would relentlessly return to the beginning again. *What more could we have done?* His mind told him the answer was *nothing*. His heart didn't necessarily agree.

"How far is it from Ysbyty Cynfyn to Caerfyrddin?" Rhys asked.

"Fifty miles or so. Why?" Llelo knew the answer because, when he'd come south at Rhys's request, he'd ridden to Caerfyrddin first before taking the high road east to Dinefwr. Once past the old Roman fort at Llanio, another road went more directly to Dinefwr, but his parents had been worried about him taking it so late in the year, since it ascended into the mountains.

Rhys gave a little snort. "Right about now your father's advice would be helpful."

"I'd like to see my father too. What would you be looking for from him?" Llelo had been thinking about his parents a great deal since the Coed Rath, while at the same time trying not to think about them at all. He couldn't help them. They couldn't help him. He was supposed to be a churchman, too, who relied upon God to do the worrying for him. Somehow, that was easier said than done.

Even more, his mind kept wandering to his brother and how he was faring. Dai was brilliant in so many ways. Maybe because of that, he was also reckless, especially without Llelo there to rein him in. Llelo kept imagining his family walking through the gates of Caerfyrddin at the same time he did. It was impossible, of course. And worse, if they ever did, Cadell would ensure they ended the day in the basement of the keep.

"I have been thinking about what my brother said: *Don't trust anyone*. What does he mean by that? Who can't I trust?" For Rhys to have been thinking wasn't the same as when other men said those words. Rhys *thought*. Very often, Llelo struggled to keep up.

"Anyone, apparently. Maybe even me."

Rhys's eyes appeared to cross. "After today, you are the one person I do trust. I have said that already."

"Maybe you shouldn't. I could be the traitor."

"You? You saved my life."

"If I was the one conspiring with Earl Clare, I would have known they were coming. I moved us just in time. I held you down rather than let you come to your brother's aid."

"If you were conspiring with Earl Clare, you would have let them have me." Rhys was almost angry now. "Why are you saying this?"

Llelo spread his hands wide. "Because someone has to. Another might, if he knew my real identity. It could be argued that

Gwynedd's best interests would be served by Cadell's death and your brother on the throne. Or you."

"That's a convoluted argument, Llelo, even for us!" Rhys made a motion with his head, in clear dismissal of what Llelo had just laid out. "Here's what I'm wondering: *why* were Gerald and the men from Tenby so anxious to depart the clearing? You saw how they were. They scavenged, as Danes would have done, but they had their wounded mounted, their dead thrown over our horses, and were heading back south less than a quarter of an hour after the last of our people hit the ground. They were supposed to search the bodies, but I think they missed that Cadell was still alive because they were so quick about it."

"Why doesn't that make sense to you? I wouldn't have wanted to be caught standing over the murdered body of the King of Deheubarth either." Just saying the words gave Llelo a moment's pause. How strange was it that it was his own father who'd been found standing over the murdered body of Anarawd, the previous King of Deheubarth and Cadell's elder brother. He'd been accused of his murder, if briefly. And it was that investigation that had brought his parents together all those years ago.

"Yes, but *why* were they worried about it? The meeting had been deliberately set for a location in the middle of the woods. It could be a month—a year!—before anyone comes across that clearing again. They had all the time in the world if they'd wanted it."

"They did have wounded men," Llelo said slowly, not sure where Rhys was going with this idea. "They needed treatment."

"Treatment that could have been better given in the clearing. Some of them were wrapping bandages around their wounds as they rode away." Rhys shook his head. "You're missing my point, which ties directly into my second concern. How did Iestyn come to be in that clearing in the first place?"

"Iestyn knew Cadell was hunting in the Coed Rath. Since he had a message to deliver from his brother, and he was not opposed to hunting Norman deer in a Norman wood, he brought his force in too."

"The forest is huge. How did he find us?"

Llelo was confident in this answer. "Lord Huw told him where to go. Head south from the standing stone, he said. And then Iestyn heard the sound of fighting." Huw was Cadell's steward, in the same way Lord Taran was King Owain's, or Gareth was Prince Hywel's. He would know everything about the running of Cadell's kingdom, and he was the one person in whom Cadell would have confided in advance about his hope of an alliance with Earl Clare. Huw surely would have had something to do with the crafting of it.

"I'm concerned about the timing. Didn't we already decide that hunting in the Coed Rath was a foolish excuse that nobody should ever have believed? It's Norman territory, plain and simple. We have plenty of places to hunt that aren't a few miles from Tenby and Carew!"

Rhys was speaking of a line of Norman castles built between Pembroke and St. Clears, and then all the way to Llansteffan. South of that line hadn't been Welsh territory in fifty years. One Welsh king or another might sack a castle, even hold it for a while, as was currently the case at Amroth and Llansteffan, but Cadell's control of those regions was always precarious at best, if one could say he had any control at all. That was the reason they were marching Cadell out of here, trying to get above that invisible line.

The Normans hadn't just built castles. In addition to invading with armies, they had brought English and Flemish settlers to live in towns associated with their castles. Tenby was such a place. It might be built on land that was originally Welsh, but only English—and English-speaking—people lived within the town walls. Over time, as the Normans consolidated their control of the area, these settlers had felt safe enough to move into the countryside. The castles weren't Norman outposts anymore. They ruled over a little bit of England, transplanted to Wales, on land which had come to exclude Welsh people. The Welsh remained in isolated pockets, like in the little village where they'd found the bier.

"I don't understand. Are you accusing Iestyn of something?"

"I don't know."

Llelo narrowed his eyes at his friend. "Yes, you do. You just don't want to say it. Or say it out loud. But this is me. You can tell me anything. What exactly are you getting at? You think Iestyn is the traitor of whom your brother spoke?"

"What if he knew there would be an ambush?" Rhys practically threw the words at Llelo. "What if he timed his arrival deliberately for the moment all the Welsh were dead and the Normans had retreated?"

"Are you actually thinking Iestyn conspired with the Tenby garrison or with Earl Clare?"

"Maybe. Or maybe Huw conspired with them, and Iestyn was the means by which he betrayed my brother."

Llelo's horror at the conclusion left him gasping. Rhys had found it difficult to encompass the notion of becoming king, but it seemed he could take treachery at this scale entirely in stride. Cadell hadn't elucidated how many of his people had known in advance that he intended to meet one of the Clares in the Coed Rath, but the circle was smaller now than ever. As far as Llelo knew, as of this moment it remained limited to Cadell himself, Rhys, Llelo, and Huw. Despite what Rhys was saying about Iestyn, as far as they knew, to him and his men, Cadell had been ambushed while hunting.

"I think the Tenby commander knew Iestyn was coming, which was why he arranged the scene as he did." And then, before Llelo could marshal a reasonable protest, Rhys continued, "Let's start over by imagining what would have happened if you and I *hadn't* been there as witnesses."

Llelo forced himself to focus. "Iestyn would have come upon the ambush, and Cadell would have told him what happened."

Rhys made another dismissive motion. "Take another step back and imagine what Gerald thought would happen if he was in league with Iestyn."

Llelo couldn't play along. "I'm lost again."

Displaying no impatience at how slowly Llelo thought, Rhys explained further, "For one, real Danes would have made sure my brother was dead. Aside from that, let's say Gerald had actually done what he'd intended and murdered my brother in that clearing. What then?"

Back on solid mental ground, Llelo was able to say, "Iestyn would have come upon the scene, found the artifacts Gerald had left, and assumed Danes had attacked and murdered Cadell, just as they once ambushed Anarawd's party."

"And then Iestyn and his men would have returned to Dinefwr with the body to tell that story."

"But to what end?" Llelo said. "I don't understand the purpose of all this subterfuge."

"For starters, if Danes murdered my brother, we would not take revenge on Earl Clare or the Tenby garrison. Earl Clare wanted my brother dead, but he is well aware of the consequences if we found out he'd done it."

Llelo's hand went to his mouth in surprise at what he'd just realized. "This ambush itself could be retribution. Sixteen years ago, Welshmen ambushed and killed Earl Clare's father. That was what set off the 1136 war that lost them Deheubarth and Ceredigion."

"Sixteen years is a long time to wait for revenge." Rhys's tone was almost admiring. "We won't be waiting that long."

"So you think not only did Earl Clare decide to turn on your brother but he colluded with Iestyn to do it?"

"If Cadell hadn't ordered us to hide, Iestyn would have come upon the scene exactly the way Gerald had staged it. What's more, he would have believed what he was seeing."

"Except, your brother didn't die."

"True."

"Why would Iestyn do any of this?"

"Silver."

Llelo harrumphed. "Cadell and Iestyn have been friends their whole lives."

"His brother is hard pressed by the Normans to the east. He might have been willing to encompass Cadell's death in exchange for easing the pressure on his family's lands. Besides, he didn't have to *do* anything, did he? Cadell hadn't asked him to come. My brother thought his own dozen men were all he needed as protection against treachery."

"So Iestyn's entire role would have been to discover Cadell's dead body." Llelo spoke slowly as the ramifications played out in his head. They had concocted Iestyn's guilt out of whole cloth. As before in the clearing, this was entirely speculation.

Rhys nodded. "Even if he wasn't out for revenge, Earl Clare must covet his father's former lands in Wales. Hywel rules there now, but his hold on the region is weak, as we all know. Clare's father died in defense of those lands, and he wants them back, likely as much as Cadell does. Just because the Normans are godless demons from the depths of Annwn doesn't mean they can't feel their losses and want revenge. You weren't wrong earlier when you explained how, with Cadell dead, Maredudd and I would be all that's left to lead. In Clare's mind, we are young and inexperienced. In other words, we could easily be overcome once he'd got rid of Cadell."

"If that's the plan, they are grossly underestimating you." Llelo let out a sharp breath. "What do we do?"

"I told you what my brother said. I can't trust anyone." He glanced at Llelo. "Anyone but you. That's why I wanted to talk to your father."

14

Day One

Gwen

Welsh monasteries tended not to be as richly endowed as many of their Norman counterparts. The abbot's quarters at Mynachlog Fawr, which Maredudd had appropriated for himself, and in which Gwen and Gareth found themselves, provided a rare exception. Between the warmth of the fire on a cold January evening, cushions for the chairs, and a substantial repast, the abbot had created a haven. Having eaten with them, he had then departed for worship in the church, leaving Gwen, Gareth, and Maredudd to talk.

Gwen was honestly surprised to be included in this conference. While she'd often played an important role in Gareth's investigations, not everyone knew that or was willing to acknowledge it. Somehow, she couldn't be surprised to learn Maredudd was an exception.

The young man in question lounged in his chair, his back to the fire, the remains of his dinner in front of him. He hadn't ordered the sacking of this monastery either, so it really might be that destroying holy sites wasn't part of his mandate. According to Prince Hywel, Anarawd had been a devilish man. As far as Gwen was concerned, Cadell was hardly better. Maredudd was fully invested in taking back Ceredigion from Gwynedd—specifically from his cousin Hywel—but he was here on Cadell's orders. She had to keep reminding herself not to judge Maredudd by his older brothers.

Nor, for that matter, by his younger one. Maredudd had been given his own command, so obviously Cadell thought him capable of leading an army. At the same time, Gwen couldn't help thinking that if Rhys had been the commander, he would not have taken over the abbot's quarters for himself and would instead have found more common lodging.

It would probably be best if she made no judgments about anyone at all.

"My lord, if you could tell us what you know, I could begin to investigate your captain's death," Gareth said. "First, I need to know why you believe him to have been murdered. And then why you decided not to tell anyone about it!"

He and Gwen were sitting opposite Maredudd, also with their plates still in front of them. Although the abbey would have laid in food supplies to last the monks through the winter, Gwen had spent enough time in monasteries to be quite sure they were not looking forward to hosting Maredudd and his men for any length of time, even if it was their duty.

Maredudd picked up a carrot and bit off the end. "Rhodri was stabbed in the back. Twice. Is that proof enough for you?" His tone was almost sneering, as if Gareth should somehow have known how his captain had died without needing to be told.

Gareth spread his hands wide. "That does seem suspicious."

Gwen laughed, because she couldn't help herself, and then Maredudd did too, belatedly, as if at first he hadn't realized Gareth was making a jest.

Gareth's lips pressed together, suppressing a smile, and then he became serious again. "Do you still have the body?"

"No."

"My lord," Gwen was not happy with the monosyllabic answer, "we need to know everything you can think to tell us and then some. That's what my husband is trying to convey. More than anything, investigations rely upon gathering as much information as possible about a great many things."

Maredudd raised his eyebrows. "What sort of things?"

"Just to start, where was the body found? When was it found? Who discovered it? How did you manage to keep the murder a secret? And then, comprehensively, we need to know about Rhodri himself, beginning with if he had any enemies. And that's just off the top of my head."

Maredudd gave another little laugh, though she didn't think he was laughing at her, just the circumstance. "I'll see what I can do." He paused for thought. "Rhodri died two nights ago in the early hours of the morning, with dawn still some time off. He had gone to relieve himself at a distance from our camp."

"North, south, east, or west?" Gareth said.

"I don't know why it matters, but he was on the north side, near the River Ystwyth. He was unguarded and alone. He spoke to the sentry on duty as he passed him. This man, after a time, grew concerned at his absence and went looking for him. After not finding him in an initial search all the way to the river bank, he was headed back to camp to raise the alarm when he stumbled over the body."

Gareth scratched the side of his head. "Where exactly were you camped?"

"South of the River Ystwyth near the church of St. Ilar. We spent the next night at a spot just past Trawscoed, also along the River Ystwyth. And now, here we are."

With that explanation, Gwen didn't have to inquire how it was they'd ended up at the commandery. From Hywel's castle, they'd taken the high road southeast to the old Roman fort of Trawscoed, and from there they'd followed the river upstream. From the bits she'd overheard since they'd been captured, after the failure of the siege, Maredudd had wanted at least some of his force to avoid the obvious routes south in case Hywel pursued.

That said, Trawscoed was an old Roman fort. Once there, the Roman road turned directly south and could have taken Maredudd's band all the way to Caerfyrddin, and then east to Dinefwr. Or, they could have followed the mountain road the Romans had also built that went by the barrows at Carreg y Bwci and the gold mine at Dolaucothi. In terms of distance, it might have been shorter to go that way. In winter, it likely wouldn't have been faster. Regardless, they were now quite a bit out of their way if getting back to Deheubarth as quickly as possible had been the goal.

"What did the guard do after he found the body?" Gwen thought the answer should be that he raised the alarm, but she wanted to hear Maredudd tell it.

"He woke Tomos, who woke me."

"And somehow you decided to pretend Rhodri died of natural causes?" Gareth said. "Why?"

"We had lost so many men to illness by then, the last thing I needed was for the men to fear an intruder in the dark. I told them Rhodri expired from the illness. Really, I believed him to have been murdered by one of Hywel's men, who'd followed us from Aberystwyth. I doubled the watch the next night. We've had no incidents since then, and the man must be long gone by now."

"If your assumption was that one of Hywel's men murdered Rhodri, why are you asking for our help?" Gwen said. "Two nights ago, you were sure this was an impossible murder to solve. What changed?"

"I have been having second thoughts." That was probably the most forthcoming statement Maredudd had offered so far. "What if, by leaving as we did, and making the assumptions I did, I have allowed a murderer to walk freely amongst my men? It's true we are at war, and men die all the time, but no death should ever be at the hands of one of our own."

"I can only agree," Gareth said.

"Where is Rhodri's body?" Gwen said.

"Buried in the churchyard before we set out that morning." Maredudd shrugged. "What else could we do under the circumstances? We weren't going to haul it with us, and we were anxious to be on our way."

"Did you fear more of Hywel's men were following you?" Gwen asked.

"Of course."

Gareth leaned forward. "Nobody else saw anything? Heard anything?"

"Not that they have said. But then, I haven't asked, have I?"

"Would your men have spoken up if they saw something untoward?" Gwen said.

"Why wouldn't they?" Maredudd turned his head to look at her. "These are good men. Experienced. I have trusted every one of them with my life."

"If you're right about Rhodri's death, one of them surely can't be what you describe, though, can he?" Gwen said. "*Someone* murdered Rhodri. He didn't stab himself in the back."

"No." Maredudd took a long drink of his wine before setting down his cup. "That would be impossible."

"Was Rhodri a popular leader?" Gwen was pushing back at all these negatives because she was trying to get a better sense of what really could have happened. Maredudd wasn't as voluble as she thought he should be for someone who wanted a murder solved.

The young prince settled back in his seat, a voiceless *ah* emitting from his lips as he acknowledged the thrust of her query. "Rhodri was a leader of men. That meant he was not always popular. Sometimes he made decisions and gave orders that men didn't want to follow. As all captains must."

"But was he hated?" Gareth said. "That's what Gwen is really asking."

"He must have been." Maredudd shrugged. "I don't doubt it. By a few."

"All it takes is one," Gareth said. "Is the man who has replaced him more popular?"

"You mean Tomos?" At Gareth's nod, Maredudd wrinkled his nose, implying a certain level of discomfort with the question. "I know what you're suggesting, but Tomos was in his bed during Rhodri's murder."

Gwen wasn't sure Gareth had actually been suggesting what Maredudd thought, but she followed up anyway. "Could he have returned to his tent secretly?"

Maredudd made a cutting-off motion with his hand. "Tomos would not have murdered Rhodri. The very idea is absurd. Besides which, his tent is always pitched next to mine. The men who guard the perimeter would have seen him. I trust Tomos more than any other man here."

After a quick glance at each other, Gwen and Gareth let it go. With that degree of certainty, it would do them no good to raise Maredudd's hackles any more than they already had. There was so much more to learn, and they could always circle back to individual suspects if it became necessary.

"What did you do after you learned of Rhodri's death?" Gareth said.

Maredudd's eyes narrowed. "What do you mean?"

"Did you scour the bushes? Did anyone think to look for tracks or footprints around the body? Did someone try to discover anything unusual about Rhodri's last days?"

"We were fleeing Aberystwyth," Maredudd said, not without a certain air of exasperation. "As I said, we decided his death had to be at the hand of one of Hywel's men who'd followed us, saw an opportunity, and took it. We wrapped Rhodri's body in a tarp right then and there beside the river, then rousted some of the men to carry him to the church, next to which we'd camped."

"Did nobody wonder at the location of his death?" Gwen was unable to hide her astonishment at this description.

"He'd had the runs, like half my army. He was one of three men who died that night. We put them in the ground at first light, then pulled up stakes and left as quickly as we could."

"What about the sentry who found him? He could have followed Rhodri, killed him, and then pretended to discover the body," Gareth said.

"I am not a complete idiot, Sir Gareth." Maredudd really was losing patience with the questions, although every one was entirely reasonable, especially considering that they were supposed to uncover this murderer after the body had been put into the ground, amongst men who hadn't been told there'd been a murder. They wouldn't even be able to determine what type of blade was used.

Gareth put up a hand. "I am just asking questions, my lord. What would you think of me if I didn't ask about him, even if his innocence seems obvious to you? The murderer has had days to cover his tracks. I am coming to this well behind. If I don't ask, I don't know."

"Yes, of course." Maredudd put up a hand of his own. "My apologies. You must ask anything you require to know about, and I, or one of my men, will answer. In this case, I spoke with the man. I had to, since I had to ensure his silence. While his hands were bloody, his personal knife was clean, as was his sword. Both of them, in fact, were freshly oiled, which he could not have done between seeing Rhodri and finding his body."

Gareth let out a breath. "As you have just discovered, the investigative process is never comfortable and rarely quick. Gwen and I may well uncover other secrets, some unrelated to the initial crime, that the bearer doesn't want exposed."

Maredudd studied him and then transferred his gaze to Gwen. "What kind of secrets?"

She wasn't sure why he was looking to her for an answer, but she gave him the first example that came to mind. "Last year, a physician at Ysbyty Cynfyn was murdered."

"I heard."

"Along the way to identifying who did it, we discovered that a number of the monks in the commandery were consuming significant quantities of the juice of the poppy without a medical need. As it turned out, the physician was murdered for a completely different reason. And yet, the commandery was censured and almost didn't survive based on a secret we learned that had nothing to do with the actual murder."

Maredudd tapped a finger to his lips. "I don't have secrets like that."

"Perhaps not," Gareth said, "but given that your captain was murdered, you can be certain that *someone* does."

15

Day One

Gareth

Maredudd took another long swig of wine. He'd had three cups tonight by Gareth's count. It was very good wine, and rich too. Potent, in other words. Maredudd might regret the indulgence in the morning. For now, it seemed to be doing its work, in that Maredudd was conveying a level of contentedness that contrasted sharply to his earlier impatience. "Your man, Meicol, will stay behind at the abbey with his family, along with the widow and her daughters. They would burden us for no reason. The monks here will shelter them until they are able to return to their homes. Everyone else must come with us."

"Does that include my father-in-law? Gwen and the children?" Gareth had been hoping to leave them behind too. It would be best if only he, or he and Dai, continued on to Dinefwr. "What about Bran and Ieuan?"

"The elder is a former soldier, and his son is an archer. Neither can be allowed to war against us." He eyed Gwen. "I know for a fact that you spied for Hywel long before you married your husband, skills I am sure you continue to employ on his behalf. Your parents also have seen too much."

Gwen gave way with a bowed head, even if her lips were pressed together, indicating she had something to say. But, like Gareth, she wasn't sure if she should say it.

For Gareth's part, he was impressed with Maredudd's manner. He had remembered the names of everyone in Gareth's caravan! That attention to detail, along with the politically astute way he'd handled Gareth and Gwen's capture, despite his hasty retreat from Aberystwyth, indicated a considerable intellect. Gareth's prior sense had been that Rhys was the clever brother and Maredudd the more physical. He told himself it would be unwise to underestimate either man in either capacity.

Maredudd accepted their silent acquiescence. "We leave in the morning for Caerfyrddin."

Gwen's head came up. "Caerfyrddin? We are not going to Dinefwr?"

"Ultimately, we are. But the road is difficult in winter and will be hard on the wagons, not to mention the men. Better to take the good road first. During the journey, you will speak to my people. I will tell them that you will be asking questions and instruct them to answer. And then you will tell me who murdered Rhodri."

"My lord, that isn't—" Gareth broke off at the hard look Maredudd sent him.

It was left to Gwen to say what needed to be said. "This murder happened days ago and miles away. What do you expect us to do at this late date? Your men will be learning of the murder only to-night! Not to mention the fact that they see us as your prisoners. Why would they consent to answer our questions?"

"Because I will order them to," Maredudd said, as if that would be enough. Clearly, he assumed it would be. "I am also offend-ed that you would call yourself a prisoner."

"Are we free to go?" Gareth said.

"No." Maredudd barked a laugh. "Prisoner it is. To tell you the truth, I expected a bit more gratitude on your part. I gave you back your sword!"

Gareth put up both hands. "I am grateful not to be in chains and that you have been so generous with my family." He paused as Maredudd bent his head in acceptance of his apology. Then he had to pick up where Gwen had left off. "But I must say that my wife is right. With no body, no suspects, no witnesses, and days having passed, you must realize there's faint hope of solving this murder so long af-ter the fact."

"And you the great Gareth ap Rhys!" Maredudd gave a laugh that was half snort.

He could have felt like he was being mocked, but Gareth chose to join in the laughter instead. He was on unstable ground with this prince of Deheubarth, and the range of emotions Maredudd had displayed in this meeting made him even less sure of his footing. "As long as you know I can't work miracles. Your first instinct still could be right that Rhodri was murdered by one of Hywel's men."

Maredudd waved a hand dismissively. "It is my turn to apolo-gize. All I am asking is for you to do what you can."

"I will." As he spoke, Gareth reached for Gwen's hand.

"My brother Rhys assures me you always do." Maredudd relaxed against the back of his chair, giving the impression the matter of his captain's death was all but resolved. He took a bite of bread and spoke around it. "My brother has also told me of your honesty, so I suppose I shouldn't have been surprised you gave Tomos your real name when lying might have better served your interests. Even now, you could have promised me the moon and dealt with my disappointment later."

"I could have. But, as you say, I try not to lie." Sensing this audience was nearly over, Gareth had one last question. "What were you really doing at Ysbyty Ystwyth? It is not on the way to Deheubarth."

"You think I know more about Rhodri's death than I'm telling? You think there's more to the story?"

Gareth was always suspicious when someone answered a question with a question. Maredudd was cagey, that was for certain, and not hiding the degree to which he was a reluctant witness. *Did he want this murder solved or not?* "I don't know. That's why I'm asking."

"You aren't a spy anymore, Lord Gareth. You should keep any questions beyond the scope of the investigation to yourself, lest I regret my largesse."

Gareth sat back in his seat, properly set down for what Maredudd clearly saw as impudence. For a moment there, Gareth had treated him like he would have Rhys.

He knew that now to be a mistake. There was nothing to say but, "Yes, my lord." The irony was that he had just finished telling Maredudd that no question was beyond the scope of his investigation.

Maredudd let out a low grunt. "Don't think I don't know the way you and your son have been ranging all over Ceredigion on Hywel's behalf."

"I am his steward." Gareth's guard was truly up now. He was going to have to tread more carefully than he had expected—and he'd already expected to have to.

"How many of my men did you kill these last weeks?"

Gareth felt himself rear backwards. "None. From what I understand, neither side lost more than a handful of men to stray arrows this whole time."

Maredudd harrumphed and spoke his next words under his breath, more to himself than to Gareth or Gwen. "Maybe my brother is right. I'm too soft to rule, and you should be in chains. Too many good men died for nothing this week."

"For nothing?" Gwen said. "Do you mean—"

"I meant because they died from dysentery." Maredudd cut her off, not admitting what had been Gareth's first thought too: marching north and besieging Aberystwyth in the middle of winter had been a terrible idea from the start.

"Of course, my lord." Gwen bent her head. "It is a scourge."

Maredudd rose to his feet and stretched his back. Gwen and Gareth hastily set down their cups and rose too, at which point Gareth decided he should try to mend a few fences. He couldn't stop

Cadell from warring on Hywel, but Maredudd didn't have to be an enthusiastic participant. "Thank you for not harming my family or me. I realize many commanders would not be so forgiving."

"Forgiving?" Maredudd scoffed. "Don't mistake me, Lord Gareth. Just because I have given you leave to move about does not mean I am pleased to find myself asking my enemy for help."

"We have never been your enemy," Gwen said softly.

Maredudd shot her a sardonic look. "What would you call cousins facing off against each other over territory?" He leaned closer, suddenly more animated, and stabbed a finger towards her in emphasis. "Territory my uncle stole!"

The territory acquired by Owain had not been held by Deheubarth for some time prior to the 1136 war. Most of the country had been taken by the Normans ten years earlier. The entire reason Maredudd's father, the old King Gruffydd, had come to King Owain in the first place to ask for an alliance was because the current Earl of Hertford's father had been ambushed and killed. Maredudd's father had left his wife, Gwenllian, who was also Owain's sister, in charge of his army, and come north to Gwynedd.

During his absence, the Normans had attacked, capturing Gwenllian in the process. Once they'd executed her, their fate was sealed. Gwynedd had joined the fight and won all of Deheubarth back for Gruffydd.

After the war, King Owain had taken over Ceredigion as part of the deal he'd made at the start. Even with the murder of his sister, he hadn't been fighting Normans in south Wales out of the goodness of his heart. These events had occurred fifteen years ago. It was only after the death of Anarawd, six years after the end of the war, that Deheubarth had soured on Gwynedd. Relations had been good enough up until then for Anarawd to be on his way to marry Owain's daughter. Additionally, if Cadell had truly conspired with Cadwaladr to murder Anarawd, Cadell's outrage at what he declared was Gwynedd's perfidy was entirely a sham.

Thanks to Rhys, they knew now that Cadwaladr had further conspired with Cadell to send an assassin to Gwynedd to murder King Owain—a tit for tat aspect of their monstrous fratricidal bargain. Unfortunately for anyone who cared about justice, even as they were uncovering this new unholy piece of treachery, Cadwaladr was prostrating himself (once again) before King Owain, begging his forgiveness and promising never, ever again to do anything that would violate his trust. By the time the news arrived that an assassin might be on his way to Owain's court, Cadwaladr had already been back in Aberffraw, restored to favor.

Nobody believed in Cadwaladr's contrition, not even King Owain. But as the other options before him were to imprison Cadwaladr indefinitely or to kill him, Owain felt he had little choice but to do what he had been doing for years: biding his time until Cadwaladr perpetrated an act so heinous he could not be forgiven.

That he'd already done so several times was not something the king wanted to hear right now. Hopefully, that final, terrible act would not actually be the murder of King Owain himself.

By contrast, Maredudd seemed sincere. He had been six years old when the Normans killed his mother. Likely, he had only ever heard Cadell's side of the story. Which meant it wasn't a tale Gareth could counter tonight, even with the truth.

He told himself to be content with what he had been able to preserve today: his family, his (relative) freedom, and his honor.

16

Day Two

Rhys

It was past midnight, after an interminable day. Rhys's feet were aching more than they'd ever ached in his life. Twenty miles riding was one thing. Twenty miles walking through rough terrain or on a muddy, rocky road was something entirely different. There was a reason knights didn't walk. If nothing else, his boots weren't made for it.

In the end, they hadn't made it the full twenty miles, either. They'd had to rest—for everyone's sake, not just Cadell's, though he was the excuse. If Rhys couldn't bear to walk another mile, Cadell couldn't stand to be carried another five feet, much less the five miles required to reach the castle at Caerfyrddin. Everything hurt, from his head to his feet, which could be viewed actually as an improvement.

Earlier, Rhys had suggested he and Llelo be the latest messengers to ride to the castle to get help. At the very least, the last leg of Cadell's journey could be accomplished in the back of a cart rather than on foot. Instead, Cadell had insisted Rhys not only stay with the company, but keep to Cadell's own fire circle. He didn't even want Llelo present, consigning him to the next fire over.

And then Cadell had ignored Rhys completely. Eventually, Rhys had lain down and pretended to be asleep. The only other person present was Iestyn, who had been ignoring him too.

Just at the point Rhys was finally drifting away, within moments of sleep, Iestyn spoke—to Cadell, not to him: "What were you really doing in the Coed Rath, my lord? And don't tell me you were hunting. My men are happy to believe it, but the more I've thought about it, the less that explanation makes sense."

Rhys was frozen beneath his blankets as he waited for his brother's reply.

"It was meant to be a meeting."

Iestyn's eyes narrowed. "With whom?"

"Roger de Clare." Cadell's words were soft. Maybe that was because his head hurt, or because he didn't want his voice to carry. Rhys thought he also might be trying to be casual about an answer that wasn't casual at all. That his brother was willing to talk privately to his closest friend with Rhys in earshot was another example of the way he was always overlooked.

Not that he was sorry to be listening in. This was the very question Rhys had brought up with Llelo.

"This is the brother of the Earl of Hertford?" At Cadell's nod, Iestyn shifted on his log. "So it wasn't by chance that the men of Tenby found you there. They were sent."

"So it seems."

Iestyn rubbed his face with both hands. "Who else knew?"

"Huw, me, several of my *teulu,* since they acted as messengers between us."

"Rhys?"

"Not until last night." Cadell made a slight motion with his hand. "What about you, Iestyn? How did you come to be in the Coed Rath?"

Through eyes barely slitted open, Rhys could see Iestyn meet Cadell's gaze, after which he answered easily enough. In truth, he *had* explained earlier. Either Cadell had been so out of his head he didn't remember, or he was pretending not to remember because he wanted to hear it again.

"My brother has been concerned for some time about renewed activity among the Normans who surround his lands. When I arrived at Dinefwr to speak to you about this and Huw told me where you had gone—hunting of all things—I decided I should follow." Now he looked a bit disgruntled. "You should have included me in the negotiations. I could have—" He broke off, shaking his head, and Rhys saw him wipe what could have been a tear from his cheek. "I am devastated I wasn't in time. My men could have made all the difference."

"Or died too. Gerald of Tenby had fifty men with him. With my *teulu* overwhelmed, your dozen could have fallen just as easily. I should have brought more men myself, but I was worried about enlarging the circle of those who knew what I was doing before it was done."

Rhys noted that Cadell hadn't actually said, *it isn't your fault.* Sometimes people said more in what they didn't articulate than in what they did.

"You were worried you might be betrayed." Iestyn wasn't asking a question.

"Of course I was."

Iestyn held still through a few heartbeats. "You never need to worry about me, Cadell, if that's what you're wondering."

"I was not wondering about you." Cadell flicked out a few fingers, implying he didn't need to inquire. He already knew. What Rhys hadn't yet figured out was if this conversation was a final test of Iestyn's loyalty ... or of Rhys's.

All of a sudden, Rhys was rethinking his assumption that Cadell was overlooking him. That he feared the motives of his allies and friends like Iestyn could explain why he had chosen to speak to Iestyn within Rhys's hearing, knowing Rhys was unlikely to be genuinely asleep. And also why he hadn't wanted Rhys to leave him for Caerfyrddin. With Rhys and Llelo gone, they couldn't watch his back. If he was dead by the time Rhys returned, nobody would have been surprised.

"What's done cannot be undone. Our concern now has to be how we proceed from here," Cadell continued. "Before I left Dinefwr, I learned from my scouts that the siege was not going well in Aberystwyth, and Hywel was likely to have held. Maredudd might be retreating south even now. If we are lucky, your messenger will reach him some time tomorrow."

"Lucky?" Iestyn's tone was morose. "We have not been lucky today."

"Clearly. Then again, I *am* alive." Cadell was enough himself to let out a sound that might have been a laugh. After which he writhed in pain.

Rhys wasn't happy about the pain, but he was glad to hear his brother speak as he was. It seemed now Cadell wanted to live as fiercely as earlier he'd wanted to die.

"Why do you think Hywel will have held the castle?" Iestyn poked at the fire with a stick. "Do you not trust Maredudd to manage the campaign?"

"I trust him. If I didn't, I wouldn't have sent him. Hywel will have held because his castle is impregnable unless one is willing to burn it to the ground to take it. The storms of the last few weeks would have ensured that couldn't happen. And anyway, I told Maredudd I didn't want him to burn it. I wanted it taken intact or not at all."

"It sounds like you tied his hands." It was a bit of censure from Iestyn. Deservedly, to Rhys's mind. It looked to Rhys like Cadell had set Maredudd up to fail.

Cadell scoffed, sounding more like himself with every moment that passed. "I don't have the resources to rebuild it. And yet, without it, I can't hope to hold Ceredigion. Hywel would have just moved back in. It has been a long time since we ruled there. Hywel is respected and has treated the people well. I do not have them on my side."

"Then why waste time and men on the endeavor?"

"I had to come up with a mission that would ensure Maredudd was far away today."

Iestyn rubbed his chin. "He didn't know you were negotiating with Earl Clare?"

"He would not have stood for it. They killed his mother."

"What about *him*?" Iestyn gestured towards Rhys, who was still lying unmoving beside the fire.

"Rhys is more pragmatic than his brother."

"Then what about that friend of his, Llywelyn? He is a newcomer. Perhaps he's the traitor. I don't trust him."

"I do. Now more than ever."

"Why would that be?"

"For one, he could not have known about the ambush in advance. And then, Rhys told me that when the men of Tenby came, Llywelyn kept them hidden. My boy, here, is brilliant, but he is still too impulsive. He tried to come to my aid. If Llywelyn had let him, they both would have died. Llywelyn saw that and contained him."

Iestyn wet his lips, as if what he was about to ask next was even more fraught than what he'd already said. Which it was, as it turned out, and couldn't have been more so: "Are you sure Rhys himself wasn't involved in this treachery?"

Rhys had been feigning sleep all this time, his eyes mere slits, focused mostly on Iestyn's face, which he could see better than Cadell's. It took every fiber of his being not to rise up at hearing his name muddied.

Cadell, for his part, gave a little chuckle, which turned into a moan. "I am certain. He despised the notion of negotiating with Clare, but not to the point that he couldn't see the need. That said, he would sooner cut off his own sword arm than betray me with a Norman. They murdered *his* mother too, you know."

The particular phrasing gave Rhys pause. Cadell had said Rhys would never betray him *with a Norman*. Was he worried about Rhys betraying him with a Welshman?

Iestyn, meanwhile, bent his head respectfully. "Please excuse my forwardness, my lord. These questions needed to be asked."

"I forgive you, Iestyn. In fact, there is nothing to forgive. A king needs men around him who tell him the truth, even truths he doesn't want to hear. You have always been that for me. Perhaps you could check on the men guarding the perimeter? I would do it, but ..." He didn't bother to gesture to his legs.

"As you wish, my lord." Accepting his dismissal, Iestyn departed.

Once he'd gone, Cadell said, speaking generally, "You heard all that, I presume."

"I did." Rhys waited until Iestyn was out of sight before replacing him on the log next to Cadell. "You told me not to trust anyone. I'm guessing that includes Iestyn?" He had to ask. Just as Cadell had told his friend, if ever there was a time to speak plainly, it was now. That the ambush in the Coed Rath wasn't the greatest act of treachery ever directed at the House of Dinefwr only emphasized the number of times and the degree to which they'd been betrayed over the years.

"No. Not anymore. And really, not ever." Again, Cadell tried to laugh and ended up breathing deeply, in an attempt to manage the pain that plagued him every time he moved his head. Even injured as he was, he'd laughed more in the last quarter of an hour than Rhys had heard from him in years. "He accuses you, and I saw in your eyes today that you were suspicious of him, too. Iestyn is well-intentioned but not devious. He has saved my life more times than I can count. If he is the traitor, I would rather not know. Just as I told him that you would never collude with Normans, I say the same to you about him: put it from your mind. He did not do this."

"He could have been an unwilling dupe."

Cadell might have just meant to laugh once more, but it turned into a cough, and then something of a fit, requiring Rhys to fetch him some water. If he was truly to rest, he needed more poppy. "Huw told him where to go. Are you saying my own steward betrayed me?"

"You told me not to trust anyone. Whom do you suspect if not either of them? Why can't the devil just be the Earl of Hertford?"

"That garrison captain, Gerald, was prepared for the numbers I brought. While it's possible he could simply have guessed correctly, he could also have been warned. I am concerned, too, about the way he prepared the scene to imply Danes ambushed me. That's a very specific ruse, one that would work only if our bodies were found quickly, when the evidence was still there, before wild animals marred the scene. Or rain."

"That's why I think the traitor is Iestyn. Or Huw. Who else could it have been?"

"Though I trusted each and every one of them, I have decided it had to be a member of my *teulu*."

Rhys wasn't happy about that. "They're dead, which means they were betrayed too. I watched the last two die; they didn't protest or beg or give any indication they expected to live."

"Thus, of the three choices presented to us, only two can be investigated."

"Three choices?"

"The first is that the traitor was a member of my *teulu*; the second, that it is someone in Dinefwr; or lastly, that he rides among Iestyn's men. Huw told Iestyn where I was, but whose idea was it that he follow me into the woods? We have too many questions and no answers." Cadell made a slight motion with his hand, and even that appeared to hurt him. "Get your friend to help."

"My ... friend?"

"Do I have to say it? I know who he is. Like father, like son, is that it?"

Rhys let out a slow breath. "How long have you known?"

"I didn't for certain until now." Then, before Rhys could properly absorb the implications of this revelation, Cadell motioned in the direction of the *dwale,* asking Rhys to pour a portion into his cup and help him drink it.

When he'd finished, Rhys said, "I would apologize for deceiving you, but I also know I would behave the same way if I had to do it again."

Cadell looked directly into Rhys's face. "I know why you summoned him. I can't be sorry about it now, no matter his ultimate allegiance. It would serve Hywel to have me dead and Maredudd or you on the throne. I would accuse Llywelyn of betraying me to that end if the idea weren't so laughable."

All Rhys could muster by way of a reply to that was to wet his lips.

Cadell nodded to see it. "You feared treachery; you didn't know who to trust. Perhaps you even feared me. I won't chastise you for it. You weren't wrong about the treachery we were facing. If only I, too, had acted sooner."

"What do you mean by that?"

Cadell didn't seem to want to answer the question, or maybe the poppy was already taking effect, because he said, "When your mother died, you were the oldest four-year-old the world had ever seen. With our father gone the next year, I sometimes feared you grew up too fast. Now, I can be grateful for it. You are going to have to steer this ship we call our kingdom, Rhys."

Thanks to Llelo, Rhys understood this time what he was talking about. "Maredudd will return—"

"Do not mistake me, Rhys. I know what I have in you. The kingdom is on your shoulders now. You are the best of us. I'm just sorry it took an ambush for me to see it. I fear this is God's punishment for how I have ruled."

Rhys made to argue, but Cadell swept his words away with a gesture. "Maredudd is a capable warrior, and he will grow wiser with time, I hope, but it is you who will make those Normans pay, not just in blood, for what they've done to me. It is upon you, Rhys, that the future of Deheubarth, and maybe all Wales, depends."

17

Day Two

Gareth

Maredudd leaned down from his place in the saddle to speak to Gareth, who was finishing preparing his wagon for departure. "I will send men back to speak to you. Einion is the one who found Rhodri's body, so he will be first. He already knows what you're about."

During their journey yesterday, they'd traveled a little more than ten miles from Ysbyty Cynfyn to reach the abbey of Mynachlog Fawr. If they took the Roman road from here, they had forty miles to travel to Caerfyrddin. Twenty miles wasn't an unreasonable distance for a horse to walk in a day, especially a Welsh horse. These tended to be small and sturdy and used to difficult tracks, which this road would not be. Men were another story. Still, these were the same men who, a month ago, had crossed all of Ceredigion in three days to get to Aberystwyth. If all went well, they could be in Caerfyrddin tomorrow evening and then in Dinefwr the day after that.

"Hywel will be worried when he doesn't hear from you, now that the siege is lifted," Gwen said to Gareth as he settled in his wagon to wait. Dai was already there, walking his horse at the exact pace necessary to maintain his position at the back. "Is there some way we can get word to him?"

"I left a letter with the abbot. He will do what he can about getting my message out."

They'd already said goodbye to the two families they were leaving behind. That left them with Bran and Ieuan and Gwen's parents. Unlike Dai and Gareth, whose swords and horses Maredudd had given back, neither Bran nor Ieuan had been allowed their weapons. Gareth was just glad they still had an extra man available to drive his wagon, while Meilyr or Saran drove theirs. Meanwhile, Ieuan stumped along beside the horse's head, keeping it in line, his eyes on his feet. Every so often he shrugged his shoulders, as if missing the quiver and bow on his back.

"You could have sent me off in the night." Dai said in a low tone, even though none of Maredudd's soldiers were within hailing distance. "Me or Ieuan."

"You know as well as I that honor wouldn't allow it, same as yesterday." Gareth kicked his feet as they hung down off the back of the wagon, a few feet above the road that rolled away beneath him.

"I do know. But I am concerned that Bran and Ieuan don't."

"Are you worried one of them will run off? So far, both have been more patient than I might have expected, enduring whatever has come their way without complaint."

Dai shook his head. "I don't know them well enough to guess what either will do in the next hour, much less tomorrow." He heaved a sigh. "At least we're together. Even Taid and Nain." He was referring to Gwen's father and stepmother by the northern terms for grandfather and grandmother. In south Wales, grandparents were more likely to go by *tad-cu* and *mam-gu*. "Though, I'm still not sure I understand why."

"Maredudd said it was because any of us could spy for Hywel. I think it more likely that Maredudd's men like music, and they could use a healer too," Gwen said. "Saran restocked last night from the abbey's supplies. We left Ysbyty Cynfyn in such a hurry she didn't get to finish her accounting. And did your grandfather tell you he has a dozen requests for songs already?"

"We've barely rolled out of the abbey grounds!" Dai laughed, and Gareth was cheered to see it. The young man was trying so hard to take every setback in stride. A boy became a man in Wales at fourteen, but that didn't mean he had an adult's perspective.

Dai was still only sixteen. "And then what? We are heading into the heart of Deheubarth. Llelo is there. Don't tell me you haven't thought of it."

"I have."

Dai wrinkled his nose at his father, reminiscent of Gwen, even though they shared no actual blood. "The children will make it impossible to keep secret that he's ours."

"If he's there, we will cross that bridge when we come to it. Somehow, I can't worry about it now. We have two days with these people; two days to discover why their captain is dead. I want you to put yourself amongst Maredudd's men. For once, there's no language barrier. Maybe you can get something out of them they won't tell me."

Dai's eyes lit. "I'll bring Ieuan with me. It will give him something to do."

A gap had formed in the caravan between Gareth's horse, which was tied to the back of the wagon, and the carts hauling supplies that came next in line. These held everything from food, to tents, to stockpiles of arrows, plus any other accoutrements necessary for Maredudd's army. In all, he had a hundred soldiers, twenty cooks and laborers, and five carts in train.

Maredudd had explained that the piece of the army that had been approaching Ysbyty Cynfyn was similarly sized. The largest contingent, consisting of nearly three hundred men, had fled south on the Roman road from Trawscoed, under the command of Cadell's most-trusted general, a man named Dafydd. Maredudd had labeled him *most-trusted* without particular emphasis. Gareth hadn't been able to tell if he was implying Cadell trusted Dafydd more than Maredudd, or simply didn't consider Maredudd a general.

Maredudd hadn't known about the sacking of the church at Goginan and had been so concerned about how that second group was faring that he'd dispatched two men to ride up the road towards Ysbyty Cynfyn to find them. They should be, at most, a day behind. All were ultimately heading for the same Roman road as Maredudd.

Tangwen came up behind her father and put her arms around his neck. "You look worried."

Trust a six-year-old to say what she was thinking.

Gareth glanced at Gwen, who gave him a rueful look. "I didn't say anything. She isn't wrong, though."

Gareth pulled his daughter around so he could hold her on his lap. He had never had cause to investigate a death while moving through the countryside. He probably should have chosen to sit in the back of Meilyr's wagon instead of his own, to better protect his family from what informants might say. "Why do you think I'm worried?"

Tangwen put her finger on a spot between his eyes. "You have a little *v* there." Thanks to Meilyr, Tangwen was learning Latin, so she should know. The last few days, she'd been finding letters everywhere. *Ls* and *Os* had been particularly prevalent.

"Someone died. I have been asked to investigate."

"Is Maredudd worried that he's going to die too?"

Gareth would have preferred Tangwen wasn't as familiar with death as she clearly was. Investigations had been part of her parents' lives since before she was born, however, and that didn't look to be changing any time soon, no matter their best intentions. "He has not said so."

"He has the same *v* between his eyes that you do."

Gareth gave a little grunt of acknowledgment. He had not noticed. Nor had he considered the possibility that Maredudd was concerned for his own life. Rhys had been, so maybe Tangwen was right, and Maredudd should be—or could be—too. Whatever Maredudd's fears, Gareth didn't want his daughter to be bothered by these things, and he told her so. Gathering up her reading lesson, he picked her up and, when the wagon slowed to navigate a narrow spot in the road, carried her ahead to her grandparents' wagon. Otherwise, she would hear every word he said today. She didn't need to apprentice as an investigator quite yet.

When he returned, Gwen bumped her shoulder against his. "We usually worry about the *why* of a murder after we have made strides discovering the *how* and the *who*. Sometimes, we can't know the why of it until the murderer confesses. But I have to ask, who gains from the murder of Maredudd's second-in-command?"

"Someone who wants to take his place. That would be Tomos."

"Whom we are not allowed to question. What if it's someone who wants better access to Maredudd himself?"

Gareth felt an chill at the back of his neck. Something wasn't right about this investigation. He could feel it. "Perhaps Maredudd's first impulse was right, and Rhodri was stabbed by one of Hywel's men, taking advantage of an opportunity presented to him. He didn't care about whom he killed, and Rhodri was simply in the wrong place at the wrong time."

"Alternatively, Tangwen might be onto something."

Gareth gave his wife a rueful look. "I don't know which is more terrifying—that someone is out to murder the heir to the throne of Deheubarth or that our daughter was the first one to think of it."

18

Day Two

Llelo

“It was with tangible relief that Cadell's party passed through Caerfyrddin's gate. As had become clear hours ago, Cadell would be unable to continue on to Dinefwr today—or maybe ever. Right after the ambush, the pain in his head had been debilitating, but he hadn't been able to feel anything below his waist. Over the subsequent hours, the feeling had started to return to his lower half. Although both legs were still a dead weight, the right had more sensation than the left.

Unfortunately, with the ability to feel came an increase in pain, which appeared to emanate from his lower spine, all the way down to his toes. Just knowing that in a few moments he could be moved from the cart and receive genuine treatment had every one of Iestyn's men sighing in relief.

As they came to a halt in the bailey, Huw, Cadell's steward, hurried out of the great hall. "Get him inside. Hurry! Hurry!" He had known Cadell would be riding these last miles in the back of a cart, but his wide eyes told Llelo that knowing and seeing were two very different things.

The bearers obeyed, even as Cadell put out a hand to Huw. "It's all right."

"All right? All right is the last thing this is!"

In Llelo's experience, such overt distress was unusual in a steward.

Caerfyrddin was not by any stretch the center of Cadell's rule, but once a second messenger had been sent to Dinefwr in order to inform them of Cadell's progress—or lack thereof—his more established advisers had traveled to be with him, bringing with them the affairs of state. Such were the king's wounds and the slowness of his journey, even during the last leg in a cart, that Huw and the others had still arrived ahead of Cadell's party.

Although originally founded by the Welsh, the current castle at Caerfyrddin had been built by the Normans early in their attempt to conquer south Wales. They called it Carmarthen, since they were incapable of pronouncing Welsh words with any kind of accuracy, and mostly didn't care to try. By now, given the influx of English settlers into south Wales, every original Welsh settlement was known more by its English name than its Welsh one.

The castle hadn't been improved significantly since its original construction, still being what the Normans called a *motte and bailey* castle. In short, it consisted of a wooden keep on a high motte with a deep ditch all around and then a wooden palisade protecting both the motte and its adjacent bailey.

Because the castle was predominantly built in wood, over the years it had been burned in the various wars that had overcome the region. Today, the flag of Deheubarth flew above the gatehouse tower, soon to be augmented by Cadell's personal banner, indicating he was in residence. Llelo didn't honestly know if Rhys had a banner of his own yet. Two days ago, everyone had liked to think it wouldn't be necessary for some time. Today, Llelo was debating mentioning the need. It was one more thing Rhys wouldn't want to think about. It probably could wait.

Probably.

Llelo and Rhys initially followed Cadell to his receiving room, but once the king's healers converged on him at Huw's command, the two of them retreated to the great hall where a meal was being served. They told themselves they'd done what they could for Cadell, which was to get him here. Rhys usually didn't care where he ate, not one to stand on ceremony or be catered to, but, this time, he found a place near the end of the high table and gestured for Llelo to sit with him. Llelo didn't recall ever sitting at a high table in his life. It felt awkward to be up on the dais, looking down on everyone else, especially after they'd spent the last day and night as two men among many.

The food provided was welcome, however. Llelo laid into it as if he hadn't eaten in days, which was how he felt.

Just as the two of them were vying for the last piece of bacon, Huw returned, pulling out the chair next to Rhys. "Tell me everything the messenger didn't tell me."

Rhys had a full mouth, but he hastily chewed the food, swallowed it, and then washed it down with a gulp of warm mead. "I don't know what you don't know." He was hedging, but they weren't sure if they trusted Huw.

The steward's expression turned fierce. "Start at the beginning and don't stop until I tell you." Then he swallowed. "My apologies, my lord. That was rude. I am not myself."

"You are upset about my brother's injuries, as are we all." Then Rhys launched into a deceptively detailed description of the events of the day before. On the one hand, when he spoke of the men of Tenby and the actual ambush, he was clear and precise. On the other hand, he kept his explanation of how he and Llelo had survived to a minimum.

On the whole, Llelo thought Rhys did a credible job of conveying trust while trusting Huw with nothing Iestyn, for example, didn't already know.

Then Huw turned his piercing gaze on Llelo. "What about you? Perhaps if you hadn't prevented Rhys from saving the king, he would not be in the condition he is in now!"

Llelo drew in a breath, stunned by the attack. "There were fifty—"

"One Welshman is worth ten Normans!"

"Huw!" For the first time in Llelo's experience, Rhys spoke commandingly to someone older than himself. "The bulk of Cadell's *teulu* had been hiding too. Though they revealed themselves to fight, they could do nothing for Cadell himself, and every one of them died in the attempt. Llelo saved my life. He should not be censured for doing so."

"Would you have preferred Prince Rhys died too?" Llelo had been watching Huw's face as Rhys spoke. Huw had backed down, but there was still defiance in his eyes.

At this query, Huw gaped at Llelo and then turned to Rhys, his eyes wider than ever. "You can't think it! I would never—"

"You weren't there, Huw." Rhys returned to his usual calm voice. "Neither Llelo nor I can banish the sight of my brother falling to the ground. I see it over and over again, even when awake. There was nothing any of us could do."

Huw clutched his robe at his chest, his expression stricken at the pain in Rhys's voice. "If I had been there—"

"You would have died too." Llelo had a further thought that made him keep going, far more bravely than he might have done two days ago. "Is some of this guilt because you helped the king arrange this meeting? Did *you* betray him?"

"No!" Huw clasped his hands before his lips. "Does he blame me?"

Rhys was quick to reply. "Is there some reason he should?"

"I didn't encourage him in this treaty. I didn't believe in it." A few stray tears leaked out of the corners of Huw's eyes. "But I went along with it because he was so determined, despite my reservations. That's why I suggested to Iestyn he follow after the king to the Coed Rath rather than wait for him to return. But he was too late. Just as my regrets are too late ..." His voice trailed off, and he bent his head to Rhys. "If you will excuse me, my lord. I will return to the king's side and make my apologies there."

The steward disappeared through the doorway leading to Cadell's receiving room. Most of the buildings in the castle bailey were free-standing, but the hall was large enough to have inner partitions. The main entry led into the hall itself, and then, at the side and back, were doors leading to other rooms. Beyond the receiving room was what the Romans would have called an office and the Welsh *swyddfa*—a private chamber for official business and for storing documents, paperwork, and treasure.

After he'd gone, Llelo said, "Given the chance, I would question him further. He is, more than anyone else here, something of a witness to these events, even if he wasn't in the that clearing with us. Do you believe he is sincere and telling the truth?"

"I want to believe he is." Rhys shook his head in a despairing manner. "What happened to my brother and his *teulu* is a tragedy. How much worse does it all become if the treachery came at the hands of a man he trusted."

"Before we talk to him again, we need to figure out if our concerns are at all valid."

"Nobody is going to want to answer questions," Rhys said. "I don't have to be an experienced investigator to know that."

"Then we are going to have to be more careful than we are already trying to be. I will begin with the youngest and lowest in Iestyn's company."

"Iestyn will be sure to hear about it."

Llelo lifted one shoulder in a half-shrug. "It depends on how clever I am about asking. If Iestyn confronts you, you are free to hang me out to dry on the washing line."

"I wouldn't do that." Rhys managed a laugh. "But it does seem I have no problem sending you to wreak havoc amongst my brother's men, while I pretend nothing is amiss."

"Then nothing's changed!" Llelo gave a little laugh of his own before sobering again. "It's you who will be doing the real work."

The thought had Rhys rising from the table. Cadell's headache might actually be improving, but it hadn't done so enough yet for him to shoulder the daily burdens and responsibilities of kingship. Huw had brought with him the letters and paperwork that had accumulated these last few days.

Llelo put out a hand to his friend. "May I suggest you first gather your brother's men, before the day gets any later, and tell them you are here to serve and to lead them. Deheubarth is still at war with Gwynedd. Suddenly, you are also newly at war with the Earl of Hertford. They need reassurance that someone is helming this ship."

For a moment, Rhys stared blankly down at the table without seeing it. Llelo could almost see the mantle of responsibility settling onto his shoulders whether he wanted it or not, whether he could carry it or not. Llelo had hated to make his burdens heavier. It was still the truth as he saw it. "I will have to speak again of retribution."

"A common goal is one of the best ways to unite fighting men. You even have a clear target."

"The Tenby garrison." Rhys's mind began to work again. He had been to battle, but never as a commander. Even if Cadell was able to rise from his bed tomorrow, it would be some time before he could lead men again.

Llelo nodded. "The Normans won't know the outcome of the events in the clearing yet, but word of Cadell's survival will spread. They'll soon know they failed."

Aghast, Rhys stared down at Llelo. "Do you fear they'll send another force to finish what they started?"

"I don't know, but we have to consider it."

"As if we didn't already have enough to worry about."

But even as Rhys considered this new problem, Llelo realized what he'd just said. For the first time, he hadn't spoken of the men of Deheubarth as *you,* or *your men,* or *Cadell's men.*

He'd said *we.*

19

Day Two

Gareth

The first soldier to arrive, as Maredudd had promised, was the one who'd been on guard duty and found Rhodri's body. He was short and stocky, with dark, curly hair, and wide brown eyes. Gareth would have put his age in his early twenties. To Gareth's relief, the man, whose name was Einion, was also a font of information, eager to please and in no way on the defensive, especially after Gareth made clear he wasn't going to accuse him of murdering his commander.

At least, he wasn't going to accuse him of that *today*. No need for Einion to know about any internal qualification. They would theoretically ford that river when they came to it, just as Maredudd's company would be physically doing today.

Gareth began: "How long was it between when you saw Rhodri pass your location and when you found him?"

"Perhaps an hour? It could have been a little less than that. You can't have always been Prince Hywel's steward, so you should know how it is when standing watch in the early hours of the morning." When Gareth agreed that he had stood guard duty a time or two in his life, Einion continued, "Time passes slowly. You try to alleviate the boredom by sharpening attention every now and then, depending on what you allow to distract you. I can tell you that the night was dark with no moon, and it was well into my shift. I was anticipating being relieved with the coming of first light, which by then was not far off."

He paused and looked at Gareth expectantly, implying he wanted confirmation that what he was saying made sense. Any further information would require prompting.

Gareth obliged. "Please tell me what you did and saw."

"When Sir Rhodri didn't return, at first I thought nothing of it. Given the way so many men had been ill, he was hardly the first to pass my position that night. I assumed he was sick as well. Everyone else came back eventually, however."

The illness he was describing could afflict any army, and was one reason why sieges were to be avoided if at all possible. Sickness flourished when men were encamped, especially if the weather was inclement, which it had been nearly the whole of the time Cadell's army had been surrounding Hywel's castle.

"This was the first night out from Aberystwyth?" Gareth asked.

"The very first."

"Had you dug a latrine?"

"Yes. Hastily. As the sun was setting." Einion looked a bit pensive. "We'd already buried fifty men by then, and we'd given up the siege because we had so many more ill. Nobody wanted to be next, nor associate with the sick, so I'm not sure anyone was using the latrine anyway. If Sir Rhodri was feeling the same, that would have been why he went off on his own, to find a spot to crouch in private."

In hearing Einion's recounting of the difficulties, Gareth had to wonder again at Cadell's decision to send Maredudd to besiege the castle at Aberystwyth in the first place. It wasn't a terrible idea to surprise Hywel in the middle of winter. Any commander could have been unprepared and unable to defend against such an assault. Within Ceredigion, the castle was the jewel in Hywel's crown. Had Maredudd captured it, the war would have ended. The supreme prize would have been capturing Hywel himself.

"I am not seeing a great deal of illness among the men here, or am I missing something?"

"Those who were the sickest were sent home with the bulk of the army directly south from Trawscoed. Those among us who fell ill between leaving the siege encampment and reaching Ysbyty Ystwyth were left there, in the monks' charge. We left a few more at Mynachlog Fawr. As far as I know, nobody has fallen ill today."

"Tell me more of Rhodri. You were explaining how you were not worried that he didn't return until after some time had passed."

"So many had been laid low, it was a natural assumption." Einion shrugged. "When he didn't return right away, at first I told myself I was mistaken about why he had left the camp and his absence had nothing to do with illness. He was our captain. He could have been walking the full perimeter, and I would not know it. But then one of the other men asked if anyone had seen him, and I began to worry that I'd failed in my duty. It occurred to me that some of Hywel's men could be out there in the dark. So I started looking, walking all the way to the river and back. In the end, he was just a few paces above the bank. Dead."

"Could you tell how long he'd been dead? Had his body started to cool?"

"Oh, I don't know about that, but I'd seen him within the hour. Initially, I thought he'd succumbed to his illness. I didn't see the blood until I returned to the bank with Lord Tomos, having run to him to tell him. I'd never—" He gave a shake of his head, in apparent regret, though some part of him seemed to be relishing the telling of the story. "All this time waiting and watching the castle with hardly an arrow fired, and Rhodri dies by treachery, stabbed in the back in the dark as we were heading home."

"Do you know who might have wanted to kill him?"

Einion shook his head fervently. "I'm sorry. No."

"I heard he was a hard taskmaster."

Einion didn't want to admit that either, but he waggled his head this time in a different way. "He was hard on us, but not unfair, at least not that I saw. Some of the younger men grumbled quite a lot."

"I'd like to speak to them. Can you give me their names?"

"Oh no!" Einion was even quicker to reply this time, not willing to sell out his compatriots. "It was just general discontent. The weather was cold, and then it was wet. Nobody wanted to be told to work in it."

Gareth tipped his head. "How long were you camped around the castle all together?"

"Three weeks."

"Was it raining the night Rhodri died?"

"Not that I remember. Come to think on it, that was the first dry night in over a week. We'd broken camp three days into that last storm. Wind and rain, then ice and snow, and then rain again." He shivered just thinking about it.

Gareth had been outside much of the last three weeks, too, so he well remembered the almost continual rainstorms and wind coming off the sea. Storms weren't necessarily unusual for Wales, but the unrelenting nature of them during the siege had been. Fortunately for Gareth, most nights he'd found shelter with friendly residents of the region, who (for the most part) looked benevolently on Hywel's rule. In truth, it wasn't difficult to be better than Cadwaladr, nor the (deceased) Earl of Hertford. When the latter had been lord of those lands, his only concern had been tithes and taxes, and he'd spoken no Welsh to boot.

After a few more questions about the sequence of events, which meshed with what Maredudd had already told him, Gareth sent Einion on his way. Then, one-by-one, Einion's fellows came. Gareth was glad he'd made no promises to Maredudd regarding his ability to solve Rhodri's murder. He'd told him he would do his best, which he would, but large elements of discovering the identity of the murderer were beyond his control. He was trying to ask good questions, in search of the right ones, putting all of his powers of observation to use in his effort to elicit any information from Maredudd's men that would point towards a culprit.

But no other man had even known Rhodri had been murdered until today. They were shocked at the news, and troubled by it. But still, every answer he received, when it came down to it, was just one more way to say *I don't know*.

20

Day Two

Llelo

Llelo had told Rhys he would attempt to speak to Iestyn's men, beginning with the lowliest, since any of these would be the least likely to question what he was about. Llelo himself had once been fairly far down the roster, more because of his age than his station (given that he was Gareth's son). He hoped they would recognize a kindred spirit in him. He had found, both from his own experience and having apprenticed to his father for as long as he had, that those with the least power tended to be the most observant of the men above them.

A guard put on the postern gate generally had the worst time of it, since he was usually alone in this duty. For that reason, the man assigned the position was the lowest ranked and the youngest. Even in wartime, there seemed little point in wasting the efforts of two men by posting both to sit by a door that never opened except from the inside.

Or, at least, that was the thinking. As with many positions a guard might be assigned within a castle, this one required constant vigilance and a tolerance for boredom. In Llelo's experience, both were hard to maintain for any length of time.

Nonetheless, the door needed to be guarded, as a defense against treachery from within or without. Hywel shared the common belief on the matter: men were weak when they were alone. Bribing a single man with wine, women, or coin was far easier than bribing two. Under other circumstances, Llelo thus would have regretted the sight of the single guard at the postern gate. Not today, since he was currently in the mind for a little bribery.

"How are you doing?" Llelo slid onto the bench next to the guard, a carafe of mead and two cups in his hands.

"I'm all right." The young man's eyes widened to see Llelo joining him, and even more as Llelo began pouring the mead into the cups.

"I thought to share a drink or two." Before the man could protest about not drinking on duty, he added, "It's very watered down. And it's warm. I'm sure you could use it on a day like today."

This was the smallest guardroom he'd ever seen. To reach it, Llelo had needed to pass behind the kitchen, which was a free-standing building next to the great hall, and follow the curve of the palisade under the wall-walk until he reached the little hut. The main castle gate faced south. The postern gate faced northeast, opening onto a track that led either north past the motte or south to the river. A Norman would find safety to the south; a Welshman to the north.

The little room didn't even contain a table, just a single bench facing the postern gate. In an alcove to the right was a brazier that burned brightly, the smoke escaping through a gap between the top of the wall and the bottom of the thatch roof. The size of the room did mean the brazier was keeping the place warm. In fact, it was warmer in here than in the great hall whence Llelo had come. All of a sudden, he was revising his ideas about the least favorite posting in the castle. Being warm counted for a great deal.

Given the age of the guard, who appeared younger than Llelo, this posting might be the best kept secret in the castle. As they sat, each with a cup in their hands, relaxed against the wall, Llelo stretched his legs out in front of him.

The young guardsman sighed contentedly, too, prompting Llelo to finally introduce himself. "I'm Llywelyn."

"I know, Father. Everyone knows who you are. My name is Derwin."

"Please don't call me *Father*, Derwin. I am not a priest." Llelo had still not grown accustomed to being seen as a churchman, never mind *being* one. How the next few weeks or months went would go a long way towards giving him a better idea of what his future plans needed to be. Did he want to stay a monk? Or was he ready to return to his father's side? He had investigated murder plenty for his parents over the years. Never had he led an entire investigation on his own.

Derwin waved away the correction as if it were immaterial. "You are a member of the Order of the Knights Hospitaller and a sworn companion to a prince of Deheubarth. We are more grateful than we can say that you saved Prince Rhys's life."

"I did nothing anyone else wouldn't have done." Rhys and Cadell had thanked Llelo several times already. And while it was true that Rhys was alive because of him, he couldn't feel particularly proud. It hadn't come about as a result of Llelo's martial prowess. He and Rhys hadn't fought side-by-side or back-to-back. Llelo had saved him by *preventing* him from fighting. There wasn't any glory to be found in that. "May I ask whom you mean by *we?*"

"All of us here." Another hand wave. "We hear that if you hadn't saved Rhys, King Cadell might not be alive either. I don't know if it's possible to repay you sufficiently, but they should if they can."

Llelo supposed he didn't know if it was possible either. A king might dispense jewelry or gold when favors were done, or land for great services rendered. For a Hospitaller knight, all such payments would go to the Church. Maybe, if at some point Cadell asked about it, Llelo could suggest that a sum of money go to Ysbyty Cynfyn or another, closer Hospitaller commandery Cadell favored. Whether or not Llelo stayed within the Order, he admired the service they were providing to the people of Wales.

He didn't want to talk about any of that with Derwin, however. That wasn't why he was here. That said, knowing that Derwin thought the men of the garrison were grateful to Llelo made him think he might get real answers to his questions.

And then Derwin added, "I just wish you could have saved my father too."

Llelo froze, horrified that he'd hadn't been thoughtful enough to inquire before coming here who exactly was sitting at the postern gate. "He was a member of Cadell's *teulu*, wasn't he?"

Derwin's shoulders slumped. "I appreciate you coming to cheer me up." He took another sip of his mead.

That wasn't, of course, why Llelo had come. He felt ashamed, but not so much that he wasn't going to take advantage of the opportunity he'd been given. "I am so sorry for the loss of your father."

"The devil take the garrison at Tenby." Derwin spat on the ground in emphasis. "May each and every man responsible rot in hell for all eternity."

Llelo didn't object to the man's passion. Like Rhys, every time he closed his eyes, he could see Cadell falling to the earth and the subsequent slaughter of his men, one of whom he knew now to be Derwin's father. He quite honestly didn't know how he was going to move past it. Or, in turn, how he could help Derwin. It felt like these events would haunt him forever.

The real test would come tonight, when he was finally able to lay his head down properly in a real bed. "Have you given any thought as to how the men of Tenby came to learn of Cadell's location in the first place?"

Llelo already knew, of course, that Cadell had brought this treachery upon himself by conspiring with the Earl of Hertford. The men of Tenby knew about the clearing in the Coed Rath because Cadell himself had told Earl Clare he would meet his brother there. But that information was not general knowledge, and Llelo was not going to be the one to speak of it.

Derwin just gave a sad shake of his head. "I couldn't say." Then he frowned. "You aren't thinking the king was betrayed by one of his own men, are you? One of us wouldn't have told the men of Tenby where he'd be!"

"I would hope not, but we have to wonder, don't we? At the very least, there is some concern that what happened in the Coed Rath is part of a further initiative amongst the Normans to take back more of Deheubarth."

"They wouldn't dare!" Derwin paused. "Would they?"

"Cadell's death would have provided an opportunity."

Derwin's chin stuck out defiantly. "Well, if they thought that, they'd be wrong."

"How so?"

"We have Maredudd, don't we? He's ready to step into Cadell's shoes if needed. And then there's Rhys."

Llelo tipped his head as if simply curious. "What exactly do you mean by that?"

"Well—" Derwin gestured to Llelo "—you know what he's like, Father. Smartest man the Lord God ever made. Well built, with a strong sword arm. We are in good hands, no matter which brother leads us from now on."

21

Day Two

Gareth

Ten soldiers in a row had produced essentially the same description of what had happened as the first. Of course, they were mostly speaking through hearsay, since none of them had been the one to find the body. Thus, Gareth decided to try a different approach with his latest informant.

This time, he was speaking with a grizzled veteran named Seisyll, who, from the moment he arrived at the back of the wagon, looked at Gareth with skeptical blue eyes. His demeanor implied that Gareth's questions were nothing but a waste of his time, but since his commander had insisted he speak to him, and he didn't have anything better to do on the march, he would answer what he could.

To start things off differently, Gareth chose to hop down from his seat at the back of the wagon, rather than having Seisyll climb up and sit beside him. Walking facilitated talking. "How long had Rhodri been your captain?"

Seisyll blinked, indicating a reorientation of his thoughts away from the murder itself, just as Gareth had hoped. "Not long. In fact, I had never met him before coming on the march a month ago."

"Is that a way of telling me you didn't know Rhodri well?"

"I suppose. I don't think anyone did."

From his questioning of Maredudd's men, that had been Gareth's impression.

"Does that strike you as unusual?" Gareth felt at times he was in some way acquainted with every man in Gwynedd. He knew it wasn't true, but he couldn't deny it was a small community. It seemed that was less the case in Deheubarth.

Seisyll shrugged. "King Cadell appointed Rhodri as Prince Maredudd's second-in-command. He was from the east. Gwent, I think. I know only a few men from that area. Apparently, he'd been serving Cadell all this time and had seen a great deal of fighting on those borders."

Gareth paused to think about the several different paths he could pursue from that comment. He wanted to ask about the fighting on the border. He also wanted to ask what Seisyll knew about Prince Maredudd's opinion of this appointment. For now, he simply said, "Did King Cadell also appoint the other commanders of the army? It sounds from what people have said that Prince Maredudd was one of several."

"Yes, that's true. And yes, King Cadell was involved in every aspect of the planning. While Maredudd is the king's brother and was in overall command, he is still young and not so experienced."

"Prince Maredudd spoke to me of the man in charge of the largest part of the army, whom he referred to as his brother's *most trusted commander*. Would he be one of the men King Cadell appointed?"

Seisyll swallowed hard, looking like he thought this question was a trap but didn't know where it was exactly or how to avoid it. "That would be Lord Dafydd. He is foster father to Maredudd's nephew, Einion, whom I believe you have met."

Gareth had to blink at that. "Are we speaking of the man who found Rhodri's body? Einion is Maredudd's nephew?"

"That's right."

"Son of whom?"

"Anarawd."

Gareth hadn't known before this moment that Anarawd had a son or that Cadell had taken the throne over him. In Welsh dynasties, kingship didn't always pass from father to son. The son had to earn it. In all his life, Gareth had never heard of a Welsh kingdom being passed to a child. The people needed a man for other men to follow. Once he was grown, if the boy was worthy, he could take the throne back from whomever had replaced him when he was younger. Like Prince Hywel, Einion must also have been born outside of marriage, since Anarawd had been murdered on the way to his wedding to King Owain's daughter.

"Einion doesn't mind such low duty?"

"Lord Dafydd insists on it. Everyone takes their turn guarding the camp. Besides, he is only twenty-one, and still learning."

Putting aside further questions on that matter, which didn't appear to be currently relevant, Gareth asked, "Had you fought beside Maredudd before?"

"Several times. And before you ask, I find him to be a good leader. He cares about his men. He isn't one to ask a man to put his life on the line when he himself isn't right there leading him. I have known commanders who waste lives because they won't listen to anyone else or in a quest for personal glory. That isn't Maredudd."

This was near to the longest speech Gareth had elicited from any of Maredudd's men, except for Einion, who'd been helpfully loquacious. Seisyll continued to trudge along beside Gareth in the manner of a man prepared to go on all day, for as long as it took, to whatever end his commander had decided. Especially if that commander was Maredudd.

"I appreciate you helping me form a picture of the command structure."

"Well, as I said, Prince Maredudd is young." Seisyll stopped.

This time, he had something of an expectant look on his face and, much like Einion earlier, needed more prompting.

Gareth took a chance and asked, "Are you thinking King Cadell doesn't entirely trust his brother to make good decisions?"

"Over the course of the campaign, he was to consult on most every matter with Lord Dafydd."

"There must be a third commander too." Gareth stopped, hoping Seisyll would complete the thought.

"Four really, if you include Sir Tomos, whom you met on the road and who has taken over as Prince Maredudd's second. It is

Goronwy who leads the last party of men." And then, before Gareth could ask, he added, "I don't know him well either."

"His men sacked a church northwest of Ysbyty Cynfyn."

"I hadn't heard that." He shrugged uncertainly. "I am surprised. We would not have done that. Prince Maredudd would never have countenanced it."

"What about King Cadell?"

Seisyll's eyes narrowed. "What are you suggesting?"

Gareth made a gesture as if to wipe away the question, abandoning any attempt to get Seisyll to say something disparaging about his king. "Do you know why King Cadell did not lead the army north himself?"

"Why would I know anything about that?" Seisyll gave something of a mocking laugh. "The king doesn't share his thoughts with the likes of me!"

"But you must have some idea."

"If I had to guess, I would say the king can't be everywhere at once. Besides, this was an opportunity for Maredudd to command."

"I'm sensing that the ending of that sentence could have been *without serious consequences if he failed?*"

Seisyll bit his lip. "The issue was never whether Cadell could trust Maredudd. From what I understand, the brothers are close. No jealousy among them! It is a question, as I said, of getting the younger ones experience before they really need it."

Gareth understood that part. The more he thought about what Seisyll was saying, however, the less sense it made to him. Prince Rhys had been at Wiston as a fifteen-year-old. Gareth hadn't seen Maredudd there too because Maredudd had been given charge of the newly acquired castle at Llansteffan, which he had helped take from the Normans. At that time, he'd been all of seventeen.

And then Seisyll offered up more information than Gareth had asked for. "If there was a negotiated surrender, King Cadell wanted to be sure things were arranged properly."

Gareth made another educated guess as to what Seisyll was really saying. "He chose Lord Dafydd to lead because he thought Maredudd would be too soft on Hywel?"

He made sure not to call him *Prince Hywel*. He was learning all the ways these southerners could take offense, and he wanted to keep Seisyll as happy as possible. He'd learned more in this one interview than from the previous ten.

Seisyll took in a breath through his nose. "Hywel *is* Maredudd's cousin. Hywel's father and Maredudd's mother were siblings. They weren't even half-siblings, like Maredudd and Cadell. Blood recognizes blood. Even if the cousins are on opposite sides of this fight, neither is really in charge, are they? Maredudd answers to Cadell and Hywel to his father, King Owain. And Cadell and Owain have no reason to like each other."

That begged yet another question to pursue, but maybe not today.

"Was it Maredudd's decision to abandon the siege?"

"Now that is a pretty puzzle." Seisyll eyed Gareth.

"I don't mean to offend, but your lord did charge me with discovering who murdered Rhodri."

Seisyll put up a hand. "No offense taken. From what I heard, it was Lord Dafydd's decision."

"Did Sir Rhodri agree?"

"Again, I can only go by what I heard, but I understand the answer to be yes." Gossip swirled around an encampment quicker than the wind. It was a wonder Maredudd, Einion, and Tomos had managed to keep Rhodri's murder a secret up until now. In fact, if Maredudd hadn't come upon Gareth and seen an opportunity, nobody else might ever have known.

"And Prince Maredudd?"

"I wouldn't know." This time, Seisyll wasn't prepared to give a real answer, even a hesitant one.

"But you could guess?"

"I'd prefer not to. These are issues above my station. I'm just an old soldier, as you can see."

Gareth didn't believe that for one moment. "Thank you for your frankness. I appreciate your patience with me."

Seisyll bent his head. "I hope you find the bastard who did this. The man was killed while relieving himself! Can you imagine a worse moment to die?"

22

Day Two

Llelo

By now, Llelo was feeling quite comfortable at the postern gate, between the brazier, the warm mead, and the talkative guard. "Given the loss of your father, why are you at this post at all?" He made a gesture that encompassed the two of them on their bench as well as the postern gate. "Is this your usual spot?"

"I'm from Dinefwr, come with Lord Huw. So, no. This particular guard post isn't usual for me. The garrison captain put me here on Lord Iestyn's orders, to prevent me from riding to the forest to retrieve my father's body."

Not so comfortable all of a sudden, and ashamed of his thoughtlessness, Llelo straightened on the bench. Derwin had spoken matter-of-factly about something that wasn't matter-of-fact at all. While they'd done their best to care for the dead, leaving each fallen man in a respectful state, they hadn't had time to bury them in that clearing. Part of the mission in sending the men to bring the bier from St. Issell's had been to inform the cleric there that men had died, and to request his care for the dead.

Each man would have to be moved and then buried in holy ground. But doing so could not have been accomplished by Iestyn's men. While the men of Tenby had taken their dead with them, Iestyn had determined, sensibly enough, that they could not be slowed down in enemy territory by the bodies of a dozen men. Not with an injured king needing to be carried on foot. The Tenby garrison had been required to travel all of three miles from the ambush site to Tenby with their three dead and half-dozen wounded. The twenty miles to Caerfyrddin had been a different challenge entirely.

"I'm sorry." Llelo felt helpless that there was nothing else to say. And he *was* sorry. "I lost my father when I was twelve years old, to illness, not an ambush."

Derwin looked him up and down. "You landed on your feet, though, didn't you? You're a knight; you're a Hospitaller!"

"Time does ease the pain, as I'm sure others have said." Llelo put out a hand to him. "Did your father say anything to you before he left?"

"About what?"

Llelo affected a shrug. "Was he worried about anything?"

"Not that he said to me, but I was on the postern gate at Dinefwr, too, just a member of the garrison, not even in training to take his place, not like my older brothers."

"Do you have many of those?"

"Three." Derwin wrinkled his nose. "Maybe I should be for the church too."

Llelo preferred to avoid that subject. "Did you note anything unusual in the days leading up to Cadell's departure?"

Derwin gave a little laugh. "Nothing ever happens at this post, Father. Maybe I should be happy about that."

This time, Llelo didn't correct the mistake Derwin made in calling him *Father*. It would have been insulting to Derwin and would serve no purpose. And Derwin might be speaking so frankly because he didn't want to lie to a priest.

Then the other man made a motion with his head, qualifying his words. "Except for that one time, I suppose."

"That one time?" Llelo was careful not to shift or sit up straighter or in any way convey his interest. "When was this?"

"A month ago now? I came on duty at the midnight hour to find the postern gate open."

Llelo tried not to crow. "Where was the man who was supposed to be guarding it?"

"He arrived a moment later, having run to the latrine. As I said, it's a boring post where nothing ever happens, and not a warm one either, not like here. We were both surprised."

"Did someone enter or did they leave?"

"We didn't see anyone. There were no strangers in the castle. When we pulled the door closed again, we realized the latch wasn't catching properly because the wood was warped with all the rain. It was a matter of a few moments' work to fix."

"And then what?"

"What do you mean?"

"What did your captain say when you told him?"

Derwin blinked. "We saw no reason to tell him. There was nothing amiss; nobody missing; no attack on the castle, clearly. We chalked it up to a heavy wind, which we were experiencing at the time." It was his turn to shrug. "It isn't as if it hadn't happened before."

Maintaining his façade of idle curiosity was hard, but Llelo thought he managed it. "When was another time?"

"Oh—" Derwin threw a hand into the air. "A few weeks before that, maybe. And then maybe a few months before that. It happens."

"Is the postern door here of a similar construction?"

"Identical, I'd say. The keep at Dinefwr is built in stone, but the palisade is still made of wood."

"May I go out myself?"

"Of course, Father. And just to remind you, this happened at Dinefwr, not here."

Llelo still wanted to have a look, so Derwin motioned as if to say *be my guest*. Llelo lifted one side of the bar off its L-shaped rest in order to let the door swing inward. Then he walked through the doorway and tried to pull the door closed again, but there was no handle on the outside, as there wouldn't be.

Llelo studied the door, hands on his hips, and then looked outward to his surroundings, imagining the situation at Dinefwr. That castle was situated on a higher hill, and the land sloped sharply down from its postern gate. The River Tywi wended its way through the countryside to the south of both Caerfyrddin and Dinefwr Castle, twenty miles away. Here in January, the landscape was not quite as green as it would be in a few months. This past hour, the sky had not been completely overcast, and, in some places, rays of sunlight broke through the cloud cover into the valley.

The peacefulness of the scene was a sharp contrast to the twisting in Llelo's gut. His parents always said that the best way to investigate was to ask questions and see where the answers led.

Well, he'd asked them.

Now he just had to figure out if they were leading him to the truth ... or astray.

23

Day Two

Dai

"We're going to keep this nice and simple." Dai glanced at Ieuan, whose mood had improved considerably since Maredudd had returned his bow to him an hour ago. The prince was keeping his word that they weren't prisoners. "We walk amongst them; we let them talk to us. Then, if given an opening, we ask questions. That's how this works."

"It doesn't seem like much." Ieuan was older than Dai, if only by a year, so it felt a little odd to be instructing him. It would be like Dai telling Llelo what to do, which, come to think on it, he did all the time. "Do you want me to talk at all, or just listen?"

It was a good question to be asking. "We are here for answers, and if something occurs to you, feel free to say it." Then, feeling a bit better about the process, and making sure to keep his tone even, without any implication of superiority, Dai added, "When questioning is done well, it doesn't even feel like an interrogation. That's the beauty of this method."

Ieuan had been moving easily beside Dai, walking with him near the front of the company of men. Since his father had sent them off, they had worked their way to this position. The idea was to encourage the marching men to grow so accustomed to seeing the two of them in their midst that they took them for granted. At the very front, four men walked abreast, setting the pace.

Keeping to the proper speed was vital to the wellbeing of the company. It would be easy to lose men at the front or off the back. Someone tall like Llelo had a tendency to outpace everyone else with his long legs and youth. By the same token, older, less fit men could fail to keep up as the weariness of the march set in. With a hundred men in the company, in roughly twenty-five rows, the line had stretched out a bit over the course of the morning. It wasn't so many men, however, that the commander couldn't keep track of the total.

Beside Dai marched two archers with bows and quivers on their backs. Despite having his own weapon returned to him, Ieuan kept eyeing their gear with what Dai read as envy. Ieuan's bow was shorter and less powerful than the ones these men owned. It was a known fact among anyone who'd been to war that the men of the south made the best archers, while those in the north knew spears. Each required years of practice. Despite being a northerner, Dai's father had taught him to shoot. Though, as the son of a knight, it was swordplay on which he had focused most of his attention.

"So you are looking into Sir Rhodri's death, are you?" This came wholly unsolicited from the archer to Dai's right, a man named

Cadfan. He was tall, thin, and older than Dai, perhaps close in age to Gareth.

"That's right. What can you tell me about him?" Dai wasn't going to waste the opportunity now that it had finally arrived.

He had already tried talking to the captain of the archers, a man named Morgan, who was distinguishable from the rest of his men by his leather hat with a feather, rather than a cap or hood. The result hadn't been much more than a few monosyllabic answers. Since then, Dai had kept his conversation general, trying to learn more about the structure of Deheubarth's army, its size, and the illness that had ultimately forced them to abandon the siege. Truly, Maredudd's men shouldn't have been speaking to Dai of these things at all, except they'd been told to be accommodating. To a man, they had not been treating him like an enemy. The mood, as a whole, had been jovial and interested. Dai himself felt perfectly welcome, and sensed no animosity among any of them.

He wondered how differently they would see him if they knew he was an apprentice member of the Dragons, Prince Hywel's elite fighting force. While part of Dai could wish for nothing more than to have Gruffydd, Iago, or Steffan with him right now, he couldn't be sorry they were safe in Aberystwyth. The presence of even one Dragon might be enough to put every one of them in chains, no matter how much Maredudd respected Gareth.

"What do you want to know?"

"Well, ultimately, who killed him." Dai saw no sense in beating around the bush.

Cadfan laughed. "If I knew that, believe me, I would tell you."

That sounded like the entire truth. At his comment, the other men around him chuckled too.

Dai relaxed a little. "How well did you know Rhodri?"

"He wasn't a bowman." Cadfan shrugged.

"So, not well?"

"Less well than some."

Since Dai seemed to be questioning the whole group of men at once, even if only Cadfan had said anything, he gestured to encompass all of the men around him. "Did any of you know him better?"

For a moment nobody said anything, even Cadfan. Dai did catch some furtive looks in the direction of a man walking with three others in the row immediately behind Dai. Finally, when the looks became too obvious, the man sighed. "I suppose you might say I did. I am Daron. He was my cousin. Rhodri's mother and my mother were sisters."

Nobody had mentioned a cousin before now. This withholding of vital information was not atypical for an investigation, and when it eventually came to light it made them all say, *why didn't someone care to mention that earlier!*

Leaving Ieuan with the first group of men, Dai fell back a pace, and those nearest made room for him, adjusting their own place in the lines of marching men. Dai began with, "I'm sorry for your loss."

The man glanced at him. "You sound like you mean it." In contrast to Cadfan, he was similar to Dai in height and weight, neither particularly tall nor thin. He was much older, however, perhaps even thirty years.

"Was Rhodri older or younger than you?"

"Older by two years." Daron made a motion with his head. "We didn't always get along."

Dai had been getting that sense. When nobody knew somebody well, that often meant nobody had liked the person in question, and, more to the point, didn't want to say so. Most people had a strong impulse to refrain from speaking ill of the dead. "Not always, or rarely?"

A man on Daron's other side spoke up. "I'd say *never*."

"Will you tell me why?" Dai said.

Daron suddenly looked a bit fierce. "Are you going to use it against me?"

"Did you kill Rhodri?"

"No!" The denial was immediate and instinctive.

Dai nodded to hear it. "I never met the man. There is no body to examine, no murder weapon, and no suspects. I don't even know what he looked like, except if he looked something like you?"

Daron shrugged. "Maybe a bit."

"And yet, my father is charged with discovering who killed him. Our place in this company depends upon it."

"I don't know about that." Then Daron mumbled something else under his breath Dai didn't catch, some southern saying he didn't know. Normally, he was very good with accents, but that didn't always mean he understood what was *said*. "To answer best I can, Rhodri had a temper. We didn't grow up in the same household, but he would come to our home when his father beat him. We were friends when we were young but, once Rhodri became an adult, he fell to drinking and ended up following in his father's footsteps."

It was a common story. Dai's birth father had been much the same. Dai and Llelo had resolved to take after Gareth when they eventually married. If they married. He couldn't imagine hurting someone he loved, and the idea of Gareth stumbling into their wagon having drunk more than his share and hitting Gwen was so horrifying as to make Dai gag. That was never going to be him. Never.

"Did Rhodri have a wife and children?"

"Just a wife. Have you not spoken to Enid yet?"

"I didn't know he had a wife until this moment. She's here?"

"She's a cook." Daron eyed him. "I wonder why nobody has said."

People have been saying everything and nothing, apparently was Dai's thought, but he didn't voice it. Instead, he said, "Until now, we didn't know about either you or her."

"Talk to her. They were married ten years. No children. I was with her when Rhodri was being murdered, so she didn't do it. You can ask her."

Dai really wanted to know what Daron meant by being *with* Enid while her husband was being murdered in the middle of the night, but he didn't feel he could ask right in this moment. He had a hard time believing Daron would openly admit to betraying his cousin with his cousin's wife. If he had been, it was one of the first secrets they'd unveiled, as his father had told Maredudd would happen.

Even if Dai wasn't going to ask about that in particular, he still had plenty of questions. He gestured again to encompass the men around them. "Are all of you part of Maredudd's guard?"

"As in, do we make up his *teulu*?" Daron said. "No. He doesn't have a personal guard, no more than does Rhys, his brother. We'd all protect Maredudd, of course, if he needed it, which mostly he doesn't."

That comment brought a general round of laughter from Daron and the dozen men who were stumping along with them. Over the course of Dai's questioning, there'd been some shuffling about as men fell back or caught up on the march.

Ieuan had remained silent this whole time, letting Dai do all the questioning, and now he unexpectedly said, "Do you mean Prince Maredudd doesn't like having someone protecting him all the time, or do you mean he doesn't need protection because he's such a good fighter?"

Daron laughed again. "Exactly."

24

Day Two

Gareth

This was one murder investigation in which Gwen had thought to have little involvement. She had a baby to look after, not to mention Tangwen and Taran, for whom the adventure of the road had already worn off. They didn't have other children to play with anymore. Despite having objected to their presence initially, now they were upset they were gone.

The news that Rhodri had a wife, however, had brought Gwen to the supply carts where the cooks and other helpers were setting up to make dinner. The monks at Mynachlog Fawr had restocked Maredudd's carts so they would be eating well. At least tonight.

And likely tomorrow, too, if all went as they hoped, since by then they might actually make Caerfyrddin. They had come close to twenty miles today through a process of marching five miles, and then resting for an hour, and then marching another five, and resting again. Gwen sensed the pace of the marching soldiers had actually increased over the course of the last leg of the journey this afternoon.

The farther they could travel today, the less distance they'd have to go tomorrow. They were close to home now, and they could smell it. They'd had a difficult time at Aberystwyth, losing good men without ever really doing any fighting. They were ready for it to be over.

Rhodri's wife saw Gwen coming and, before Gwen could introduce herself, or really say anything at all, she thrust a spoon towards her lips. "What do you think?"

Instinctively, Gwen tasted … and then smiled in surprise. "It's delicious. You're Enid?"

The woman went back to her fire, stirring the pot of stew from which she'd served Gwen. "Yes. And you're Gwen. I heard you might be coming to speak to me. You or Lord Gareth." She glanced at her. "Are you here instead of your handsome husband because he thinks a woman might better gain my confidence?"

That was exactly what Gareth had thought, and Gwen didn't deny it. "Yes."

Enid barked a laugh. "You're probably right." She eyed Gwen up and down. "A woman with a baby strapped to her chest is a very different prospect than a knight from Gwynedd."

"We do just want to know about your husband."

"My dead husband, you mean." And then, maybe as a means to soften her bluntness, she came closer and touched Angharad on the nose. "Aren't you a pretty one. Just like your mother."

"Thank you. She is beautiful."

Enid went back to her cooking. "I meant what I said about her mother, too." She glanced over her shoulder at Gwen. "What do you want to know?"

Gwen had been intending a more gentle approach, but Enid's manner was anything but gentle, never mind her kind words about Angharad's and Gwen's looks. "Rhodri's cousin had some warning words to say about your husband."

"You mean that he had a temper. That he beat me."

"Yes."

Enid allowed herself a grunt. "He's not wrong."

"Why didn't you leave him?"

In Welsh law, a woman had a right to compensation if her husband beat her, and could divorce him under specific circumstances. The laws weren't always followed, especially in Norman territories, where it seemed women had no rights at all, but Enid and Rhodri were Welsh, serving a Welsh king. Enid shouldn't have had to put up with beatings.

Enid was silent for a long moment, at first making Gwen fear she had still been too blunt. But then Enid's expression softened slightly. "I loved him, in my way, and I know he loved me as well. He was a good provider; he didn't put me aside for failing to give him a child. He was often away at war, and we would have the best times when he returned. It was only bad when he fell to drinking."

It was an old story, one Gwen had heard a hundred times before. She had personal experience with the type, too, since her own father had fallen to drinking, though he had never once raised a hand to Gwen or her brother. If Gwen had known Enid before this moment, if they'd been friends, she would have tried to help her before now. Her husband was dead, however, and all that was left were questions.

"Daron says he was with you when Rhodri died."

"I know what you're thinking." Enid let out a snort. She'd already emitted an admirably wide range of sounds during their short interaction. "I hope he didn't imply we were rolled up together."

"He didn't say one way or another."

"Well, that's something." Enid grunted again. "We camp together. There's a dozen of them, plus me. I cook for them." She gestured to the pot hanging above the fire. "Tonight is unusual because we have foodstuffs from the abbey. Every small company brings their own cook and is responsible for their own sustenance, you see. That changes when the lord forbids foraging. Like tonight."

"Is foraging forbidden because we have crossed the River Teifi and are back in lands King Cadell holds? It was all right to *forage,* as you say, before then, when we were in Ceredigion?"

The River Teifi flowed almost directly east to west at this location. The bridge here wasn't the only place to cross the river, but it was by far the best. A Norman lord had put up a motte and bailey castle on the other side of the river, but it had been destroyed during the 1136 war and had not been rebuilt. Since Gwynedd had taken over Ceredigion, the river had provided a rough border between Hywel's lands and Cadell's. Both lords might be regretting not rebuilding—and holding—that castle now.

Enid gave her a dark look. "You should watch how you speak. How would we fare in Gwynedd, do you think?"

Gwen put up a hand, glad she hadn't shared any of her real thoughts. "My apologies. Prince Maredudd has been generous in allowing us to remain unbound."

"He has a soft heart."

Gwen had entirely lost the thread of the conversation, and she had to take a breath to reorient herself. "How well do you know Lord Maredudd? Your voice became quite gentle when you spoke of him."

"I was his nanny, once upon a time. His and Rhys's."

Obviously, some digressions were a good thing, which she should remember in times to come. "For how long?"

"After their mother was killed, until they no longer needed one. I had no children of my own, you see. And, before you ask, I married Rhodri afterwards, not while I was with them."

"What about Daron, Rhodri's cousin? Does Lord Maredudd know him well too?"

"Well, of course. We are all family, really, aren't we? Daron's father served old Gruffydd as his valet practically his whole life. After Gruffydd's death, he went to Anarawd and then Cadell. He died two years ago."

"Does that mean Lord Maredudd knew Rhodri well too? It was my understanding that King Cadell appointed him and he wasn't Maredudd's choice."

Enid wrinkled her nose. "I suppose that's true. Obligations, you see. Despite his temper, Rhodri had earned it. It was his turn."

"Did Lord Maredudd resent his brother telling him what to do?"

"Not that I heard. Rhodri didn't imply that. And it isn't something I would talk to Maredudd about."

Gwen made sure her voice was particularly gentle for the next question. "Do you know who killed your husband?"

Enid stirred the pot through a count of ten, acting as if she hadn't heard Gwen speak, though she must have. Finally, she shook her head. "It had to have been a servant of Hywel, trailing after us, and then taking advantage of an opportunity when it presented itself."

It was a nice thought; it would make things easier for this company, and it was exactly the reason Maredudd hadn't told anyone Rhodri had been murdered in the first place. In past investigations, it had been common for people to hope, or, in fact, assume, that a culprit came from outside their circle, as if wishing could make it so. In this case, it could even be true. "Do you know why Prince Maredudd suspects otherwise?"

"I don't know that he does."

"Then why would he ask us to investigate?"

"What kind of commander would he be if he didn't?" This was essentially what Maredudd had said to Gareth and Gwen earlier. To Gwen's mind, he was right to be worried about a snake amongst his people. That first murder was like crossing a threshold. A second was easier. Gwen had also seen that many times. "You shouldn't be asking me any of this. Ask him."

"We have. It is my understanding you didn't know Rhodri had been murdered until today. How do you feel about Maredudd keeping it a secret?"

"What difference does it make now?" Enid shook her head. "I have no reason to look farther than what's right in front of me. My husband is dead. Let him lie."

"You don't want the murderer caught? As Rhodri's wife, you should be owed *galanas*." That was the word for the payment required when one man murdered another. In Wales, once guilt was established, the family of the murderer was required to pay the family of the victim. If they then chose to inflict some further punishment on their own guilty family member, that was up to them and not for the court to decide. Only among Normans were men hanged for crimes. The Welsh weren't that wasteful of a soul God had created.

"If I could get it; if it could ever be proved. Best not to hope for it; best to get on with living." She glanced over at Gwen, this time without a smile. "And now, if you don't mind, I have hungry men to feed. I'd best get on with the cooking."

25

Day Two

Gareth

"Enid's last words to you sound like a dismissal if I ever heard one," Meilyr said.

"It did seem that way." Gwen said. "One moment we were talking pleasantly, and the next she was telling me to leave, just like that."

Gareth was sitting with his family around a campfire he and Meilyr had built to a respectable height. Despite the fear and difficulties of the journey, Meilyr had been in good spirits all day today, as if something within him had been set loose. It was Saran's opinion that he had missed being on the road. For him, this current journey was like the best of both worlds. He got to experience the day-to-day diversions of itinerant singing while remaining secure in the knowledge that he was King Owain's chief bard and the most renowned bard of his generation. Plus, he had a comfortable place to sleep every night! Back when he'd been a true itinerant bard, he and his family had transported their belongings in an old cart and slept in tents. They'd come a long way in eight years.

Moments ago, Meilyr had returned from singing before Prince Maredudd and a large crowd of gathered men. Such events always brought about a heightened state of good humor in Gareth's father-in-law. Even among strangers—and potential enemies—his music was appreciated.

This time, to the great delight of everyone in the audience, Tangwen had joined her grandfather for a song he had been teaching her. Thus, the performance had concluded with uproarious cheers. Gareth wasn't entirely sure he was in favor of his daughter performing at six years old—or maybe ever—before a hundred veteran soldiers, but he couldn't fault the result. Even now, he could hear Tangwen plunking away in their wagon on her child-sized *crwth*, even though she was supposed to be going to sleep.

Taran, who should also have been asleep, was singing along with her in a voice of such purity, even at his tender age, that Gareth was getting chills. Every now and again, Meilyr shot a look of such pride and genuine joy towards the back of the wagon that Gareth's heart contracted, too. It just went to show how it was possible to be happy even when the world around him descended into chaos.

Meanwhile, Dai was lying on his back, his head pillowed by his clasped hands, to all appearances unmoved by the joviality in his elders. "Let's lay out what we know. Do we even have a grasp yet on what we're looking at, here?"

Normally, it was left to Gareth to ask that question, but he could be content with the reversal of their usual roles. "Why don't you tell us, son."

Dai obliged. They had an investigation, and he wanted to talk more about it before the night got any older. "Rhodri, Maredudd's second-in-command, was stabbed twice in the back by an unknown assailant, near the riverbank, in the early hours of the morning the first night this company rested after fleeing Aberystwyth. Rhodri had a wife, a cousin, and a bad temper that made the rest of the men here avoid him, if not actively dislike him. King Cadell chose him for this command." He broke off, glancing towards his parents.

Gareth had the sense he was wondering if he should continue, or maybe he feared he had overstepped. As Dai's father, it was Gareth's job to nip that idea in the bud. "Your tone tells me you have more to add."

"I do, not the least of which is to point out that, other than his temper, we have very little sense of Rhodri as a person. Did he gamble? Did he keep a woman on the side? Did he have any children not with his wife? The descriptions of him I heard today are so nonspecific, at one point I wondered if Rhodri ever existed at all. Could this be the first investigative failure for the great Gareth ap Rhys?"

"Son—" Gareth put out a hand to him, made suddenly uneasy by Dai's mocking tone.

But Dai grinned. "That was the way Maredudd referred to you. I don't even disagree! But I can't help thinking there's a remarkable lack of urgency in everyone involved. Rhodri was murdered, and nobody cares."

"Not even Enid," Gwen said.

"It reminds me, and not in a good way," Saran said, speaking for the first time, "of our experience investigating at Ysbyty Cynfyn. Nobody wanted to know the truth there either."

"They were hiding an entirely unrelated secret," Gwen said. "So what's the secret here?"

"*I* can't help thinking it has something to do with how happy Maredudd was to see us," Saran said. "It was the sight of you, in particular, Gareth. I can't dismiss the way his eyes lit when you gave your name, like he couldn't believe his good luck. Was that really because he wanted Rhodri's murder investigated?"

Gwen nodded. "It is that idea which makes me consider once again why Maredudd brought his men this way when they could have taken the high road straight south from Trawscoed, just like the largest part of the army led by Lord Dafydd. I know what Maredudd said about leaving the ill at Ysbyty Ystwyth, but there are other religious houses between Trawscoed and Caerfyrddin. His band could have outpaced the slower and the ill. They could have been at Dinefwr by now."

Gareth gave a shake of his head. "We can't know, and I don't feel at this point that I am able to ask. Tomorrow night when we reach Caerfyrddin, whether or not we've solved Rhodri's murder, I will talk to Maredudd about when we can leave. In the interim, we have one last day to learn as much as we can."

"What if the killer really was one of our men?" Meilyr said. "Hywel could have sent any number of people to follow Maredudd's army, to ensure everyone really left Ceredigion. Rhodri died the first night out. Enid could be right that one of them saw his chance and took it."

"It would be a convenient solution, one that requires no investigation at all," Gareth agreed. "Rhodri's death would be just one more casualty of war. I wouldn't be sorry to know it."

"But if that's not the truth, the killer is among us," Dai said. "If I were he, I would just lay low for these few more hours. Once we reach Caerfyrddin, our chances of finding him go from slim to nonexistent—"

He broke off as a shriek rose up from the woods to the north of them, near the river. They swung around, peering into the darkness beyond their fire circle. After another few heartbeats, Gareth made out the figure of Bran hobbling towards them, waving his hands to get their attention, as if by the time he was this close they could possibly miss seeing him.

He limped the last few feet to stop in front of Gareth, breathing hard. "He's dead! He's dead. I swear to you, he's dead!"

26

Day Two

Gwen

Gareth put a hand on Bran's shoulder to steady him and looked directly into his face. "Who's dead?"

Up until this moment, Bran had affected the attitude of someone who'd seen everything and could no longer be surprised by any event, no matter how horrific. Over the last two days, he had given the impression of being entirely capable and worldly. He'd fought in battle and been wounded. He'd survived on his own for decades. But as he gazed up at Gareth, his eyes were wide, his face pale with shock, and he looked well on his way to full-blown panic. "I don't know! I couldn't see!" He managed to take a full breath, after which he was able to explain. "I tripped over someone in the dark coming back from the river."

Then Bran looked down at his right hand and his face paled even further at the blood on his palm and fingers. He started wiping at it with a cloth he'd been carrying, meant for drying one's body after bathing. As his motions became increasingly desperate, Gwen took the cloth from him, dunked it in the water bucket kept near the fire, in case it needed to be put out quickly, and slopped the water over Bran's hands. Cleaning off blood wouldn't normally be the most important thing she could think to do after learning of a dead body, but she could see the way Bran calmed as the blood was washed away.

"You're all right now," she said. "Look, it's all gone."

Bran shook himself. "My apologies. I don't know what came over me."

"You have lived through war and tragedy," Gareth said. "Something like this can bring it all back, especially when it comes as a surprise."

Bran nodded jerkily. "I'm better now. I'll take you to him, and you can see for yourself."

By then, since it was impossible for anyone within fifty feet of their campfire to have missed Bran's arrival, Gareth motioned to one of the onlookers, the behatted captain of the archers, Morgan, and spoke with the same clarity he'd directed at Bran: "Find Tomos and Prince Maredudd, if you will. Tell them someone else is dead near the river, and I am going now to investigate."

Morgan bent his head in acknowledgment and ran off without needing further instruction.

Then Gareth grabbed a burning brand from the fire, Dai took a second, and they set off in the direction whence Bran had come. Gwen followed with Bran, walking at a slower pace, since his legs were shorter than Gareth's, and the leg wound was obviously bothering him.

"What were you doing by the river on your own?" Ironically, the best time to ask questions was when a witness was most agitated and upset. It was then she was most likely to get truthful and spontaneous answers.

"I wanted to wash off the dust of the road." Bran's hair was cut very short, but as he shook his head, he scattered drops of water. "Today was difficult for me. It reminded me so much of past marches—" He broke off, unable to fully articulate what he was thinking, his mind still too full of death. "And now this." His eyes were almost hollow. "It doesn't get easier. You would think it should, but it doesn't."

Gwen would have liked to know more about his past, but questions along those lines might actually do more harm than good in this moment. Instead, she stuck to the mundane. "I myself bathe nearly every day." In point of fact, Gwen's hair was still wet, too, from when she'd gone in the river shortly after Enid had sent her away, Gareth keeping watch and the two of them taking turns. Being clean was well worth a few minutes of chill, and Bran was right that it was a good way to wash away the troubles of the day, along with the dust from the road. Blessed were the times when she could bathe in warm water, like at King Owain's seat at Garth Celyn. Otherwise, any ocean, river, or lake was good enough for her. The River Teifi had been flowing robustly, and running water always helped her think. "You even had your own towel."

"Oh, that?" Bran's already hobbling step faltered. "The cloth wasn't mine. It was on the ground next to the body. I hadn't even realized I'd picked it up until I reached your fire circle."

Maredudd had ordered the camp set up in a field just off the main road they'd come down. Cattle filled the next field over, grazing on what grass had put up shoots over the winter. They would mostly be fed from stores until spring was in full bloom. Meanwhile, this particular field had been left alone. The dead grass was a bit long in places, and the closer they came to the river, the boggier the ground, coating Gwen's boots in muck. She could have stayed at the campfire with Angharad, but Saran was perfectly happy to hold her granddaughter for an hour while she slept on her shoulder, and Gwen wanted to see whatever this was with her own eyes. Gareth might need her perspective later.

"Did you murder this man, Bran?" Gareth glanced over his shoulder, speaking gently and without urgency. The question was forceful enough.

"I did not, my lord. Why would I?"

"Lord Maredudd wanted to blame one of Hywel's men for Rhodri's death. You are one of Hywel's men. You have made no secret of it."

"I wasn't anywhere near the place where Rhodri died!"

"How can any of us know that?" Gwen said. "You didn't join our company until yesterday."

Where before Bran had been sick with horror at the murder, now he was shaking with rage at being accused of it. "You think I murdered Rhodri and then decided to murder someone else while I was at it?"

"We have to ask," Gwen said. "We won't be the only ones wondering."

Perhaps it was unfair to immediately turn the one who found or reoprted a murder into the primary suspect for that murder. And yet, to have the murderer *discover* the body of the man he'd just killed was a good way to deflect attention. Bran was obviously shaken by the death. But was it, rather, that he was shaken by the murder he'd just committed? In the eyes of the southerners who surrounded them, he was the perfect culprit. He was an outsider who had joined the company only yesterday. As far as they knew, he could be anyone.

A saving grace for him was that murderers, unlike arsonists, didn't tend to want to stick around to watch the aftermath of their work.

Bran swallowed hard, and then he nodded. "Yes, I see that now. So I will say it again. I did not kill this man. I did not bathe in the river, commit murder, and then decide I'd better cover my hands in his blood so you wouldn't suspect me once I reported it. I can't be any more clear than that. Some other man did this. We have a camp full of possibilities. The men of Deheubarth are all traitors anyway."

Gwen understood that Bran's defenses were up as a result of being accused of murder. She also knew why Bran might hate the men of Deheubarth. Turning them into minions of the devil made killing them easier. It still didn't make them anything other than human.

"Prince Hywel wouldn't agree with you," Dai said from his place beside Gareth. "He didn't ask for this war. He doesn't want to fight his own cousins. He certainly doesn't want to be responsible for harm coming to either Maredudd or Rhys."

Bran latched on to Dai's defense of Hywel as a distraction from what he himself might have done. "He has faced down his own relations before. He has put Cadwaladr in his place."

Bran wasn't wrong about that, though Gwen wasn't going to concede anything in this moment. They had accepted Bran as one of their party as a matter of course, spreading a protective cloak over him from the start like he was their own cousin. To do so had been right and practical. She wasn't sure how she felt about any of their decisions now.

When nobody countered him immediately, Bran walked a few paces more, taking deep breaths as he did so. As soon as he was able to speak calmly once more, he said, "I don't want to argue with you. Please believe me that I didn't kill this man. I will swear it before the altar."

By then, they had only ten yards to go to reach the woods above the river bank. Gareth and Dai took a few last strides to reach it first, but with the darkness under the trees, they then waited for Bran and Gwen to catch up. Taking the lead now, his shoulders high and tense, Bran showed them the way, following the very trail along which Gwen had walked a few hours earlier when she had gone to bathe in the river. A dozen feet farther on lay the body of a man, lying face down in the dirt.

Gareth bent to him, his torch lighting up the area. The man wasn't wearing armor. Nor was his hair wet. If he'd come to bathe in the river, he'd been murdered before he'd had the chance. That's why the cloth Bran had picked up had still been dry. This man's only protection from attack was his shirt of undyed wool, which meant he'd had no protection at all.

The killer had stabbed him twice in the back. The wounds were bloody and wide, indicating they'd been struck with force and anger.

At Gareth's nod, Bran and Dai rolled the body over to reveal the face of Tomos, Maredudd's new second-in-command, who'd replaced Rhodri.

Gwen crossed herself. "Peace be with him."

"And also with us." Gareth couldn't have looked more grim. "Dai's advice was good, but it seems our culprit has no interest in laying low. And he has developed a taste for murder."

27

Day Two

Gareth

“This is is more like it.”

Gareth’s head came up at Dai’s words. “Dai.” He made his tone flat and thus censoring. Dai had obviously thought it safe to speak his mind, now that Gwen was headed back to the encampment in order to tell Maredudd where to go to find them and Bran was vomiting his guts out by the river.

“What? It’s just the two of us to hear. You were thinking it too.”

Gareth sent him a sideways look. “If you’re right that I was also thinking it, to do so was equally wrong of me.”

Dai pointed a finger at him. “But you *were* thinking it.” He didn’t actually grin. That really would have been inappropriate.

Gareth made a grumbling sound deep in his throat. “I am torn between wanting you to remain your honest self and wondering where I went wrong in raising you. Yes, this changes everything. Maybe I’m sorry about that, too. I liked Tomos, what I knew of him, and if this hadn't happened, we could have arrived at Caerfyrddin tomorrow and put aside this entire investigation. One attack on the first night of a retreat can be encompassed or explained away, especially when nobody seemed to like or miss the dead fellow in the first place. But not a second murder, using what appears to be the exact same method, within Deheubarth territory. We are in for it now."

Dai took a step closer and lowered his voice so the sound wouldn't carry. "Do you think Bran murdered him?"

Gareth wrinkled his nose. "I saw the anguish in his eyes when he arrived at our fire. He was genuinely horrified by the murder. That doesn't mean he didn't do it, but I won't accuse him again without proof."

Then Gwen came down the path with Maredudd in tow. As the prince encompassed Gareth and Dai standing over Tomos's body, he picked up the pace and arrived in something of a huff. Halting some five feet away from Gareth, his chin jutted out as if they were about to have a fight. Or, at least, Gareth read in his posture that he wanted one. "What happened to Tomos?"

"We don't know anything more yet than you yourself can see, my lord." As he spoke, Gareth gestured towards Bran, who had also returned, wiping at his mouth with the edge of his cloak. The older man was trying to convey his usual stolidity, but he was still visibly quivering from the vomiting and the threat against him that hung in the air. Whatever else might be thought of him, this murder had affected him deeply. "While Bran was coming back from the river, he stumbled over the body."

Hands on his hips, Maredudd looked Bran up and down. The weather had turned cold, and Gareth could see the prince's breath in the torchlight. The leaves underneath were a little crunchy, too. "Give me your knife."

Bran blinked, his eyes moving to Gareth. At Gareth's nod, Bran removed his knife from its sheath, reversed it, and handed it to Maredudd. He had learned enough from the earlier accusations to do as he was told and not protest.

The prince studied the blade with a fierce expression. In the torchlight, Gareth could see how clean it was. That proved nothing, really. A clever murderer would never use his own knife. At the very least, he would dispense with the blade he did use. If Bran had been intelligent enough to murder Tomos and then pretend to discover the body, he wouldn't be carrying around the knife that did the deed.

After Maredudd handed it back to Bran, he turned to Dai. "What about you, boy? Did you kill him?" He was still on fire, glorying in his anger and knowing to the very core of his being that he had every right to it. He'd lost someone close to him. Lashing out at witnesses was inconsequential by comparison.

Dai appeared so shocked at the sudden accusation that he laughed. Gareth was ready to defend Dai where he hadn't Bran, but Dai was able to collect himself a half-breath later and say, "No, my lord. I did not."

Maredudd's manner remained one of aggression. He spoke loudly and thrust his body forward, as if trying to put those facing him on their back foot. Maredudd was a leader of men, however. One day, he might be King of Deheubarth. He needed to learn that he couldn't, or shouldn't, lay blame where it wasn't deserved, no matter how overwhelming his grief. Gareth might not be the best man to teach him this lesson, but he was the man Maredudd had. Especially with Tomos dead. "My lord, my son is not—"

Before Gareth could complete his sentence, the fire left Maredudd like water poured on a hearth. "Forgive me. I know this is not your handiwork." He made a helpless gesture with one hand. "Find out who did this, Lord Gareth."

"I will try, my lord." Gareth spoke with the same lack of emphasis he'd used at the start of the conversation when he'd said Dai's name.

It was a night for deep breaths, it seemed. Maredudd visibly reoriented his thoughts like the leader of men he was. "Whatever you need to do the job, Lord Gareth, you may have. I, along with any of my men, are at your disposal."

"Thank you for that. For now, I would request a litter to move the body into the back of a cart so I can examine it. Do you hope to be on our way again first thing in the morning, even with this death?"

"This murder, you mean?"

"Yes, it is murder. He was stabbed, as you can see, just like Rhodri."

Maredudd pressed his lips together before replying. "Will spending another night here aid your investigation?"

"I won't pretend we wouldn't benefit from revisiting the scene by the light of day." Gareth spread his hands wide. "That said, as long as I have space to work in the interim, and I can get to work right away, we wouldn't have to stay here another whole day."

"Then I would just as soon get my men home."

Gareth wondered if he should point out again what he'd said by the fire—that when they did get home, Maredudd's men would scatter. They had families to see to. It had been a difficult campaign; one they had, to all intents and purposes, lost.

But, for now, he had other worries. "My lord, you must be careful." He put a further degree of urgency into his voice. "You have had two men murdered, both very close to you."

"You fear for my life?"

"I do, my lord." He didn't mention that his six-year-old daughter had been the first to see it. "Do you have someone you can trust to guard your back?"

"As I told you last night, that is what you are here for." In an abrupt motion, Maredudd strode away, back towards the encampment.

Gwen had been staying in the background throughout Maredudd's conversation with Gareth and Dai. Now she looked at Gareth, eyebrows raised, and he gave her a quick nod. "If you could."

"I'll see what I can do. Maybe my parents can help." She motioned to Bran. "Come with me, Bran. You don't need to be here for this."

Bran startled, as if not expecting to be addressed, but then he acquiesced. They both started up the path after Maredudd.

Gareth watched them go and then, like Dai earlier, said what he was really thinking. "That right there might be the bigger task, in the end."

"What task is that?" Dai asked.

"Saving Maredudd from himself," Gareth said.

28

Day Two

Llelo

Rhys met Llelo at the entrance to the great hall and shoved a quarter of a loaf of bread into his hands. "You need to eat."

Men were still awake even at this late hour. Dinner would have been served shortly after sunset, so he'd missed it long ago. Llelo took a bite of the bread, finding it fresh and chewy, warm enough to have melted the butter Rhys had spread on it.

"Thanks." He spoke around a full mouth. "I was talking to one of the guards whose father died in the Coed Rath." He swallowed, already feeling better to have something solid in his stomach to soak up the mead he'd drunk. "I'm not sure I learned anything useful. Time will tell."

The truth he was loath to admit was that he wasn't enjoying investigating on his own quite as much as he'd thought he might when he'd started. By now, based on his investigations with his father, he felt like he should have learned a more telling piece of information than that someone *might* have been in and out of the postern gate at Dinefwr. It could be important, especially in light of the ambush and death of Cadell's men. But it could equally be quaintly irrelevant, signifying either that the wood was warped, as the guards had assumed, or at worst that some person in the castle had gone to meet a lover. These events were in the past. How they could be relevant to this week's treachery couldn't at this late date be determined.

Given that Dinefwr was twenty miles away, too, it didn't seem to be the best use of his time to set a watch on this postern gate, not when guards were already posted there. He had asked Derwin to let him know if he encountered anything unusual during his watch, or heard about something from others. That left him with nothing obvious he should be doing and no new thread on which to tug. The more he considered the matter, the more likely it seemed to him that the traitor, if there was one, had died at the hands of the Tenby garrison, himself betrayed by the men with whom he had conspired.

Rhys made a motion with his head. "Finish the bread. We need to talk to my brother."

Llelo found his step faltering. "We?"

Rhys just shrugged and led the way. Cadell had insisted he not be left in his bedchamber in the keep, even if he might have rested better there (which was the concern of his healers). He wanted instead to stay in his receiving room off the great hall, so as not to be isolated from what was happening in the castle. Everyone had endeavored to please him. Cadell had been coherent at the time, and he was still the king. If Llelo had been the one so wounded or had only a few hours (or days) to live, he would have wanted to be with people, too.

Regardless, Cadell's proximity to the great hall made it easier not only to tend to him, feed him, and see to his every wish, but to visit him when he wasn't asleep. Rhys had been doing exactly that all day, while at the same time going through the papers and affairs of kingship, which Cadell was leaving undone. It was exactly as Llelo had warned: if Cadell wasn't capable of making the decisions that needed to be made, then it was Rhys who had to.

"Is something the matter? I mean, more than the obvious?" Llelo asked from a pace behind his friend.

"I don't actually know. It's you he wants to talk to."

Llelo raised his eyebrows. "Me? Why me?"

"That is, more or less, the same question Huw asked, except it was *you want to see* him*? Why* him?"

Llelo made a face. "I don't want to get on Huw's bad side." He already knew the steward had spent the day assuring Cadell that he would be on his feet in no time and that, in the interim, Huw would take care of everything. Cadell had replied the same way each time, "My brother needs to learn. You have to teach him, since I no longer can. God has given me this momentary grace. We need to make the most of it."

Rhys let out something of a mocking chuckle. "It is impossible to count all the things Huw has been disgruntled about today. I have ended up ignoring him most of the time. You should too."

Llelo thought that was all very well and good for Rhys to say. He was a prince.

However, when Llelo and Rhys entered the receiving room, Cadell was talking to Iestyn, without Huw present. At the sight of the two young men, the king dismissed his friend and, in the same motion, waved Llelo closer.

Just Llelo. He sent Rhys back to work. Not that Rhys still couldn't hear everything they might say, since he returned to the table rather than be banished from the room.

Up until Iestyn's men had realized Rhys might soon be the heir to the throne—if not the actual king—they'd treated him like any other eighteen-year-old amongst their company. He'd been encouraged, tolerated, and dismissed all at the same time. They didn't appear to hold him in particularly high esteem, other than according him the same respect as anyone of a higher station. None of the men had consulted him anymore than any other soldier, which meant *not at all*. Mostly, they'd ignored him.

Which was why Llelo honestly hadn't expected to hear Rhys spoken of so admiringly by a soldier he didn't know personally. Llelo had long since come to see how remarkable Rhys was. Anyone who spent any time in his company should know it. On the one hand, a casual approach to Rhys's abilities while he'd been growing up should have been better for Rhys, since it wouldn't do for him to feel continually chuffed about his worth. On the other hand, it was less good if it meant he underestimated himself. Rhys didn't naturally put himself forward nor take a leadership position. The time had suddenly come, however, when everyone around him expected more. So far, Rhys had not disappointed them.

In fact, Huw had assigned him two personal guards to follow him everywhere. Rhys was not well-acquainted with the two men, but he had decided to give them a day, maybe two, before reassigning them and conscripting two others of his own choosing.

In retrospect, the older men's approach had reflected Cadell's attitude, right up until Cadell suddenly had to rely on Rhys for something more than hiding in the bushes. Cadell had said all sorts of nice things about him since then, on top of openly stating to Rhys that he saw the ambush as a sign of God's wrath at how he'd governed Deheubarth all these years. He'd been so convincing that Rhys was no longer suspicious of his brother. An as-of-yet unspoken truth in Llelo's mind was that this change of heart on Cadell's part would not last.

Cadell lay on a proper bed, rather than a pallet on the floor, indicating the people who cared for him had gone to some effort to keep him here. It was far easier to tend a man who was raised up from the floor, anyway, since the healers wouldn't have to kneel or crouch to do their work. It also allowed Llelo to sit on the stool which Iestyn had been occupying.

Feeling uncertain to say the least, Llelo waited, his hands between his knees, for Cadell to finish his examination of him. Throughout, Llelo endeavored not to sigh, twitch, or look away, and thus give the impression he was uncomfortable under the scrutiny. Cadell, in fact, was looking better in this moment than he had since before the ambush.

Finally, Cadell said. "Rhys told you that I know who you are."

"He did."

"Did he also say that he told me the reason he summoned you was because he was worried that the threat against him was coming from me?"

"Is that what he said?" Llelo answered Cadell's question with a question which, if he were doing the interrogating, would have immediately raised his hackles.

Cadell guffawed, which was a bit terrifying to see, as his face became all teeth and the humor never reached his eyes. "That was a test, Sir Llywelyn. Rhys has told me no such thing. I know it to be true, anyway. Why else summon you, the son of my enemy's steward? A man would have to be desperate to do that. More than desperate."

Llelo didn't know what to say. It seemed impossible that he wouldn't give himself or Rhys away by even a simple nod of the head. Twice now, Cadell had made a comment as a way of confirming a guess. However much poppy he had imbibed, his mind was still working. That meant Llelo couldn't trust anything he said not to be a trap.

At Llelo's continued polite expression, Cadell's mouth twisted. "So, tell me, why do *you* think you are here, Llywelyn?"

"Because your brother asked me to come."

"And you don't know why?"

"It wasn't necessary to know why at the time. Of course, we have discussed his reasons, but you'll have to ask him about them. Certainly, by now it seems it was a good decision. Prescient, even, one might say."

"You saved Rhys's life. If you weren't already a knight, I would dub you one." He made a slight scoffing sound. "Though, your knighting came from the hand of Prince Henry himself. It would be hard to imagine a greater honor."

Llelo bent his head, acknowledging the truth of Cadell's words without speaking.

Cadell wrinkled his nose as an indication of dissatisfaction. "Not a talker, are you?"

"That would be my brother," Llelo said, maintaining his seriousness. "I have learned the hard way that my mind never works as quickly as his, so it's usually better to say nothing at all and see how the conversation develops."

"A skill you are using on me, I see."

Llelo had to shift in his seat. "You asked to speak to me, my lord. I will answer truthfully any question you put to me."

"Like father, like son, is that it?" Now Cadell tsked under his breath. He was so much more animated than yesterday, Llelo could imagine him rising from his bed tomorrow. "Tell me: if your father were here, would he be as worried about my life and Rhys's as I can see you are? Would he be seeking answers, as you have been on my brother's behalf?"

Llelo wasn't immediately sure how fully he should reply. He didn't want to spar with Cadell. That was, in fact, the last thing he wanted. At the same time, he sensed that if he didn't show a bit more spark, Cadell would think less of him, maybe even limit his access and attachment to Rhys. It had become clear over the months Llelo had lived in Deheubarth that Cadell was ruthless in his opinions and didn't suffer fools. That he was currently confined to his bed was irrelevant.

So, while Llelo's impulse was to fade into the woodwork, for once, maybe, the circumstances called for something different. "You mean if my father walked through that door behind me today, and you didn't instantly toss him into the dungeon?"

"If that." Cadell's tone couldn't have been more dry. "If we had a dungeon here."

"Then, yes."

In all this time, Cadell had barely moved his head, letting his facial expressions do all the work. Now, he tsked under his breath and said, "Yes ... to what?"

This might be a test again. Llelo didn't actually think Cadell had lost the thread of his questioning. Llelo certainly had not. "Yes, he would be worried about your life and Rhys's. Yes, he would be seeking answers."

With that, Cadell contemplated Llelo for another long moment. It was so long, in fact, that Llelo felt the need to review what he'd said, wondering what trap had been sprung on him while he wasn't looking. Then Cadell said, very softly, "Why would that be?"

"Because he could do nothing less."

29

Day Two

Dai

They hadn't brought a real bier, just two long poles with a tarp tied between them. It would be difficult to carry the body very far on it, but then, they didn't have far to go, just to one of the carts parked near the road. Even now, some of Maredudd's men should be unloading its contents into another cart to make room for Tomos's body.

As they watched the men work, Gareth spoke low in Dai's ear: "Footprints."

As when Gareth had fit an entire conversation with Gwen into a few words, no further instruction was necessary. By now, everyone in the family knew the routine. The immediate ground around the body, since it was just off the path, was torn up by all the people who'd walked this way tonight, heading to the river and back. That was where Gareth and Dai had been looking up until now. Next, they'd have to ask the sentries about what they'd seen, just as they'd done with their investigation into Rhodri's death. Until Gareth examined the body, they couldn't really know how long Tomos had been lying there. Plus, with the cold weather, the body would have cooled more quickly than in summer.

None of that was Dai's charge at this moment. He bent to the ground, some three feet away, and stepped carefully, worried about disturbing what little might be left to find. Beginning on the trail itself, he first circled around to the east, towards the main road. The encampment was just off it to the west, so directly south of Dai's position.

Then he crossed the path closer to the river, to the north of the body. He only managed a single step before he saw, right there in the mud, a distinct boot print. And then another. "Father." He didn't raise his voice, not wanting to distract the men around Tomos's body.

Dai and Gareth had worked together often enough these last months that Gareth knew what that particular tone of Dai's meant and left off what he was doing. When he arrived at Dai's side, they both lowered their torches so they could see the ground better.

"From the length and shape, it's a man's boot, but it's hard to tell much else about it, given the mud." Gareth placed his own foot next to it. "My size, near enough. A person's foot is bound to slip every now and then because the soil is so damp."

"Your feet are bigger than mine." Dai compared his foot to the boot print, too. If he squinted, either his own or his father's could have been a match, with Gareth's foot slightly larger and Dai's slightly smaller than that of the man they were seeking.

"In order to be sure ..." Before the men carrying the makeshift bier could leave, Dai pulled off one of Tomos's boots and compared it to the print. The size of Tomos's foot proved to be significantly smaller than that of whoever had made the print, even accounting for the squish of the mud that might make a man's foot look larger than it was.

"Did you notice Maredudd's feet?" Gareth said. "They were small too."

"What I saw was his expression when he looked down at Tomos," Dai said. "I don't think he believed Tomos was really dead until he saw his face. I don't think he killed him, either."

Gareth let out a low laugh. "Well, that's three of us we can exclude. Only a hundred more men to go."

"Bran's feet are much larger than mine. I made a point to check before he left, in case we got this far." In truth, after Maredudd had accused Dai of murder, Dai had felt a little more sympathy for Bran.

"I saw that too." They'd been fooled on this matter before. A great deal depended on how far in advance the murder had been planned. "The toes of Bran's boots were particularly pointed as well, which those in this print aren't."

"I will look for more footprints and follow where they lead."

"Thank you," Gareth said. "Not for the first time, I am grateful you're with me. It's going to be a long night."

It would be a dark one too, with heavy cloud cover threatening rain once more. It brought Dai flashing back to his very first investigation. He'd been all of ten, merrily consenting to help his parents, though they hadn't been his parents at the time.

As he walked along, at first Dai was worried the darkness would make the footprints difficult to spot, but as long as he kept his torch low to the ground, he had no trouble following them. Even this far under the trees, the soil was saturated from weeks of rain. In many places, the bootprints were sunk deep into the mud. At another time, muddy boots would have been something to look for once he returned to camp. But Maredudd's men had been living in mud for weeks. No wonder everyone wanted to get home as quickly as possible. They could cope with yet another night in wet tents if it was the last one.

To be on the safe side, Dai walked slowly, his eyes on the ground, not only watching for the prints but for other signs someone had passed by here. Gareth had been adopted too, after the death of his parents when he was five. His uncle had taught him to be a tracker. In turn, Gareth had taught Dai to look for broken sticks on the ground, indicating someone had walked on them; bits of fabric caught on spiny bushes; and, in some cases, drops of blood.

The footprints curved back towards the encampment. Dai really would have liked to find the avenue the murderer took on the way to murdering Tomos, not just the one he'd followed after the killing. If these were even his prints in the first place. Since none of them faced the opposite direction, Dai had to conclude that the man who'd made them had walked along the main path, waited for Tomos, killed him, and then fled by this route.

He hadn't run from the scene, though. The steps were evenly spaced and solid. In fact, they looked remarkably like Dai's own in their ponderous progress.

Dai had helped his father with plenty of investigations, so he was happy to help again, but he missed the Dragons and wondered if he would ever get back to working with them again. He had been paired with his father most of the last year as it was. That was fine by him, on the whole, but he wouldn't want his friends to forget about him. When Hywel had sent Dai and Gareth out one more time, hours before the arrival of Maredudd's army, Dai hadn't openly protested. As they were leaving, however, he had privately made his discontent about what he viewed as his banishment known to Gruffydd. He had wanted to stand and fight with him and the other Dragons.

Gruffydd had demurred most strongly, saying, "Hywel doesn't need more fighters. What he needs is men who can think on their feet, as you can. You are a born scout. Actually, I heard the prince the other day call you a *natural spy*. Don't think you're missing out here. You aren't being sent away as some kind of punishment or because you don't belong with us. We need you out there more than in here. The rest of us are jealous of *you!*"

Since then, Dai had rolled the words *natural spy* around in his mind and on his tongue. In his family, there definitely were worse things to be.

A piece of a cloak snagged on a branch banished his thoughts of past and future. In the darkness of the woods, Dai couldn't tell the color at first, but when he brought the torchlight closer, it looked black or maybe a very dark gray. That would be typical for any man's cloak, since the color was an easy one to dye and hid dirt well. The Cistercians and the Templars wore white cloaks of undyed wool, indicating both austerity and purity. White cloaks were also impossible to keep clean, and every Cistercian monk of Dai's acquaintance had a rim of grime along his hem no matter how often his garments were washed.

Then Dai spared a thought for how Llelo was doing wherever he was. His cloak, as a Hospitaller, would be black. Regardless, Dai wished Llelo were here right now so he could tease him about his attire. And they could follow this investigation where it led together.

Dai came all the way up the river bank, out of the woods, and walked straight into a sentry.

Both of them were surprised, the sentry brandishing his spear in Dai's direction.

Dai put up both hands. "It's just me, Dai ap Gareth."

The man tipped up the spear point and blew out a breath. "My apologies. Lord Tomos is dead! We are on high alert."

"As you should be." Dai couldn't blame him for his fear. The killer could be hiding up a tree, watching them work, and they wouldn't know it. Most of the trees didn't have leaves this time of year, but here and there was a pine or a spruce. Even were a man in a tree without leaves, it wasn't as if Dai would have noticed. His eyes this whole time had been on the ground. The thought was a good reminder that occasionally it would be wise to look up. "It is I who should be apologizing. I should have been whistling or humming a tune so you would know I was friendly."

Here was another lesson Dai had learned over his years as Gareth's son: it never hurt to apologize. A real man had enough sense of his own self that he could encompass his mistakes. Or even take the blame for ones that weren't.

Dai was rewarded with a brief smile from the sentry. "Were you—" He paused and tried again. "Were you the one to find Tomos's body?"

"Not me, but my father and I have seen him, since the man who did stumble over him came to us first." Dai paused. "Did you know Tomos well?"

"He was kindly to me. My mother's cousin. I'm Gronw. How was he killed?"

Dai kept his eyes fixed on Gronw's face. What he saw was genuine grief. "He was stabbed in the back."

"That's how Rhodri died."

"Yes. So now someone has killed two people."

Gronw looked away, towards where Tomos's body had been found. "Is that what you're thinking? The same man did both killings?"

"It would be a great coincidence to have two men, both Lord Maredudd's second-in-command, die in the exact same way within days of each other within the same company of men and have it not be the same person responsible for both murders."

Now, Gronw looked down at his feet and dug into the dirt with the toe of his boot, like a boy chastised for misbehavior. "It could still be someone from outside the camp and have nothing to do with anyone here. Coincidences happen."

"They do." Dai endeavored not to openly scoff. "But I wouldn't want to bet my life on it."

Gronw sighed. "Nor would I."

30

Day Two

Llelo

"You're telling me your father's honor is such that it would not allow him to let me die if he could do something to stop it?" Cadell asked this question in a mocking tone. With every moment that passed, he was sounding more like his old self and less like a man suffering under God's punishment. "My death would make Hywel's life easier."

Unexpectedly, Llelo found laughter bubbling up in his throat. He had put forth the very same idea to Rhys while they were on the march. "That may be true, but I also don't see it as that simple. Prince Hywel doesn't want you dead. He wants you to accept the bargain your father made with his father."

Cadell dismissed that observation as if Llelo hadn't spoken. "What if I told you I didn't want any investigation into the circumstances surrounding the ambush in the Coed Rath, and that you are to stop what you are doing?"

A chasm opened before Llelo's feet. This really had become an interrogation—except instead of Llelo questioning Cadell, it was Cadell attempting to extract from Llelo information, or some response, that Llelo couldn't predict. And Llelo was definitely a recalcitrant witness. Worse, Cadell appeared to know it or he wouldn't have been testing him this way.

"I am here on Rhys's behalf. I would want to hear any order like that from him."

"That is far too diplomatic an answer. I am telling you right now as the King of Deheubarth: stop investigating."

Llelo gazed at Cadell, thinking through all the possible replies and not liking any of them. At the very forefront of his thoughts, even though this time Cadell hadn't asked about Gareth, was *what would my father say?*

"If that is your order, I would obey it."

"But you wouldn't like it? And you would express that thought? You think you should have the power to go your own way, do you?"

Llelo knew the answer to that question. "I am responsible for my own soul. If you died and I had done nothing to stop it, even were it in my power, wouldn't I be culpable before God?"

Cadell harrumphed. "You think every man should be his own master that way?"

"Every man *is* his own master that way," Llelo had to smile, "whether he knows it or not."

Unexpectedly, he was feeling far better about this whole conversation. Never before had he been required to stand on his honor the way he knew his father once had. Back then, Gareth had refused a direct order from Prince Cadwaladr and been ejected from his position. He'd lost Gwen's hand in marriage in the bargain, since Meilyr couldn't countenance their union when Gareth no longer had a lord to serve.

Throughout this conversation, Llelo had, in its essence, been laying out for Cadell what had become, for him, a central tenet of his faith. It was not a faith to which he'd been born. Even as Gareth's son, he could have gone many different ways and still been of service. His parents would still have loved him. He'd chosen this one. He'd just never had to articulate it so overtly before. "The only part of a man's life which he truly controls, when it comes down to it, is his own soul. I hope to stand upright before God for what I have done with mine."

"I forgot I was speaking to a churchman," Cadell said, again with a bit of mockery in his tone. "Some would say that to follow an order given by your lord, no matter what you think of it, is doing God's Will."

"Some would say that."

Cadell persisted. "To defy your lord's order is, by definition, to defy God. Is it not better to stand in unity with your fellow men than to create disunity by going your own way?"

During Llelo's growing up with Gareth and Gwen, discussions like this had been a regular part of any mealtime. What was honor? How did one stay true to oneself? How does one decide what is right and what is wrong? What if there wasn't always a clear path? For his family, finding that path was the necessary thing.

Cadell seemed to think Llelo wouldn't have thought of all this before. He wanted to be the devil on Llelo's shoulder. He might not even believe in what he was saying.

Still, he *was* saying it, and he seemed intensely interested in Llelo's answers.

"Is that not, in the end, how we arrive at tyranny? Do we not hear from Psalms, *Shall the throne of iniquity have fellowship with thee, which frameth mischief by a law?*" Llelo made a motion with his head. "When good men ignore what their hearts are telling them is right and do what their overlord commands, even when they know it to be evil, they do evil, too."

"Surely, a lesser one." Cadell's tone was almost sneering now. Llelo didn't sense that was because of the specific content of Llelo's argument. It was more because he had become uncomfortable with Llelo's sincerity.

Sincerity was something else Llelo had chosen. And really, he struggled with being anything but sincere.

Trying to right the ship of this conversation, Llelo said, "Your brother asked me here to watch his back, and I have done that. If I believed standing down would jeopardize Rhys's life, I would be remiss in anything one could call my duty to ignore that feeling. It's what kept Rhys alive in the Coed Rath."

Cadell contemplated Llelo's face once more. "If others knew who you really were, they might fear you were spying for Hywel."

Even more than before, Llelo found himself with a need to call upon his inner *Dai*, the braver, more outspoken version of himself. "You don't seem like a man to worry overmuch about what other people think."

"Touché, my young friend!" Cadell actually let out a bark of a laugh. "You are correct. I have been baiting you, and you have risen to the occasion. I have questioned your honor, and I apologize. But I needed to know who and what I was dealing with, given that your honor didn't stretch to telling me who you really were."

Llelo tried not to openly sigh in relief. When Gareth had stood up to Cadwaladr, he had been cast into the wilderness. While traumatic at the time, in retrospect, it had been the best thing that could have happened to him. Even if the same might be true for Llelo, he had been hoping he wasn't going to follow in Gareth's footsteps in that. At the very least, he would prefer not to experience the dungeon Cadell claimed not to have. He was also intensely thankful Cadell wasn't his lord.

Rhys had been listening this whole time from his desk on the other side of the room, and for the first time felt moved to intervene. "That was my doing, brother. Don't blame Llelo for that. The only way he would agree to come was if he never had to lie."

"A lie of omission, though ..." Cadell's voice trailed off. He was back to testing Llelo, and by this point Llelo found his temper rising to see it.

But Rhys scoffed. "I don't discuss with everyone what I had for breakfast, nor the state of my digestion. That doesn't mean I am lying to them about how I feel. It was you who taught me to mask my true self when knowledge of it would impede my aims or do my listeners no good. With Llelo, we didn't discuss his background. And before you complain that it was the one thing you would have liked to have known, and that it was relevant, I still beg to differ. Llelo's parentage is not important because Llelo is not here to spy for Hywel. He is in service to the Hospitallers, and he is here as my companion, to watch my back, as he has so ably done."

Llelo felt like applauding, but Cadell's eyes narrowed further. This was by far the most animated he had been since his injury. His head couldn't be hurting him as much if he was able to have such an extended conversation. "As to how you became acquainted in the first place—"

Rhys cut him off with a wave of his hand. "Llelo and I met years ago during the attack on Wiston, where you brought me, as you must recall. We have been fast friends ever since. Just because I didn't tell you about it, doesn't mean I was lying either. Do you need to know about every person I meet?"

"Only when one of them gives you a child. I want to know then." Now he looked back to Llelo. "Hywel is going to know soon enough that we were ambushed by the garrison at Tenby—and that I have not yet been able to walk properly. I can already sense his glee from here."

"As before, I beg to differ, my lord. Hywel does not wish you ill. Nor dead." Llelo chose not to repeat what Hywel actually did wish, knowing Cadell didn't want to hear it again. Instead, he said, "Though I hear you can feel your toes now. That surely is a good sign. And your head must be much better too."

"Just in the last hour or two I can feel life returning." Cadell waggled both feet back and forth. "I can even do this." He pushed up abruptly, prompting Rhys to leap to his feet.

"Brother! Stay where you are." And when Cadell persisted in swinging his legs out of bed, Rhys hurried closer. "What are you doing?"

"What I can. What must be done."

Before Rhys could stop him, Cadell reached for Llelo, who had no choice but to catch his arms and help him rise. "Now, we are going to walk around this room if you have to drag me between the two of you the entire time."

In point of fact, Cadell did better than that. He was able to lift his right leg, not normally but on its own. He could even stand on it and it would hold him up. It was his left leg that dragged.

It took a quarter of an hour, but they made it around Rhys's desk and back to the bed. When Cadell was finally lying down again, sweating profusely and exhausted, he said, "So, what are we going to do about Tenby?"

Rhys gazed down at his brother. "We will give Maredudd another two days to get here. If he doesn't arrive by the end of the week, and Llelo hasn't discovered a traitor within your ranks who's still alive, the three of us will make a plan." He paused. "And then Llelo and I—and every man of Deheubarth who is capable of bearing arms—will carry it out."

31

Day Two

Dai

The sentry, Gronw, chewed on his lower lip. "If the murderer really is one of us, how is poking about in the woods going to help you find him? I thought Tomos was murdered closer to the road?"

"I was following footprints that might have been left by the man who did the murdering."

Gronw's eyes widened. He wasn't that young—not as young as Dai—but he had the expressive face of an eight-year-old. Or maybe the boy Dai had been at ten, even having lost both parents. That first investigation with Gareth and Gwen at Newcastle-under-Lyme had been nothing but an adventure in Dai's eyes. Until the very end, that is. Adventure was something he'd longed for but had seen very little of up until then. Perhaps that made him the same as most boys, and what was different was that he'd met Gareth and Gwen and had his world transformed. "Did you see anyone come out of the woods like I just did at any time tonight?"

"No. There has been nobody about here since I came on duty."

"Which was when?"

"Several hours ago."

"Really, nobody? You've seen nobody at all?"

"Well, I mean, nobody who shouldn't be here. Nobody new."

With that, Dai realized he had to redefine what he was asking. *Nobody* to Gronw, meant a stranger, someone whom he thought could have murdered Tomos. "Who did you see otherwise?"

Gronw rubbed his chin as he thought. "My friends Marc and Pedr came by with a cup of warm mead, just to keep off the chill. Cadwgan was here briefly. He's the watch commander. Then he went back to his tent. There was a steady stream of people walking to and from the river all evening. I think I did see your uncle, the older man. The path is some distance away, so I couldn't be sure, and *oh!*" This came out as a real exclamation. "Not long after that, I saw what must have been Lord Tomos walking towards the river."

"Must have been?"

"I wasn't sure if it was Tomos or Maredudd. But that can hardly help. Lord Tomos didn't stab himself in the back."

"No, it does not seem so. Was it dark by this time?" Dai felt it best to keep his questions coming quickly, before Gronw had time to think about answering.

"Yes. He was leaving the encampment with a cloth over his arm. I assumed he intended to bathe. That would have been an hour ago?" Gronw waggled his head as he thought about the series of events. "I almost called out, since, if it was Lord Maredudd, he was without a guard. When I realized it was just Tomos, I let him go, thinking we didn't have to worry about him anymore."

It had already been at least an hour since Bran had found Tomos's body, which had been warm and not stiff when Dai had first touched him. Bran had picked Tomos's bathing cloth up from the ground and brought it to the fire, where Gwen had used it to wipe the blood from his hands. Given the body's location, Tomos couldn't have been dead long, not with being so close to the path. From Gronw's observation, Bran had gone to the river first and might have been bathing already by the time Tomos followed. Tomos was then killed before he could reach the river, and Bran found him on his way back up the path.

Then Dai focused on Gronw's last word. "Anymore? You didn't think you had to be worried about him *anymore*? What does that mean? Why were you worried about him before?"

Gronw's mouth opened and closed, taken aback by this line of questioning and not wanting to answer. Eventually, however, he had to succumb to the pressure of Dai's steady gaze. "Tomos was too old to be on the march with us, really. He'd come only because Lord Maredudd asked for help with this command. He had been to war as a younger man, but that was fifteen years ago. We were glad to have him anyway because he cared about us more than some."

Dai nodded his understanding. Some captains believed that in order to get the best out of men, harsh discipline was necessary. Others thought they could do more with clear rules and a little understanding. Dai personally preferred the latter. Really, he'd just described the difference between his birth father and Gareth. "How does this lead to worrying about Tomos?"

"He'd been married, with two grown sons, but his wife died, and then both his sons died—one from sickness and one in battle two years ago. Just before that second death, Tomos remarried. All of a sudden, he was a new man. But then his new wife and child died in a sickness, around Easter time last year. He was devastated. She and the babe had become everything to him. For some men, even old men, they never recover from grief, and he had so much to recover from. Maredudd was trying to give him purpose because he didn't care about his life anymore. He started drinking too much."

Dai pursed his lips. "Sometimes that makes men reckless, not just with themselves but with the men they lead."

"That wasn't Tomos. Well, he wasn't our commander until a few days ago, was he? He was a leader in this company, but more as an adviser to Maredudd. He always knew how to say the right thing. It was like we were all his sons. He didn't ask men to do anything he wasn't willing to do himself." Gronw shook his head. "I can't believe he's dead. Lord Maredudd must be devastated."

"Why in particular do you say that?"

"Well, Tomos was his foster father, wasn't he? After Lord Maredudd's parents died, it was in Tomos's household that Maredudd was raised."

Once again, it would have been nice to have had this piece of information earlier. "Him and Rhys?"

"Yes, at first, anyway. Eventually, King Cadell brought Rhys back into his household, so he could have better tutors, once the king realized how quickly Rhys learned. A scholar and a warrior, is our Rhys." For a moment Gronw's voice had swelled with pride. Then, his brow furrowed again. "Maredudd and Tomos even look alike. That's why at first I thought he was Lord Maredudd on his way to bathe. Now, I wish I had called out anyway. If I had stopped Tomos from going to the river alone, he would still be alive."

32

Day Two

Saran

After a few breaths to take in the scene, Saran walked straight up to Maredudd, sat herself beside him, and put her arm around his shoulders. "I am so sorry to hear about the loss of Tomos. I have just learned what he meant to you."

Maredudd might have shrugged her off, pretending he wasn't grieving as profoundly as he was. Alternatively, he could have thanked her politely and sent her on her way. Both options would have confirmed the idea that he wanted to be alone. It wouldn't necessarily have been true, but he was a prince and a leader of men, and she would have given way.

What he did instead was swivel on his log in order to put his face into her shoulder. As she brought both her arms around him, his arms came around her waist, and he began to weep. He was quiet about it, but she could feel his shoulders shaking. He had to know that every one of his men was watching him sob in her arms. He was enough of a leader, and enough of a man, not to let that stop him.

With Gareth examining Tomos's body, Dai finding other men to speak to, Gwen with the children, and Meilyr playing lullabies to soothe everyone to sleep, Saran had seen an opportunity—and a need—to get close to Maredudd. The young prince might have rejected any notion that these deaths were directed at him, but it would be dangerous for anyone else to assume it. Both dead men had been his second-in-command. One of them looked like him. To her mind, it was a short step to the idea that Rhodri and Tomos had died to make it easier to murder Maredudd. Or, more concerningly, it was Maredudd whom the murderer had intended to kill tonight.

Either way, he was vulnerable and alone.

She had found him sitting at his fire circle with his head in his arms. He had been surrounded by other men, in that his tent was set up in the middle of the camp. But while every one of them was keeping a constant eye on his hunched form, none had been closer than ten yards away.

Saran knew herself to be opinionated, but she wasn't usually one to impose those opinions on others without real cause. Even if her advice seemed needed, she would find a way to know her recipient's mind before trying to help him. It was one of the many practices she'd picked up over the years that made her such an accomplished healer. Healing had to take place in the heart and mind as well as the body. Any practitioner who dealt only with the physical being was forgetting an important part of what allowed a person to heal.

His men had been thinking Maredudd needed to be left alone in his grief. On the whole, the Welsh were more demonstrative than Saxons or Normans, but warriors required a certain level of stoicism in order to stay on their feet. Maybe Maredudd had even been the one to send everyone else away.

But Saran had learned a bit about the minds of young men over the years, not just through her two step-grandsons. Maredudd might have been sitting by himself on his overturned log near the fire because he thought he wanted to be alone in his grief. If that were truly the case, he would have retreated inside his tent. In point of fact, what Maredudd needed more than anything in this moment was his mother.

His mother was dead, however, as was his foster mother. Though never having given birth herself, Saran was still the next best thing. Dealing with the grief that was a natural result of murder was the hardest part of Gareth and Gwen's investigations. Grief was a universal experience, but also singular to every person, and a path each person in the end had to walk alone. But that didn't mean Maredudd needed to *be* alone. Not if Saran could be there for him.

"I should have gone with him! I had planned to be with him."

Saran made sure to stay relaxed so as not to distract from his story. "At the river, you mean? Was it your intent to bathe tonight?"

"I told him I was going to."

"When was this?" Saran asked softly.

"Earlier, we were in my tent, talking. But then I fell asleep. Tomos must have decided to go without me."

Saran could easily picture the murderer witnessing a man wrapped in a cloak against the chill of the evening leave Maredudd's tent in order to head to the river to bathe—and assume it was Maredudd himself.

As Maredudd continued to sob, his men began filling the seats around the fire circle at which he and Saran were sitting. They weren't tentative now so much as respectful. Meilyr was among them, strumming quietly on his *crwth*, not to draw attention this time, but as part of the background, to ease the conversation around the fire.

The leader of the archers sat on the opposite end of the log from her and put a hand briefly on Maredudd's shoulder. "I remember the day Anarawd asked Tomos to take you on, you and your brother. Tomos was like a stunned ox, stuttering his gratitude at the honor, while at the same time overwhelmed by the responsibility. Old King Gruffydd had wanted to keep the boys close after their mother died, but he was dead just months later, and Anarawd couldn't see raising you boys himself while trying to learn how to be king."

"Oh, but Tomos was pleased, he was." Another man, this one truly gray in his beard, spoke from the other side of the fire circle. "He loved you the moment he took your hand in his. And you know Catrin loved you as much as her own boys."

Saran hadn't heard the name *Catrin* before, but she gathered from the context and the nods all around that she had been Tomos's first wife, the one who'd died years ago. With Tomos's death, these men had lost one of their closest friends too.

"He sounds like a good man," Saran said.

"He truly was." This speaker wore a hat with a feather, and she remembered Dai giving his name as Morgan. "I knew Tomos my whole life. I will miss him." For a moment grief overcame him too, and he dug viciously in the dirt in front of him with a stick he was holding. The man next to him bumped his shoulder, intending comfort.

The conversation had eased Maredudd's tears, and he pushed upright. "I'm sorry—"

"Don't be, boy." That was Morgan again. "There is no sorry here." He made a gesture to encompass everyone sitting with them. "Tomos had his troubles of late, but he was a father to you, the only one you really remember. And Catrin your mother."

"Not a one of us thinks any less of you for weeping," the older bearded man said. "More, really."

"He was like an uncle to me." This came from a younger man with a shock of blond hair. Tears glistened on his cheeks in the firelight. "I don't know if I would have survived these last weeks, if not for him."

Other men nodded their agreement.

The older bearded man spoke one more time. "We grieve with you, my lord."

Tears rolled unchecked down Maredudd's cheeks. Seeing him, Saran realized she had been weeping, too, in sympathy and shared sorrow. She wiped at her cheeks with her fingers. Nobody looked askance and she felt no judgment.

What's more, Maredudd's back, and even more his soul, were no longer bowed. These few moments of shared grief had been exactly what he needed.

33

Day Two

Gareth

Gareth was struggling to tug off Tomos's shirt when Ieuan arrived at the back of the cart, taking a spot Saran had occupied earlier when she'd told him her plan to talk to Maredudd. Peering into the depths, Ieuan said, "You're here alone?"

Gareth might have allowed himself a laugh. "Except for Tomos."

"Who's Tomos?"

Gareth gestured to the body. "Our latest murder victim."

Ieuan gazed at Gareth and then at the body with something akin to horror. "I heard someone had been killed, but I didn't hear who. This is Maredudd's second-in-command?"

"Sadly, yes."

"How did he die?'

"The same way as Rhodri. Stabbed in the back."

Ieuan absorbed that news with a bit of a slack jaw. "We have a real demon on our hands."

"It does seem so."

And then Ieuan asked a genuinely insightful question. "Why would anyone want these two men dead? From what I have gathered since we joined this band, they had little in common."

"Other than being Maredudd's second, of course."

Ieuan bit his lip. "So you think the aim is ultimately to attack Maredudd?"

"What do you think?"

Ieuan gave himself a little shake. "Should you really be trying so hard to solve these murders at all? Maredudd is our enemy, isn't he?"

Gareth grunted. "I don't see it that way."

Ieuan looked to his right, mumbling under his breath as he did so, in a manner that reminded Gareth of Dai when he had thoughts he didn't think he should say out loud but wanted to say anyway. What came more clearly was: "He did take us captive."

"You have come to no harm." As they'd been talking, Gareth had stripped off the rest of Tomos's clothes. It had to be done before burial anyway, in order to wash the body.

Ieuan watched him do it and then asked, a bit more tentatively. "He looks a bit like Maredudd, doesn't he?"

"So others have noted." This time, Gareth's tone was dry. Maybe the killer had intended Tomos to die, for reasons as yet unknown, but with Maredudd in camp, Tomos was a strange target. They couldn't afford to think otherwise. "I am not liking the thought."

"That would mean the wrong man is dead." Ieuan's mind was proving to be far more agile than Gareth might have expected, given his common beginnings and poor gear. "If so, what does that say about the death of Rhodri? From what people have said, he was tall, thin, and red-headed."

"I have no answers as of yet." Gareth eyed the young man again, deciding that just because Ieuan was seventeen didn't mean he shouldn't be questioned like everyone else, the rounds for which were going to begin again first thing in the morning. "Where have you been this evening that you just heard about the death?"

"Mostly, I was sitting among some of Maredudd's men. You came over to speak to several of them at one point."

"I remember." That had been after Gareth had bathed but before Bran had arrived at the fire circle and upended their evening.

Ieuan looked a little rueful. "I stayed with them after that, thinking about Rhodri's death, and hoping I could contribute something, too."

Gareth gave a grunt, feeling a bit pleased, actually, that something of what his family cared about seemed to be rubbing off on the boy. Ieuan really could be like any other youth: not so much prickly as wary among strangers. That was understandable, given where they were right now.

"And then I was in the latrine for longer than I liked."

Gareth looked up at that. "Are you well?"

"I think so. I feel fine now." He put a hand to his belly. "I'll be glad to be in Caerfyrddin tomorrow."

"If you aren't fine in the morning, talk to Saran. She should be able to give you something to help."

"May I ask why you are—" He waved a hand to encompass the body. "You said you know how he died."

"Come on up, and I'll explain."

Displaying real eagerness, Ieuan trotted up the steps that led into the cart and crouched beside Tomos's body. At that point, Gareth proceeded to examine every inch of the corpse, looking for bruises, rashes, or other indications of harm, beyond the wounds to Tomos's back, and explaining to Ieuan all the while what he was doing. As Gareth had determined when they'd been beside the river, someone had stabbed Tomos twice. The first thrust had penetrated the meaty part of his shoulder and would have brought him to his knees. Gareth didn't think the angle was right to have killed him. Death had come from the second wound, which had entered lower down, the blade shoved between two of his ribs straight into his heart.

Although Ieuan had climbed into the cart with evident enthusiasm, this detailed explanation caused him to pale a bit and visibly swallow. Unlike Bran, he didn't actually vomit. "Poor man."

Gareth eyed him, still taking his measure. "Some might say Deheubarth's offenses against Gwynedd justify this murder."

Ieuan shook his head. "Tomos might have been a lord, but we all answer to someone, don't we? We all have orders. Everyone but Maredudd."

"As I understand it, Maredudd led this army on Cadell's orders. Nobody here is entirely his own man." But even as Gareth spoke of Maredudd and Cadell, he was thinking of Llelo and Rhys—and the reason Rhys had summoned Llelo to him.

Rhys had been afraid for his life.

Maybe the life he should have been afraid for was Maredudd's.

34

Day Three

Dai

Even though it was past midnight, Dai had decided he needed one last look at the place they'd found Tomos. He feared not only rain overnight that would mar the scene but also that the murderer might have second thoughts about leaving traces of himself behind and beating him to the discovery of any evidence. To that end, he headed back into the woods, admittedly with his sword in one hand and a lantern in the other. He could be diligent without being stupid.

Tomos had been discovered on the bank above the bathing spot located not far from the bridge over the River Teifi and the main road. Dai had come to see, having ranged all over the terrain tonight, that the killer had taken an enormous risk being seen. He really must have wanted Tomos dead.

And then, just as he reached the spot where they'd found the body, an arm came around his shoulders, and he found himself pulled backwards against a larger man who had a knife pressed to his throat. "Didn't I teach you better than this?"

"Steffan!" In a matter of a dozen very rapid heartbeats, Dai went from fear to fury to joy. He counted himself lucky he hadn't actually jumped out of his boots. Or lashed out with his sword, even if ineffectually.

Before he could apologize, exclaim further, or really say anything at all, Iago appeared from behind a tree, grinning like a madman. Once Steffan sheathed his knife, Iago wrapped Dai up in a bear hug. The man was huge, twice Dai's size. And yet, he'd been able to sneak up on Dai as easily as Steffan, who had made sneaking about a way of life.

When Iago finally released him, Dai knew better than to make excuses and, sheathing his sword, went straight to contrition, else he'd never hear the end of it. "I should have known better than to be so unguarded."

"Yes, you should have," Steffan said. "It is unbecoming in a Dragon."

Dai hunched his shoulders. "It won't happen again—"

"Let him be, Steffan. No harm done." Iago clapped Dai on the shoulder and shook him in a fatherly fashion. "Besides, it isn't as if we came upon him by accident. We've been watching him for some time, waiting for our moment."

Dai would have continued to apologize if he hadn't at that moment glanced towards Steffan and seen him chuckling.

"It will be a good story when we finally get you home."

Each of the Dragons brought certain characteristics and skills to their service to Hywel. For example, Cadoc was a supreme archer, while Steffan was immensely capable with all sorts of knives. He was also never very far from Iago, who was built on the scale of Goliath. As a team, they were nigh on unbeatable, as they had proven yet again tonight.

Once Steffan stopped laughing, Dai looked from one to the other, their faces softly illuminated by his lantern, which he kept low to the ground. "The real question here should not be about my behavior, but yours. What are you doing here?"

"Our job," Iago said.

Dai stepped closer to grip his friend's arm. "Have you been following Maredudd's band this whole time?"

"Of course. Once Cadell's army retreated, the prince sent us out in pairs to shadow them. Steffan and I followed Maredudd and his men; Aron and Evan went after the band that took the northeastern road; and then Gruffydd and Cadoc rode south from Trawscoed. Honestly, I wanted to be among those who followed the more northerly route because I thought we might be more likely to encounter you."

"We left Ysbyty Cynfyn as soon as we heard about the sacking of Goginan," Dai said. "That part of the army had reached the crossroads by that time. When we left, we were only a mile or so ahead of them."

The two other men exchanged a glance, and then Steffan said, "We didn't know about any of that. Nobody has mentioned sacking churches. Maredudd has done nothing of the kind and would never allow it."

"Cadell, on the other hand ..." Iago's voice trailed off.

Dai nodded. "Father was worried we might be the cause of retribution against the monks at Ysbyty Cynfyn, which is why we left when we did."

"That was wise." Iago said. "But you didn't know Maredudd was riding towards Ysbyty Ystwyth, then, did you?"

"We did not. Anyway, our choices of which direction to go were limited. South was really the only option." Dai let out a quick snort. "And now look at us."

"You are in one piece," Iago didn't hammer on Dai's shoulder again, but merely shook it, "and we are here."

Dai was suddenly feeling a bit distraught again. From what he could see of his friends, they were both significantly worse for wear, dirty and exhausted after so many days on the road sleeping rough. "You really shouldn't be here. What if you were caught? It is one thing for us to be Maredudd's prisoners, but you are both genuine Dragons. Everybody knows it."

"You are a Dragon, too." Iago made a dismissive motion with his head. "Besides, we have been careful, as evidenced by the fact that we are standing before you. You are talking to us now only because we made ourselves known to you."

"About that—" Before the conversation could go any further, he gestured for his friends to follow him farther down the path that ran along the river. Dai was suddenly fearful that his friends had killed Tomos, even though that wouldn't normally have been their way. Steffan was very good with knives, but it would be unlike him to stab a man in the back.

Regardless, they shouldn't stand here to talk about it. The sentry to whom Dai had spoken earlier that evening was posted some fifty yards farther west from where Tomos died. Sound traveled more easily at night, so Dai urged his friends to walk another hundred yards along the river and then up the bank to arrive in a field. They were more exposed here but, at the same time, would be able to see another man coming long before he was upon them. Dai didn't want to be surprised again in the same way he had been surprised by Steffan and Iago.

Once they reached a wooden stile over a farmer's stone wall, he turned to the two Dragons. "Did you kill Tomos? Tell me right now if you did. You can be on your way, and I can pretend I never saw you."

"Is that what you think?" Iago looked a bit offended.

Dai glanced in the direction of the encampment. Maredudd had sent sentries to watch the perimeter, but he didn't have men scouting farther out. Maybe that was an oversight on his part, or maybe he was simply worried about losing any more men. "You don't know how hard it was for me to walk you this far without asking that question. I don't want to think you did it, but we are investigating a murder, so I have to ask. Tomos seemed like a good man, but I won't be more than momentarily troubled to let you go. If you killed him, you were following Hywel's commands and not subject to Cadell's or Maredudd's." Dai would have to think later why letting them go would be so easy to square with his conscience. Maybe that was part of being a *natural spy*.

"We didn't kill him," Iago said flatly.

"That is a relief. You are here, though. A man is dead. Talk to me."

"We had nothing to do with his death," Steffan said, "but we did see him die."

"That's why we decided to risk speaking to you now," Iago put in. "It was kind of you to make it easy for us."

"Don't tease him. He's on a mission, and he has every right to be." Steffan elbowed Iago's ribs. "I have killed men in my time, but I have never witnessed a death quite like this one. The man who murdered Tomos has ice in his veins instead of blood."

"Can you describe him?"

"Unfortunately, as you well know, it was dark." Iago's expression was rueful. "We saw a man in a cloak. A hood covered his head."

Like Iago, Steffan had been part of their investigations before, so he knew what Dai was going to ask next before he asked it. "The killer was too large to be a woman. Too strong too. With the first blow to his back, Tomos went down hard. Then the man stabbed him again. A moment after that, he was gone, away west on the path you followed. It was so quick—" He broke off at the memory, which must truly have been a troubling sight to give Steffan pause.

"Did he return to the camp?" Dai held his breath.

"We didn't see," Iago said regretfully.

"How long was it between Tomos's death and when Bran found him?"

"That man you've been traveling with?" Iago wrinkled his nose. "Not long. We'd seen him pass earlier, heading down to the river."

"Could the killer have *been* Bran?"

The pair had to think about that. "I heard him singing at one point while he was bathing," Steffan said slowly. "It's hard to see how he could have done it."

"Honestly, neither of us were able to determine from which direction the killer came. He might have come up the path from the river, but he could have just as easily been hiding in the woods. He appeared out of nowhere." Iago's lips were pursed as he thought. "If I were Bran and set on killing, I would have gone down to the riverbank and stripped off my clothes. Wearing only my cloak, it would have been a matter of moments to walk back up the path in order to lie in wait for Tomos. Once I killed him, I could then have disappeared into the woods to the west, reentered the water, and then made my way back upstream to the bathing spot as if none of it had ever happened."

"Was Bran wearing a cloak when he went down to the river?" Dai asked.

They had to think again. "No," Iago finally said.

"And not when he found the body either," Steffan said.

"Doesn't mean he couldn't have planted it by the river earlier and then discarded it afterwards," Iago said. "All he'd have to do then is wash off whatever blood from the murder got on his skin, clothe himself, and then 'discover' the body of the man he'd killed. It would have required planning, in addition to the foreknowledge of Tomos's decision to bathe, but it isn't impossible."

Dai had to pause then, thinking how to ask his next question without sounding accusing. "I assume you didn't stop the murderer from leaving the scene because you couldn't?"

"We were up a tree." Steffan said a little sourly. "Even Iago."

"I could have dropped down on him. Maybe. But he'd just killed a man in cold blood. Stabbed in the back!" Iago puffed out a breath. "I couldn't risk getting caught myself."

"We are here now because we did, in fact, have second thoughts about just letting a dead man lie," Steffan said. "And now, I'm sure you do too."

35

Day Three

Dai

Dai put both hands to his head, thinking about the order of events his friends had just described. "Let me get this straight. If you've been following Maredudd's band this whole time, did you witness our capture, back at Ysbyty Ystwyth?"

"We did see it," Iago said regretfully, "but we were as impotent to stop it as the murder. We were glad Meilyr had the sense to put away the banner of Owain Gwynedd."

"How did you get that close?"

Again, it was Iago who answered. "By then, we knew their patterns, and we were able to reach the monastery enough ahead of Maredudd's army to warn the abbot they were coming. We were among the monks when you arrived. I am sorry we couldn't let you see us."

Dai made a rueful face. "It would have been nice to have known we had real allies sooner, but I understand why you had to stay hidden."

"Steffan wanted to come to you that first night at the abbey of Mynachlog Fawr. I talked him out of it. You weren't hurt, and Gareth knows what he is doing."

"We didn't want to interfere with his strategy," Steffan amended.

Dai let out a laugh. "My father almost always knows what he's doing, but I'm not sure *strategy* is really the right word in this instance. We have been making it up as we go along."

"Be that as it may, we had no good way to reach you without risking all of us," Steffan said. "You weren't in chains. Maredudd even gave you and Gareth back your swords. It looked to us as if he had decided to trust you. Our best option remained simply to follow."

Dai realized he had to back up again, this time because this tale was directly relevant to their *first* investigation. "If you witnessed Tomos's murder, did you see Rhodri's too?" He didn't ask if they had been the one to kill him. On the whole, it seemed unlikely, and they would have told him if they had. He'd had to ask them once already, and he didn't want to accuse them unnecessarily. Just because Maredudd and every other man in his party had been hoping Rhodri and Tomos were murdered by an outsider didn't make it true.

"Who is Rhodri?" The furrow in Steffan's brow was visible by the light of the lantern Dai had relit, once they were on the other side of the wall, where it couldn't be seen from the direction of the camp.

Dai spread his hands wide. "We are here because Maredudd asked us to discover who murdered his captain. His name was Rhodri, and he died on the first night out from Aberystwyth."

"Murdered how?" Steffan asked. "And where?"

Dai was suddenly feeling wary—not of his friends, *per se*, but of where this conversation was taking him. "He died the same way as Tomos. He'd left the encampment to relieve himself by the river and never returned. He was found some time later near the bank, stabbed twice in the back, just like Tomos."

Iago scratched at the back of his head. "Tell me again when this was supposed to have happened?"

"The first night out from Aberystwyth."

"And you said by the river?" Steffan said. "After he relieved himself?"

That they were repeating Dai's answers as if he hadn't been clear the first time was worrying. "So we were told."

Both men were frowning now. "By whom?" Iago asked.

"Maredudd. And then the sentry who found the body, a man named Einion." Dai looked from Steffan to Iago and back again. "What is it? Why do you two look like that?"

"Nobody was murdered that first night out from Aberystwyth," Iago said.

"Are you sure you would know?" Dai said. "It happened in the early hours of the morning. Maybe you were asleep."

That question prompted a disgruntled look from Steffan that Dai would question his professionalism. "We were watching the camp, just like tonight. The goings on had our full attention."

"Were you close enough to the river? Could it have happened in a place you couldn't see?" Dai said. "Even you two can't be everywhere at once. You didn't see where Tomos's murderer went."

Iago scoffed. "If someone was murdered as you describe, don't you think we would have noticed an alarm being raised?"

"They didn't raise the alarm," Dai said. "That's the whole point. In fact, Maredudd didn't tell anyone that Rhodri had been murdered until after he asked Father to investigate it."

"Then, I'm not sure what we're talking about," Iago said.

Steffan pointed a finger at him. "We did see a man die by the river. We thought at first he'd gone to sleep because he just laid down on the ground. Then one of the sentries found him, left again, and returned with two other men. They wrapped him up in a tarp and carried him away."

Dai nodded vigorously. "So you did see it! That's exactly what Maredudd told my parents had happened."

"Except it didn't," Steffan said. "Since it was the first night of our vigil, we were paying even closer attention than we were tonight. Hywel was concerned Maredudd was only pretending to have abandoned the siege. We were watching, believe me."

Iago took up the tale. "We were afraid they were going to break camp in the middle of the night and return to Aberystwyth in order to catch Hywel by surprise, as they failed to do the first time, thanks to you and your father. The salient point here is that both of us were close enough to this Rhodri fellow to have murdered him when he came down to the river to relieve himself, but we did not, and I would swear on any relic you gave me that nobody else did either."

"He just died," Steffan said. "The sentry found him, and ran for help. They wrapped him up and carried him away. There was no murder. He collapsed and died all on his own."

Dai chewed on his lower lip. "But someone really did stab Tomos, right?"

"Twice." Steffan's tone was more than a little dry. "That isn't something either of us could mistake."

"Nor Maredudd," Iago said. "It was impossible to miss."

It wasn't like Dai didn't believe what they were telling him, but he could not reconcile their story with Maredudd's. "We were told they buried Rhodri the next morning in the churchyard of St. Ilar's."

Iago laughed outright, quickly cutting himself off because laughter, in particular, carried easily in the night. "Sure they did. I admit to that. Actually, they buried three people that morning, all of whom died in the night. None of them were murdered, either. This army has been beset by the sickness, you know. They lost two more the next day."

Dai rubbed his chin. "I don't understand any of this."

Iago shrugged again. "I'm not saying there was no such person as this Rhodri. All I'm saying is that neither he nor anyone else was murdered that first night out from Aberystwyth, especially not in the same manner as Tomos. I couldn't tell you why Maredudd would mislead you in this way. I don't know how it's possible to say that someone was murdered when he wasn't. We can tell you only what *we* witnessed."

"I kind of like this Maredudd, though," Steffan said, as something of a *by the way*. "Imagine making up a murder! And why? Because he wanted Gareth to agree to join his company?"

"Not that I blame him for that," Iago said. "Women, children, bards. Even soulless men of the south don't want to see any of you harmed."

Dai stood with his hands on his hips. "You think Maredudd lied because he wanted my father to come with him willingly?"

Steffan turned both hands upward. "That's what it looks like to me."

"Why would he do that?" Dai said.

"Your guess is as good as mine," Iago said. "Maybe better, since you've been in the middle of this company for two days."

Dai was suddenly feeling very unhappy. "We are meant to reach Caerfyrddin tomorrow. What's going to happen then?"

Steffan gazed at him. "Be assured we have your back."

"No, you don't. Or you shouldn't. You two need to head home immediately. The deeper we travel into Deheubarth, the more dangerous the journey will become for you."

"You are worried for us?" Iago dismissed the notion with a wave of his hand. "We are not leaving you. I would think, rather, that it is you who need to come with us."

Dai bent his head, contemplating the logistics of what they were asking. "We can't. We'll never get away without being seen, not with the children. We are going to have to face what comes as it comes." He looked up. "But you two are a different story. Hywel needs to know what has happened to us—and you are the only ones who can tell him.”

36

Day Three

Gareth

"Are you finished with what you needed to do?" Maredudd came to a halt in front of Gareth. When they'd first found Tomos's body, Maredudd had been holding back his grief with anger, looking for someone to blame. Now, he just looked tired.

Gareth had come around the back of the cart, having sent Dai to bed after hearing the story of his encounter with Iago and Steffan and having himself finished his examination of Tomos's body. He had found nothing new that stood out to him. Tomos had been an older man, who'd lived a soldier's life. He'd survived battle, only to die in the dark.

From beside Maredudd, Saran, who should have been in bed long since, too, shrugged, as if to say, *sorry about this. He didn't want to wait until morning to talk to you.*

Gareth had a great deal to say to Maredudd. For now, he just answered the question Maredudd had asked: "Yes."

With that one word, the four men who had also come with Maredudd flowed around the cart and into it. They'd brought another makeshift bier by which to transport the body. Gareth knew without asking that they were taking Tomos's body to prepare it for burial. As with Rhodri, the funeral would take place at first light, in this case in the church they'd passed on the other side of the River Teifi. He was happy to leave the details to Maredudd and his men to sort out.

Gareth leaned his head back against the side of the cart, his eyes on the prince. It was hard to believe that just two days ago they'd been at Ysbyty Cynfyn. He was short on sleep. It didn't look as if he would be getting more than the minimum any time soon, not with a prince of Deheubarth planted in front of him, holding on by a thread.

Maredudd waited until the four men had set off towards the bridge across the river before speaking again. When Saran had suggested she visit Maredudd, Gareth had thought it a good idea to try to reach him. Now, it seemed she'd worked her usual miracles. "Can you tell me who killed Rhodri and Tomos?"

With a much diminished prince before him, Gareth found the truth easy to say, despite the vast chasm of duplicity between them that still needed to be addressed. "I cannot, my lord."

Maredudd bowed his head. "I assumed not, but I had to ask."

Gareth couldn't leave it there. "I had thought to wait until morning for this, but I realize now I need to speak. We have learned that you have deceived us as to the manner of Rhodri's death. He was not stabbed in the back. In fact, I have every reason to believe he was never murdered at all, but died of the same sickness that took so many of your men these last weeks."

Maredudd's head came up. "What are you saying?"

"I am saying there was no murder, at least of Rhodri. You lied to me."

Maredudd wet his lips. "I don't know what you're—"

"You're lying again." Gareth was too tired to be anything but blunt.

Maredudd stared at the ground, though Gareth didn't think he was seeing it. "I should have known I would not be able to maintain the pretense for long."

"The question before me now is *why did you try?*" As Gareth waited for the answer, he had a stray thought that this was, without a doubt, the most unusual investigation in which he had ever been involved, and he'd been involved in plenty of strange ones.

Maredudd looked around him, his manner not so much furtive as assessing. Seeing that it was still only the three of them present, he said, "Because I needed you to come with me, and I couldn't tell you why, not in front of my men."

According to Dai, that had been Steffan's guess. "You had a chance, back in the abbot's quarters at Mynachlog Fawr, to tell me the truth."

"By then, the board was laid. I thought it best to play it out."

"And now?"

He let out a huge sigh. "What I couldn't have you know was that I have been acting on my brother's orders. In short, he is worried about treachery within his ranks and wanted you to come to his court to ferret it out."

Gareth's first hopeful thought was that Maredudd was referring to Rhys, but the phrasing wasn't right. Rhys didn't give orders nor have ranks. Maredudd meant Cadell. It was on the tip of Gareth's tongue to mention that Rhys had asked for Llelo for the same reason, but that might be giving away too much right at the start. If confidences were going to be shared, then Maredudd needed to be the one to go first. "How so?"

"I don't entirely know, but if it was at all possible for me to find you, he asked that I get you to come. My brother assured me you can uncover any villain, any murderer, any secret, as you have just done."

Gareth might have quibbled by stating that he hadn't, in fact, found the murderer. For now, this failure was adjacent to the current point. "How did Cadell suggest you convince me to come? Was a false murder his idea?"

"It was mine." Maredudd gave a bit of a laugh. "My brother can be more, shall we say, straightforward than I am."

"He would have had me in chains, in other words, and worried about the cooperation part later."

Maredudd made a qualifying motion with his head. "His words were *convince him to come with you. I don't care how.* Making you think Rhodri was murdered seemed like the easiest way to go about it."

"Is that why you sent that other company of men east from Aberystwyth? Were they looking for me too?"

"No, actually. That was smart tactically. We didn't want to lose the whole army if Hywel decided to pursue, which it appears he did not."

Saran spoke for the first time since she'd brought Maredudd to the cart. "I'm interested in how you convinced your people to go along with this deception."

"Who did I have to convince, really?" Maredudd shrugged, dismissing as of little import what was truly an enormous indication of trust on the part of those he led. "Most of what I told you was true. Only Tomos and the sentry had to be given clear instructions as to what to say, and all that I required from them was to pretend Rhodri had been murdered—rather than dying of natural causes on the same spot. He did die near the river, after all, and we did bury him the next morning at St. Ilar's."

Gareth clasped both hands on the top of his head, still shocked at how casually Maredudd had lied to him and how easily he'd been duped. "Unfortunately, you now really do have a murderer amidst your company."

"Is Tomos's murder my fault, then?" Maredudd rubbed his palms on his thighs. "By calling upon the devil, did I allow him entry into this world?"

"The blade that killed Tomos was real. I have no reason to think the killer isn't human. For now, I am far more concerned about the *why* of it than the who. Tomos was murdered by the exact method you told me Rhodri died: two stab wounds to the back. Except, Rhodri didn't die that way. Which means whoever killed Tomos wants us to think he murdered both men in the same fashion, when really, he murdered only one."

37

Day Three

Gwen

When the gray light of dawn began creeping into the wagon, Angharad woke and refused to nurse back to sleep. Given that she had slept through all the tumult in the night, Gwen couldn't resent her fussiness. Gareth had joined them in their wagon sometime in the early hours of the morning, stepping over sleeping children who, fortunately, hadn't woken as he came to find his bed.

Gwen had sent Tangwen off to sleep with Meilyr and Saran. It was a treat for her and left more room in the wagon for Dai, who had come in after midnight with the story of meeting Iago and Steffan.

All Gareth had said before he'd closed his eyes was, "Stabbed in the back, as we thought. Twice. I've had a talk with Maredudd too. I'll tell you the rest of it in the morning."

And then he was asleep in that utterly exhausted fashion that meant if he lay on his back he snored. Several times, she had reached across to poke him. She hadn't wanted to wake him, but she also knew if she didn't get adequate sleep herself, she would be worthless in the morning. Thankfully, he'd rolled onto his side eventually. And slept there still.

As it wasn't really morning yet, she left him alone. She wasn't so self-effacing that she didn't recognize her contributions to their investigations, but she also knew it was Gareth who was keeping their family together on this perilous journey. He deserved every moment of sleep he could get. Gwen's hands had been full with the children, anyway. That was usual for her, but never more so than this week.

Gwen stepped over Dai, who was so deeply asleep he didn't stir, either. And Taran, darling boy that he was, slept on, too. Fortunately, now that she was up and moving, Angharad had quieted, interested in where they were going.

With people starting to rise from their beds all around the encampment, it was hard to believe Tomos had died a matter of hours ago and yards away. It seemed impossible that someone would snuff out a life like that, casually, as if he counted for nothing. Steffan and Iago had described no frantic struggle, no hesitation, just two stabs, one right after the other, and away the killer had gone.

Gwen had assured Gareth when they started this journey that she would not wander off by herself. At the time, they'd been thinking of Rhodri's murder. Now, they had Tomos's genuine one to worry about. With a hundred men in camp, the tents were spread throughout the field, giving Gwen plenty of space to walk safely. All appeared quiet in the center where Maredudd's tent was pitched. The structure was in no way a grand pavilion, just the shelter in which the prince slept. Gwen was mildly concerned to see nobody sleeping on his threshold.

To her mind, the three sentries posted around the perimeter were not enough either. Their primary job was to look outward, not inward. From Iago and Steffan's testimony, the man who'd murdered Tomos was not a stranger. He was here in their camp with them. Somewhere.

Angharad loved to be walked about and soon rested her head on Gwen's chest. As the light grew in the sky, more people woke, though still not Maredudd. He'd had as late a night as Gareth. Everyone else was preparing to continue the journey to Caerfyrddin, wanting to be packed and ready to go immediately after Tomos's funeral. The cooks prepared breakfast, others began taking down tents, and still more stowed gear in the carts.

Because Gwen was dithering on the margins, she was among the first to hear hoofbeats coming up the road from the south. The urgency of the rhythm was unmistakable. When the rider appeared, it was only one man, so she simply stepped off the road into the grass to make sure she stayed out of his way. By the time the horseman reined in at the entrance to the encampment, two of Maredudd's men were there to greet him. The rider made himself known to them, and then one of them escorted him at a jog towards Maredudd's tent.

By then, even Maredudd, exhausted as he must be from the events of last night, couldn't remain unaware that something was happening. Thrusting open the tent flap, he appeared fully clothed and with his sword already belted at his waist. Perhaps he'd slept in his clothes like Gareth.

The newcomer bowed deeply before speaking. "I bring news, my lord, from your brother."

"Cadell?"

"Rhys."

"Tell me."

The messenger looked around at the men (and woman, Gwen) (and baby, Angharad), who'd gathered to listen. Dai was suddenly among them too, stepping into place opposite Gwen, and, to all appearances, included by the other men as one of them. "Pardon, my lord, but may I tell you alone first?"

"These men have been through the fire with me. Your news is obviously urgent. Speak."

"Your brother Cadell has been grievously wounded in an ambush by men from Tenby. They left him for dead. Prince Rhys does not know if he will survive. He needs you to come home now.

38

Day Three

Dai

Even as the men around Maredudd gasped, Maredudd didn't blink. In fact, he didn't show any emotion at all, nor did he look around to catch anyone's eye. It was as if, despite what he'd said about wanting everyone to hear, he and the messenger were alone.

Dai met his mother's eyes through the sea of faces. She had to be barely breathing, the same as him. He reminded himself that, if Rhys had sent the message, then he, at least, was alive. That should mean Llelo was too. Could mean. *Please God let it mean what I need it to. I can't lose my brother today.*

Maredudd was fully aware of his audience, however, because he waited to speak until the initial wave of consternation had swept through his men and settled down. "How did you come to bring this news to me? Were you there? Is Rhys himself well?"

He could have simply asked, *what happened?* but that was too vague a question. Dai had learned from his father that when

- 243 -

questioning informants, it was often best to be specific when it came to details. He'd seen exactly that last night when he'd been talking to the sentry. Maredudd had learned this too and was already thinking clearly enough to act accordingly. And, like Dai, he had a brother in peril. Brothers.

"The lord Rhys is well. He was not even injured in the ambush." To Dai's utter relief, the rider answered the last question first. And then he further explained, "I am sorry to report that except for him and his Hospitaller companion, every member of the king's *teulu* was killed. I am part of Iestyn ap Meurig's retinue. We arrived too late to either witness the event or to avert it."

Externally, Maredudd continued to respond to the messenger's news with hardly any change in expression. Internally, he had to be cheering to know his brother was alive and well, just as Dai was. It was such a relief to have the weight of Llelo's absence lifted off his chest. Obviously, the greater news of the ambush and Cadell's injuries might be dire for Deheubarth, but Dai couldn't fundamentally worry about that in this moment. His family came first.

From the day he'd been born, Llelo had been a constant. These last months without him had been more difficult than Dai liked to admit. They'd been separated before, but never for this long, and he had struggled daily with not knowing if Llelo was well or ill. He couldn't count the number of times he'd surveyed Maredudd's encampment around Aberystwyth, hoping to see the figure of Llelo walking by—while at the same time praying he was far away. As it turned out, Llelo had been protecting Rhys all along, as he'd promised.

"Where did this happen?" Maredudd was still managing to keep his tone level, on display in a way he may never have been before. Dai had lived in a royal court for enough years by now to know that every twitch and tremor in a lord was noticed by his men. His behavior, good and bad, reflected on them. They took pride when he did well, and cursed when he fell short.

"As the king was hunting in the Coed Rath."

Dai blinked, and some of the men beside him shifted, indicating he wasn't the only one suddenly feeling uncertain.

"Where are my brothers now?" Maredudd asked this instead of the more immediate query, which would have been, *what in the name of all that is holy was Cadell doing hunting* there? While the deer were plentiful, the land was all Norman, with the castles of Tenby and Carew within striking distance. And that was just to name the first two Norman castles that came to mind. Given the unlikelihood of Cadell choosing to go hunting so deep into Norman territory on a whim, either the rider wouldn't know the answer to Dai's question or, if he did have an answer, it wouldn't be the truth.

"When I left, they were walking north."

At last, Maredudd faltered, even as a murmur of protest grew among his men. "Walking? Cadell too?"

"Not the king. I do not know the details, in such haste were the lords Rhys and Iestyn to send me to you, but such were the king's injuries that he was unable to walk. Lord Rhys's intent, as I understood it, was to make for Caerfyrddin." He bit his lip. "They were carrying King Cadell in a makeshift litter."

"Caerfyrddin is twenty miles from the Coed Rath!" One of Maredudd's men spoke out of turn, but he'd said only what everyone else was thinking. "Was he alive when you left?"

"Yes. He was alive." The messenger spoke with a certain emphasis, as if to assert that Cadell *was* alive when he left, but he wouldn't make a guess as to whether or not he was alive *now*. Then he hesitated yet again, this time wetting his lips before speaking. "My lord, I must confess, that he didn't look good. When I left, King Cadell was unable to feel his legs."

If the king's injuries were that severe, he wouldn't be alive by the time they reached Caerfyrddin. Maredudd would know this for a truth without anyone saying it. As this reality began settling on Maredudd, it settled visibly, too, on everyone around him. At last, Dai began seriously considering exactly what the consequences of this ambush to Deheubarth might ultimately be. If a man couldn't walk, it was hard to see how he could lead men, even if he did survive.

Cadell had no heirs of his own body. Maredudd had been the heir to Deheubarth before today, but now everybody was thinking they were looking at a king instead.

Maredudd glanced around him, maybe also noting the way his men were subtly shifting their stances. A few of the more senior stepped closer, protectively, as if he was under threat just as Cadell had been. Up until now, Maredudd had discouraged this kind of attention, viewing it as coddling. Having served as a guard for a prince for several years, Dai could have told him his men's attentiveness had nothing to do with Maredudd's own capabilities. Nobody wanted a dead lord on their watch. Protecting him was their job. The more he protested, pushed them away, or, at the extreme, evaded their efforts, the worse everyone's life would be. Including Maredudd's.

Others among the group were taking a moment to glance outward, wondering if the Normans could have penetrated this far north. They usually were content to remain in the southern lowlands.

Morgan, the Welsh captain with whom Dai had marched the previous day, had arrived at Maredudd's fire circle at the same time as Dai. His tent was by Dai's family's wagons, which was how he'd been on hand last night for Gareth to send him to find Maredudd. Dai hadn't considered the practical consequences of Tomos's death at the time, but his loss might have inadvertently elevated Morgan in rank. At least, he was the first to speak now.

Bowing before his prince, a little more deeply than was usual for him, he said, "My lord, what are your orders?"

Maredudd released a sharp breath. "Send a rider on our fastest horse to Caerfyrddin to say we are only a day away. We will march through the night to get there if we have to."

Morgan turned immediately to do Maredudd's bidding. The messenger, however, cleared his throat. "Caerfyrddin, my lord? If the king dies—"

As a younger brother of the king, Maredudd had been a person whom older men could occasionally second-guess. No more, which Morgan, rather than Maredudd, made clear by a sharp cutting off motion with his hand. "You heard him as well as I. We are headed to Caerfyrddin."

Although at first Dai didn't understand the problem, Maredudd managed to both thank Morgan for his intervention and calm the messenger with the same twist of his lips. "It is in your mind that Cadell might not live to reach the castle. If that turns out to be the case, then riding to Dinefwr to claim the throne would be politically astute, in order to prevent another claimant from gaining supporters before I arrive. I hear your concern. But my brother is still alive. Thus, there is no throne to usurp. I will go where my brother said."

Nobody else argued with him, and with another wave of his hand, he got them moving away from the fire circle, back to their duties, which were now more urgent than ever. Very quickly, the only people left in Maredudd's vicinity were Dai and his mother—and little Angharad, of course.

Maredudd let out another breath, this time allowing his shoulders to sag. "Before today, I would not have thought any Norman lord would have the temerity to ambush a sitting King of Deheubarth."

Gwen glanced at Dai and then said what anyone remotely partisan had to be thinking: "Fifteen years ago, the Normans hanged your mother from the ramparts at Kidwelly. You, of all people, should never forget that Normans are capable of *anything*."

"First Tomos; now Cadell." Maredudd allowed himself another sigh. "I see now why you fear Tomos's murder was meant for me."

Gwen gave him a sad smile. "I would hope by now, my lord, that you would fear it too."

39

Day Three

Meilyr

Leaving a small number of men to guard the wagons, supply carts, and horses, the rest of Maredudd's company, including Meilyr and his family, recrossed the River Teifi on foot. Since Tomos's body had already been carried to the church, all that was left was to hold a mass and burial. Over the course of Meilyr's life, he had sung at more funerals than he could count.

Tomos's funeral could have been perfunctory, given the urgency every single one of them was feeling about their upcoming departure. But Maredudd had loved Tomos. While he never would have wished him to be buried so far from home, he was going to give him all the care he could, under the circumstances.

The church of St. Pedr, like so many churches in Wales, was set within a circular graveyard. Ysbyty Cynfyn had been a holy site before the coming of Christianity to Wales, if the standing stones incorporated into the churchyard wall were anything to go by. It was comforting to Meilyr to think about the generations upon generations who'd lived and died here. Churches were primarily built for the living, and this church, located as it was at the crossroads of kingdoms and peoples, had seen its share of life. In truth, this was hardly the first army passing through that had asked for a man to be buried in holy ground. The church itself was sturdy but needed new thatch in its roof. As they'd come into the graveyard, Meilyr had caught Maredudd eyeing it. If he became king, perhaps he would donate a coin or two towards its upkeep. Meilyr might even suggest it if he had the chance.

Although it was January, the ground was not frozen, and the endless soaking rains they'd experienced these last weeks allowed the gravediggers to dig a grave deep enough to accommodate Tomos's body. The village priest, after a short consultation with Maredudd, delivered an appropriate sermon as if he'd known the deceased. He'd even collected a number of his parishioners to round out the substantial crowd to witness the burial.

And then Meilyr sang the eulogy. *A blessing I will dare to ask, a blessing I will pray for, and thus will I bind myself thereby ...*

Meilyr had learned this song, as he'd learned so many songs, in the ancient past of his youth. In this instance, as was often the case these days, he hadn't actually planned what he was going to sing, but sang whatever came to him in the emotion of the moment.

Once he finished, the laborers lowered Tomos's body into the ground, and the onlookers began to disperse. Meilyr didn't begrudge their speed, not as long as they accorded Meilyr himself the appreciative pause of silence after his song had finished. They didn't have time today for prayer and contemplation, not if they were going to make Caerfyrddin before midnight.

Maredudd made appreciative noises in Meilyr's direction, after which he took a few more solitary moments beside Tomos's grave. Since the messenger's arrival, he had barely been able to take a step without one of his men, as directed by Morgan, at his side. But with the rapid movement of people back towards the encampment, none had noted Maredudd's hesitation. In short order, except for the gravediggers, somehow only the two of them remained. Even Gareth, Dai, and Gwen had headed off, assuming, along with the rest of Maredudd's retainers, that someone else was keeping an eye on the lord.

Still with his eyes closed, Maredudd said, "Your wife came to me yesterday evening to provide comfort after the news of Tomos's death. Thank her for that for me, if you will."

"Everyone else is concerned for your safety. What is always of concern to her is your heart."

"I had a mother, and lost her. And then I was fortunate to have another mother," he nodded towards the grave, "Tomos's wife, and lost her too."

"You need a wife of your own."

Maredudd scoffed. "Not you too. It is a constant refrain of my brother. But only Rhys is betrothed. Perhaps the sooner we marry him off, the better. Deheubarth men don't seem to be all that good at marriage and family."

Finally, Morgan had looked over his shoulder and seen them standing alone. He stopped in the entrance to the churchyard and waved several other men back to their posts.

"You'll find your way." Meilyr spoke the platitude really just to keep Maredudd talking. "How are you now? With this news, you may soon be King of Deheubarth."

Maredudd made a cutting off motion with his hand. "None of that, either. We won't talk of the kingship until it happens."

Meilyr had sung for kings since he was fourteen years old, so the conversation wasn't overawing. Rather, he was glad to be able to take the measure of the man. Although Cadell had been found wanting long since, and Rhys was a power in his own right, up until this week, Maredudd had been an unknown quantity. If he was to be King of Deheubarth by the end of the day, the men of Gwynedd needed to know him.

None of this did Meilyr say, even if, as the premier bard of Wales, he could speak the truth without penalty. It was practically his job. Instead, he spoke of different truths. "That shows an admirable loyalty to your brother, but you also need to be prepared. Losing a king in battle is one thing; losing him to treachery is quite another."

"I repeat. I am not a king."

"You heard the messenger. He, at least, believes you will be." Meilyr had learned all about the conversation from Gwen and Dai.

Now, Maredudd eyed Meilyr with a jaundiced eye. "Not to be blunt, but I'm surprised you care."

Meilyr gave a little shake of his head. "How is it that the men of Deheubarth came to think the men of Gwynedd hate them? It isn't true. None of us wish ill upon you. In fact, we wish you the best. We know how fortunate we are to have been born in our mountains, safe, for the most part, from Norman incursions. It is you and Powys who bear the brunt of the Norman advance. What we would prefer is for you to fight them instead of us!"

They had started walking slowly towards the entrance to the graveyard. Morgan and his men fell back, forming a wide circle around them, already understanding that not every conversation of their new king, if that's really what Maredudd was to be, was meant for their ears.

Maredudd spoke now in a musing tone. "Some have become convinced that fighting you is the only way to have peace with the Normans."

"They would be wrong to believe that." Meilyr gave a little snort. "Your brother should have known that before the ambush. Certainly, he should know it now."

For a moment, Maredudd's stride hitched. "You are brave to say that to me."

"Not brave. Just old."

That garnered him a laugh. "Gwynedd hasn't always been steadfast. Anarawd died on the way to his own wedding."

"That was Cadwaladr's doing, as you well know, not Owain's." It was on the tip of Meilyr's tongue to tell Maredudd, who apparently didn't know, that Cadell had conspired with Cadwaladr to murder Anarawd so he could take the throne. He didn't. Really, that tale was Rhys's to tell. "I admit Gwynedd and Deheubarth have had their differences over the years. Still, Prince Hywel wishes you no ill."

"So I have been told." Maredudd gave a little tsk. "Such pride! Such righteous certainty of your place in the world. You always do the right thing, too, do you?"

"Of course not. Hardly ever." Meilyr realized he had goaded the other man, and thus had no right to take offense himself. "That would be my son-in-law. Doesn't mean I don't try."

"Well said." Maredudd stopped abruptly in the path. "Which I should have expected from you. I see now how much like Rhys you must have been when you were young. Quick on your feet. That has never been me. You have my apologies for doubting your intentions. Much of what you say, Tomos taught me, even if my older brothers would have the world a different way. I wasn't so young when my parents died that I don't have memories of both. My mother was intelligent and willful; my father indulgent of her and demanding of his sons, even me, who was only six. And then, of course, they died." He looked down at his feet. "Everyone died."

He was not speaking only of his parents, Gwenllian and Gruffydd, but of two more full-blood older brothers, Morgan and Maelgwn, both of whom had died at the same time as Gwenllian. One had been killed in the battle, and the other had been executed by the Normans alongside his mother.

When the news came of Gwenllian's death, the men of Gwynedd had descended on the south, and the battle cry *remember Gwenllian!* continued to rally them to this day. Too bad the men of Deheubarth had forgotten the reason why.

Cadell had lived by treachery; no surprise, then, that he might die by it, too.

40

Day Three

Gareth

Within moments of Maredudd's return to the encampment from the funeral, he ordered the party to march. Then he summoned Gareth to him, to ride beside him at the head of the company. It was the best place to be, in general, since anyone behind would be eating the dust of those in front. Gareth was glad to avoid that, though he might be less happy with Maredudd's renewed scrutiny. Gareth was keeping secrets, more than before. He feared Maredudd still was, too, despite the revelations of last night.

Their conversation started out casually enough, with Gareth asking about the milestones they would see along their way. He might have traveled parts of this road before, but he wasn't actually sure.

Maredudd related what he knew, and then, out of the blue, said, "Why haven't you asked to be set free?"

Gareth was quite sure he didn't want to have anything to do with this conversation. He had been thinking Maredudd had called him to the front to demand he explain his failure to uncover the murderer. As far as Gareth was concerned, his only failure had been to be so slow in realizing Maredudd's duplicity.

The truth Gareth had been forced to confront last night was that he had been prideful. Maredudd had appealed to that part of Gareth that wanted everyone to marvel at his reputation—both for honesty and for solving murders—and he hadn't been able to see the way Maredudd was using that pride against him.

Only in retrospect did he understand that the tale Maredudd had related that first evening in the abbot's quarters could never have been the whole story.

He didn't feel like saying any of that to Maredudd, however, future King of Deheubarth or not. "Are you saying I am released from your service? If I were to turn around right now and ride away with my family, you would let me?"

"I would."

Gareth made a sound that was meant to convey the full measure of his disbelief. "You could have mentioned this to me earlier."

"I was afraid you would take me up on it."

"And now?"

"Now, I'm sure you won't."

Something that might have been real laughter bubbled up in Gareth's throat. "Why is that?"

"Because you are the man I assumed you to be."

Gareth rode another dozen yards before replying. "I am not happy that you deceived me."

"But you understand the reason why, and thus, you have already forgiven me. I saw that in your face last night. Whatever the reason I asked you to come with me in the first place, you can't walk away now."

Once again, Maredudd had seen right through him, and Gareth wasn't so proud he couldn't admit that, too. Even so, there was more to Gareth's decision to stay in Maredudd's company than what they'd discussed so far, not the least of which was some concern about retracing his steps. Maredudd had spread his cloak of protection around Gareth's family, but two other portions of this army were headed this way, by now coming down this very same road, fleeing the siege of Aberystwyth. Their leaders might not take as kindly as Maredudd to discovering Gareth and Dai roaming freely through Deheubarth.

Besides, Llelo should be in Caerfyrddin. Gareth had seen the joy in Gwen's face at the idea they could be reunited. Although she went about her daily life as if nothing was amiss, a constant shadow hung over her, and Llelo's absence was like a weight on her heart.

Maredudd didn't need to know any of that. It was another secret that would be revealed—or not—in time. "You are not wrong. I gave you my word that I would try to discover who murdered Rhodri. Now that we have a real murder to investigate, I don't feel less of an obligation. I took you at your word that you meant me and my family no harm. We all have been to your brother's court before. I investigated a murder at Dinefwr. This doesn't have to be any different."

Maredudd made a motion with his head. "That's one reason you're coming. You are also worried about me. You've said it. Your wife and son reminded me of it this morning."

"Someone murdered Tomos; possibly someone close to you. Having had a night to think on the matter, do you have an idea of who that might be?"

"None at all." Maredudd shot him a look out of the corner of his eye. "When I first invented the idea that Rhodri had been murdered, I also implied it would make sense for him to have been murdered by one of Hywel's men, who trailed us to our encampment and took an opportunity when it came. Could such a man have murdered Tomos?"

"If Rhodri had actually been murdered, then that an outsider had come upon him would not have been an unreasonable conclusion. That's why I took you at your word. I am far less open to that idea when it comes to Tomos. We are far from Aberystwyth. In light of your brother's situation, I feel confident Gwynedd didn't do this." That Gareth *knew* Gwynedd didn't do this had to remain unsaid, for now.

"So you see the link too," Maredudd said, "between Tomos and Cadell?"

"Not to put too fine a point on it, my concern is that Tomos was killed either to get to you, or because the killer mistook him *for* you. Your brother feared treachery within his ranks. This looks like the very definition of treachery."

Maredudd sighed, for the first time admitting what couldn't be denied. "Do we really look that much alike?"

"In the daylight? Yes. In the dark, even more so. You have the same height; the same shape. Last night under the trees, it would have been hard to tell the two of you apart."

"That would mean Tomos died for nothing."

"He died for you."

Maredudd made a frustrated motion with his whole body. "But in entirely the wrong way. He didn't stand back-to-back with me in battle! He was killed in the dark."

"I know. And I'm sorry. At the same time, I see this death as a grave mistake on the killer's part. Not only did he murder the wrong man, but, going forward, he has made it that much harder for him to get to you. You are not going bathing by yourself ever again. In fact, I am quite certain that none of your men are going to let you do *anything* in the future without at least several of them in attendance."

That prompted a real snort from Maredudd and the comment, "Ridiculous."

"Is it? How freely can your brother roam about?"

"Too freely, apparently. Though—" he made another motion with his head, "—he had his *teulu* at his side and look what good it did him."

"He was ambushed by a larger force from Tenby," Gareth said. "That is a very different situation than a single man slipping a knife between your ribs in the woods."

This wouldn't even be the first murder in Gareth's personal experience where mistaken identity came into play. Prince Cadwaladr had arranged for Gareth's death in an ambush but instead killed Prince Rhun, his brother's eldest son, because Rhun had been wearing Gareth's helmet. Cadwaladr had been forgiven for his treachery only because Owain had no choice, given the politics with England and Cadwaladr's close ties to Owain's enemies. Owain had been able to accept him back into his court because Cadwaladr hadn't done the deed himself, nor intended it to happen.

However, Rhun's accidental death in no way altered the fact that Cadwaladr hated Gareth passionately and wanted him dead. If Tomos had looked anything like Gareth, Gareth would have looked in Cadwaladr's direction for the murderer.

Had Gareth been walking, the thought would have brought him up short. As it was, he just twitched a little in the saddle.

Had he just discovered the real reason Cadell had sent Maredudd to find him?

Cadell had done Cadwaladr's bidding in the past, or attempted to. They'd plotted together to murder Cadell's older brother, Anarawd. Rhys was convinced they were currently plotting together to murder King Owain, though nothing had come of those plans as yet. The pair had also been in league in this latest war against Hywel. It could even be that Cadell was feeling threatened by his younger brothers and was scheming with Cadwaladr to eliminate them. That would make whatever was happening here all of a piece.

That said, Gareth couldn't see the sense in Cadell killing his brothers. He had no heir of his body. His brothers *were* his heirs. No matter their growing maturity and power, Deheubarth would be nowhere without them. Gareth would need more evidence than he currently had collected to convince him Cadell meant to murder either of them.

Murdering Gareth was an entirely different matter. As far as Gareth could tell, Cadwaladr so far had done all the work in this unholy alliance with very little tangible gain for himself personally. Meanwhile, Cadell had become King of Deheubarth.

From where Gareth sat beside Maredudd on the road to Caerfyrddin, certain facts had suddenly become undeniable:

First, Cadwaladr had allied time and again with Cadell.

Second, Cadwaladr wanted Gareth dead.

Third, Cadell had asked Maredudd to find Gareth and bring him south.

It was not inconceivable that Cadwaladr had told Cadell he would aid him no more until he got *something* of what he wanted—namely Gareth's head on a pike.

And Gareth, fool that he was, was set to ride straight up to Cadell and say *here, take it.*

41

Day Three

Rhys

Rhys poked his head into the small cubby off the receiving room where Llelo was helping to organize Cadell's papers. He'd continued the work even after Rhys had decided to take a break. "A messenger from Maredudd has arrived!"

The papers in question included everything from estate accounts to documents outlining border disputes or proposals for alliance, plus a flurry of well wishes from every lord in Cadell's domain who'd heard of his misfortune. Nowhere to be found was any letter from Gilbert de Clare, the Earl of Hertford, and Cadell had no recollection of what he'd done with it. Likely, it had either been in Cadell's gear when Gerald of Tenby had stripped his body of everything valuable or in his saddlebags, which the Normans had also taken, along with his horse.

Regardless of the missing letter, the documents that formed the foundation of any kingship had become Rhys's responsibility until such a time as Cadell was able to deal with them. They could not be put off even for a day. There was nothing wrong with Cadell's mind some of the time, but he still didn't remember the hours leading up to the ambush, and he'd needed a bit more poppy today to stave off the pain in his back and legs. After yesterday's coherence, everyone had been hoping he'd turned a corner. Perhaps they were asking too much too soon.

Llelo rose from his chair. "Are you sure you want me present to hear it?"

Rhys scoffed. "You still have to ask? I need you to advise me. These older men have no trouble expressing their opinions about the right thing to do. I have made so many decisions today for which I feel woefully unprepared that I can't discern anymore what is best for Deheubarth and what is self-interest—either mine or theirs."

This was essentially the same thing Rhys had been telling Llelo ever since he had arrived in Deheubarth. Throughout his life up until now, Rhys had been left to his own devices most of the time. All of a sudden, he was bombarded by what everyone else wanted him to do or say.

The leader of this small group of wise men was Huw, Cadell's steward. Seventy years old if he was a day, he had served Rhys's father and elder brother in the years before Cadell had ascended the throne. Huw knew the workings of Deheubarth inside and out. But even with his long years of service, he felt uncomfortable deciding everything on his own. The rest still needed the approval of his lord.

The rider Maredudd had sent stood in the middle of the receiving room, waiting for Rhys to reappear. Huw had brought him in here instead of into the hall, not only because it was where Cadell was being cared for, but also in case they didn't want to share whatever he had to say before they were ready.

The messenger didn't seem to know to whom he should be addressing his message. His eyes went first to Cadell, his king, upon whom he was accustomed to relying. At his somewhat slack expression, he looked at Huw. To the steward's credit, by way of reply, he made a slight motion with his head in Rhys's direction, and so the man turned finally to him.

"My lord Rhys, I come from your esteemed brother, Prince Maredudd. Your message found him a single day away. He instructed me to say he will be here tonight, no matter how many hours they have to walk in the dark."

The relief Rhys felt to hear this was impossible to measure. "Was he already on his way to Caerfyrddin?"

"Yes. He had just crossed the River Teifi at Llanbedr, with twenty miles remaining to march."

Cadell had overheard, and now he rasped out, "He gave up the siege, did he?"

"Yes, my king." The messenger cleared his throat, nervous to be speaking directly to Cadell in his condition. "Too many men had died."

Rhys suppressed his impulse to raise his hands to the heavens in gratitude. His prayers for his brother's deliverance from war had been fervent. He hadn't been able to help praying also for Hywel and the men and women around him, including Llelo's parents. He didn't dare glance into Llelo's face to see how he was taking this news. His friend had been unhappy when he'd learned Cadell planned to send men marching north. Now, they might be looking at a total victory for Hywel.

"Why did Maredudd not bring this message himself?" Cadell continued. "He could have ridden here with you."

"He did not feel it wise, under the circumstances."

"And what circumstances are those?" Even in Cadell's stuporous state, he could make his tone desert dry.

"After hearing the tale of the events in the Coed Rath, he thought it would be unwise to travel with too few men, even in his own lands. We are a company of a hundred. The men of Tenby wouldn't challenge so many."

Cadell's laugh had a touch of madness behind it. "Look at that. Maredudd is already thinking like a king." Then he moaned and put his hand to his head.

"Don't say such things, my lord." Huw hastened closer to help him drink from a cup of mead. "You are better today. We can all see it."

Rhys wasn't so sure about that, but he was impressed by his brother's wit and that he was still capable of it despite his pain and the way his mind had been stewing continually in poppy juice. Because Cadell continued to moan, with Huw making clucking sounds in commiseration, Rhys returned his attention to the messenger. "Thank you for your service. You must be exhausted. There is food and drink for you here."

"My lord—" The man's eyes flicked towards the king and back again. With Cadell and Huw distracted, he took two steps closer and lowered his voice to barely above a whisper. "Your brother—Lord

Maredudd I mean—wrote you a letter, for your eyes only." He held it out.

Rhys accepted the letter, but then kept the messenger a little longer. "You were there, were you, at Aberystwyth?"

"Yes, my lord."

"You said too many men had died. Was there battle—"

"The bloody flux, my lord. And rain. So much rain. We couldn't get dry, and then we were sick." He dropped his eyes to the floor.

"How long did we maintain the siege?"

"A matter of weeks, my lord, before those in charge deemed the situation impossible."

"Those in charge?"

"Lord Maredudd wanted to stay, to do his duty, but he was overruled by Lord Dafydd." Now, the man bit his lip. "My deepest apologies for saying this. I hope you understand, my lord, that we were miserable and dying for nothing."

Rhys dismissed the messenger. By the end of the day, Rhys was going to be able to have this conversation with his brother, so he didn't need to hear it from a third party. The thought of speaking to Maredudd again brought a wave of comfort. It was as if Rhys had been holding his breath ever since the first swing of a Norman sword in the Coed Rath. Suddenly, for the first time in three days, he was able to fill his lungs properly. He let out that breath, took in another, and then opened the letter.

Llelo stood silently at Rhys's shoulder while Rhys read the few sentences explaining how Tomos had been murdered. Rhys swallowed down tears he didn't want to shed, not here in the receiving room in front of Huw and Cadell. Tomos had been Rhys's foster father, too, even if for a shorter time. Rhys wished he'd saved the reading of the letter until he could retreat to the wall-walk with Llelo. It had started to rain, which could have masked his tears. Standing in the receiving room now, he longed for the ceiling to open up and drench him. For a single moment, Rhys had felt able to breathe, knowing his brother was safe and on his way. And now this.

Llelo put a hand on his shoulder. "I am sorry, Rhys."

Blinking away his tears, he turned to his friend. "Thank you. Tomos's murder is hard for me to encompass. For Maredudd, it will be more so. It would have been one thing for Tomos to have died in battle, but murder? It doesn't make sense."

Then Llelo frowned to see further writing on the back of the page Rhys still held in his hand. "What's this?"

Rhys flipped over the paper and found himself swallowing down a bark of surprise at Maredudd's further news, equally succinctly stated, that he was riding to Caerfyrddin with Llelo's whole family. "Is it too strange that I am more astonished to learn of the murder of Tomos than the fact that Maredudd has roped your father—not to say your entire family—into finding his killer?"

Suddenly, Llelo was grinning. "We wished to consult with my father, and now he is coming to Caerfyrddin. He will get to the bottom of everything."

"If only wishing could make more things so." Rhys glanced towards Cadell, whom Huw had managed to settle, finally, with more poppy.

Once he saw where Rhys's attention had gone, Llelo sobered, and now spoke in an undertone, "Like your brother able to walk on his own again, even ride a horse and lead men into battle?"

"We need a true miracle for that to happen." The weight of Rhys's responsibilities settled on him once again. Cadell was injured, potentially beyond healing, and Tomos was dead.

Then he squared his shoulders. This was his life now. The sooner he accepted it, the better. And really, things could be worse. They had been worse. He had lived through the death of his brothers and his parents. After that, any grief could be encompassed.

Especially now that Maredudd was coming home.

42

Day Three

Gwen

As they entered Caerfyrddin's bailey, Gwen searched for Llelo. But when her eyes passed over the group of men who'd come to welcome them, she didn't recognize any of them but Prince Rhys. Then she looked again and realized he was there. He just hadn't looked like himself in the black robes of a Hospitaller and the quite respectable beard he'd managed to grow. He *looked* like a churchman now. While she would, of course, be honored to have a son in the Order, she didn't know if it was the right thing for him and, as a mother, she missed him.

Back straight and chin held high, Rhys greeted Maredudd formally, not as a brother but as if Maredudd were already king. Then, a heartbeat later, he dropped any pretense of ceremony and wrapped Maredudd up in a fierce hug. The pair held on to each other through a dozen heartbeats. Tears pricked at Gwen's eyes to see it and to have confirmed what she had already assumed—that neither of them would ever conspire to hurt the other.

"You could have died." The brothers spoke at the same time, the shock of which was enough to get them each to take a step back and look at each other fully.

That was also a signal to the crowd around them that the formalities were over. The whole of Maredudd's party was by now within the bailey of the castle. Already, Maredudd's men were fewer in number than they'd been a few hours ago, one by one asking permission of their commander to depart as they drew closer to their homes. And who could blame them? It had been a hard campaign, and their families would want to know they'd survived.

Because of it, none of the petitioners had been denied, as long as they promised to return if—and when—they were needed again.

Gwen imagined they would be. If the garrison at Tenby really had ambushed Cadell, Rhys and Maredudd would be wanting to raze the English town to the ground before summer, if they could manage it.

The onlookers began to disperse, most moving towards the great hall where a meal would be waiting for them, even at this late hour. The company had kept going in darkness, knowing they could sleep safely at the castle if only they just kept walking.

Gareth had watched Maredudd greet Rhys a few paces nearer than Gwen and the children. Now, Maredudd cast about looking for him, and when he saw him standing a few yards behind him, he motioned him forward. "Rhys, you must meet the great Gareth ap Rhys."

Rhys stuck out his arm for Gareth to take. "Glad to see you again. Hopefully, you can help get to the bottom of all of this."

"What do you mean, *again*?" Maredudd asked. "You know each other?"

"We met at Dinefwr four years ago." And then Rhys's eyes went to Gwen, Dai, and the children, who hadn't yet come closer.

"There you are! Welcome to Caerfyrddin." He strode forward, parting the crowd that was left. Stopping, he bowed his head to Gwen but didn't hug her, not like last spring at Ysbyty Cynfyn when he'd held on to her like he'd just held his brother. Not here for all eyes to see. Next, he grasped Dai's arm, and then chucked Taran under the chin.

Tangwen had been jumping up and down, trying to see over everyone's heads. "Where *is* he?" Despite their best efforts not to speak about what was happening in her presence, she had discovered that Llelo would be here, and her anticipation was at a fever pitch.

"Right here, Tangwen." Llelo had followed after Rhys, a smile as wide as the River Dee to see his family.

Tangwen squealed in happiness and threw herself at her brother, who scooped her up in his arms. Then Llelo kissed Gwen's cheek before moving on to hug Dai. "I can't tell you how glad I am to see you all."

"Will someone please tell me what is happening?" Maredudd was looking from one to the other, his hands on his hips.

Rhys waved a hand airily. "Sir Llywelyn is Gareth's son. I summoned him here a few months ago to aid me. You might remember meeting him briefly before your departure to Aberystwyth."

Although Rhys had greeted Maredudd formally earlier, implying respect for his brother's station, never had Rhys looked more regal than when he introduced Llelo with a casual wave of his hand, like the earlier tale of his identity had been nothing, not even a deception. Whether or not he meant to, Rhys was telling the world that his decisions were not to be questioned.

Maredudd had never displayed quite that degree of arrogance.

For his part, Maredudd scratched at his chin, with no recourse but to accept what by now was a given. Meanwhile, the members of Gwen's family were all talking at once, with huge smiles on their faces, their joy overflowing.

Eventually, Llelo came back around to her, and Gwen was able to hug him properly. "When we heard about King Cadell—" She couldn't finish the sentence.

"I'm fine, Mam. So is Rhys."

"He saved my life," Rhys said, overhearing. "You need to know the truth of it. Don't let him tell you different."

"I see there is much that has gone on behind my back." Maredudd's tone wasn't even sour. Then he introduced Gareth to Huw, Cadell's steward, who had been waiting a respectful five paces away. They had met at Dinefwr, too. Looking directly at Gwen, Maredudd then said, "My brother and I must speak to the king, and then we will join you in the hall. Please, make yourselves at home. You are our guests."

"Thank you. We appreciate it." Gwen bent her head. "Truly."

Gareth nodded, too, and took a step back, evidently thinking he would stay with Gwen and the children. But Maredudd laughed out loud. "Oh no, you don't. Now that you're here, you won't get off the hook that easily." Flapping a hand between Llelo and Gareth, he added, "You two come with us."

Tangwen was unhappy to be parted from Llelo so soon, but Dai pulled her back. "They won't be long." And then, under his breath, he said to Gwen, "Will they?"

"One would presume." Gwen took Tangwen's hand while Dai swung Taran onto his shoulders. After the meal, the children would need to be put to bed. Fortunately, home was their wagon, which Bran had parked near the stables beside Meilyr's wagon.

There was room for both wagons—and a hundred men, if they still had them—within the bailey at Caerfyrddin because it was enormous. While the Normans had conquered the entire southern coastline of Wales, Caerfyrddin was located at the northern edge of the territory they'd carved out for themselves. As part of their conquest, and their attempt to hold the land they'd conquered, they'd brought English and Flemish settlers into these regions to displace the native Welsh. Prior to the arrival of the Normans, the Welsh hadn't built or lived in castles, since, in general, their kings didn't have to protect themselves from their own people.

The Normans, by contrast, were trying to impose their will on an overtly hostile populace. They feared attack. For that reason, they'd built a castle here with a bailey large enough, and defensible enough, for a significant-sized army to assemble inside.

Before she and Gareth had acquired their wagon, they might have found a place to lay their heads at the Augustinian priory located along the river. Their family had a long history of staying in monasteries, which tended to have relatively comfortable guesthouses. It would have removed them from Llelo's environs, however, which wouldn't have made Gwen happy tonight.

"What's next for us?" Meilyr spoke in a low voice near her ear, his eyes on the princes' retreating backs.

"I have no idea." And she honestly didn't. "Our warm welcome was a relief. Gareth genuinely feared we might end up in the dungeon."

"Don't get your hopes up too high." Meilyr remained in good spirits, despite the uncertainty. "I imagine there's still time."

43

Day Three

Rhys

Having led the way to the receiving room, Huw hesitated at the door, a finger to his lips. "We have much to discuss." Once inside, he went immediately to the table where his ledger and pen lay abandoned. He closed the book before turning back to Maredudd, who had his full attention. "It is so good you are here, my lord Maredudd. We have been doing our best, but we have been quite bereft."

Rhys chose not to take this as an insult. He, too, would be happy to offload the burdens of kingship onto his brother.

For Maredudd's part, his smile held an overtone of grimness. "I realize we have matters of state to see to, but, first, I must speak with the king." He paused, his gaze on Huw, and when Huw didn't take the hint and depart, he added, "Please use this next hour to rest and eat. I will find you when we are finished."

"Of-of course, my lord." Huw stuttered at the dismissal. Then, glancing to where Cadell lay asleep, he said, "Are you certain you want to wake him? He has had a hard time of it."

"I don't intend to wake him."

Huw didn't seem to know what to do with that either. He was being encouraged to leave the four of them alone with the king, and it was clear from his dubious expression that he didn't like the idea of any conference that didn't include him. He would feel that nothing should happen within the king's vicinity he didn't know about. Up until now, other than the ambush in the Coed Rath, nothing had.

So whether or not he meant to imply this, Maredudd was telling his brother's steward that things were going to be different if he became king. It was a lesson in dealing with retainers Rhys thought he would do well to learn.

"Of course, my lords," Huw's eyes tracked from Maredudd to Rhys, and then swept over Gareth and Llelo. "Please try not to tire him."

"We will do our best." Maredudd was firm and implacable in a way Rhys had not been able to be with Huw since they'd arrived at Caerfyrddin.

Huw swallowed hard, realizing now how far he had overstepped. "If I may, it is a relief to see you well."

Maredudd canted his head. "Thank you. Where, by the way, is Lord Iestyn?"

"He was here earlier. Once he learned of your imminent arrival, he removed himself and his men to the priory rather than take up any quarters at the castle."

"I would be grateful if you could send for him in the morning. As it is late, there's no need to disturb him tonight."

Huw bent his head. "Of course, my lord. I will arrange for food and drink for you all." He left.

Immediately upon the steward's departure, Maredudd walked to the bed and stared down at Cadell. He looked for long enough, in fact, that Rhys was about to suggest he move away because the intensity of his gaze was permeating the room.

And then Cadell woke anyway. At first, he shook his head as if he was disoriented, making no actual acknowledgment of Maredudd's presence. Then, he attempted to swing his legs out from under the covers, like he had yesterday with Llelo and Rhys. For the moment, Gareth and Llelo stayed where they were, visible to Cadell were he to turn his head, but not in his direct line of sight.

For his part, Rhys hustled over to the bed. "Don't get up."

"I must." Every time Cadell had woken so far, he'd bitten the head off of anyone within hearing distance. Rhys felt bad that he hadn't warned Maredudd what might be coming. Llelo had been the target more than once, though Huw had taken the brunt of Cadell's anger and pain. Everyone was trying to be patient, as they would have to be. For a man as vibrant as Cadell, who before the ambush had been nothing if not vigorous, his current state was intolerable. To say he wasn't taking it well was to woefully understate the case.

Rhys reached the bed just as Cadell managed to get one foot on the floor. He glanced up at Maredudd, glaring at first, and then his expression softened as he recognized who was looking down at him. "You're here. I've waited so long for you to come."

It wasn't true, but Rhys understood why he might feel that way.

"Yes, brother. I came," Maredudd said.

Cadell grunted. "My other leg still isn't moving on its own accord."

"I'll get it."

With some no-nonsense encouragement, Maredudd got Cadell sitting on the edge of the bed, at which point Cadell said matter-of-factly. "I need to use the chamber pot."

He hadn't greeted anyone else yet. Maybe he couldn't. Maybe, except for Maredudd, his eyes weren't clear enough to see. His head wound remained serious, the pain coming and going in an unpredictable fashion.

With utter aplomb, Maredudd pulled out the chamber pot from under the bed. His subsequent glance at Rhys said *help me* without voicing the request out loud. Rhys obliged, and Cadell managed to do his business with a minimum of fuss. At that point, he collapsed back onto the bed. "Thank you. It's shameful I can't do even this for myself. I am grateful to the two of you. This situation is humiliating enough without having to call a servant every time I need to move."

"We are here for you, Cadell." With a few more easy movements, Maredudd adjusted Cadell's pillow and covers. Then Maredudd himself sat on a stool near the head of the bed and held his hand. "Can you talk?"

"That appears to be the only thing of which I am capable." He snapped his fingers towards a side table. "Poppy first."

"You will rise from this bed again," Maredudd said. "You will live to fight another day."

"If not for this headache, I think I might actually believe that." Cadell didn't turn his head, but he waved a hand to point past Maredudd. "Who else is here? Didn't I see Gareth and his son a moment ago?"

At that, Gareth moved into view, Llelo just behind him. "We are here, my lord."

"So, you found him. Good." Cadell relaxed back against the pillows.

"As you hoped," Maredudd said.

Rhys was lost now. "What are we talking about?"

Cadell gave something of a snort. "You were not the only one who didn't know whom to trust and did something about it."

"You mean—"

"I have wanted to see Gareth ap Rhys in my court for some time. Maredudd was sent north with specific orders to find him and bring him to me, by any means necessary." He was speaking as if Gareth and Llelo weren't in the room.

Rhys found himself on the edge of laughter. "And then what did you hope would happen?"

"Once Lord Gareth learned of my need, I knew he would do as I asked. Unfortunately, we were just a bit too late." Cadell's guffaw became a moan as his hand went to his head. "At least he's here now."

"I am here, my lord, and would ask what you need from me." Gareth took another step closer to the bed.

Cadell's eyes were closed. "I will say to you what I said to your son: if my own people have plotted against me, I need you to discover it."

"Do you have reason to believe the treachery goes beyond Earl Clare and the men of Tenby?" Gareth could see as well as everyone else in the room that there was no point in not speaking frankly with Cadell in this condition. "Is there someone in particular you suspect?"

"I suspect everyone." Cadell found the strength to toss one of his smaller pillows onto the floor in his frustration.

Maredudd picked it up and used it as a cushion for the stool. "A name would help."

Cadell bared his teeth. "At one point I was worried the two of you were conspiring against me."

Rhys reared back. "How could you even think that?" Since, of course, his concern had been the other way around.

"You brought Llelo here because you feared my intentions, but it never occurred to you that I might fear yours?" Now, Cadell peered through half-closed lids at Maredudd. "Please believe I had no designs on you and had nothing to do with Tomos's death. You are my heir. I would never seek to harm you." He closed his eyes and his whole body relaxed as the poppy began to work within him.

Maredudd held Cadell's hand still, but his gaze went to Rhys, both understanding what they'd just heard. Cadell had sounded entirely sincere in his pledge to Maredudd. What echoed in the room was what he had left unsaid—namely, that he could give no similar assurances to Rhys.

44

Day Three

Gareth

Whatever Gareth had expected upon his arrival in Caerfyrddin, it hadn't been for him and Llelo to accompany Maredudd and Rhys to see the king. That conversation had been a revelation, to say the least, one that in many ways was not easy to digest. Maredudd appeared to think so, too, because, after the king fell into his poppy-induced sleep, he motioned them all towards the table where servants had begun laying out a repast. "I want to hear everything that's happened since I last saw you, Rhys."

A quarter of an hour ago, Gareth might have been hesitant to take a seat with these two princes. Now, he pulled out a chair at the table as if he routinely ate meals in the presence of a king, asleep or not.

And then, as if Maredudd's query had lifted a sluice gate to release a torrent of water into a mill race, Rhys started talking. Llelo nodded every now and again from beside him to confirm his story.

While Gareth couldn't be more proud of the way Llelo had risen to the occasion, the details of the ambush were stomach-curdling.

Once Rhys finished, Llelo gave a regretful shake of his head. "The truth is, I have never been so afraid in my life. I felt like such a coward, watching Cadell's men die while keeping Rhys down. All I knew was that I had to prevent him from getting killed too."

"It was your job," Maredudd sat flatly. "We can't thank you enough for it." Then he looked at his brother. "Though I wish you had felt you could confide in me."

"I didn't know what to believe anymore," Rhys said simply. "For me, it was like the sun in the heavens was no longer moving along its proper course. We were never in the same place for more than a day. It was hardly something I could write in a letter. And if I genuinely had something to fear, I couldn't draw attention to myself by traveling to see you."

"So instead you sent for a total stranger." The moment he spoke, Maredudd waved a hand as if sweeping crumbs off a table. "Clearly that isn't what he is. You know this family. And you trust them."

"I do."

"God help me, so do I."

"I can't even apologize," Rhys added, "because I would do the same thing again, given the same set of circumstances. On top of which, with you undertaking the siege at Aberystwyth, it seemed unfair to burden you with my fears when you had so many concerns of your own."

"One of which should have been fearing for my own life, as it turned out." Maredudd motioned to Gareth. "Tell them about Tomos's death."

Gareth did as he was bid, after which there was a long silence as each of them thought about what they knew and the implications of that knowledge.

Then Llelo said, not without hesitation, "So ... how did you come to join the prince's party in the first place, Tad?" He looked at Gareth. "King Cadell asked Maredudd to find you, and he did. But then ... what? You agreed to abandon Prince Hywel and come to serve Cadell because he asked?"

Gareth would have answered, but Maredudd spoke first. "Do not doubt your father's integrity, even for a moment. My brother asked me to bring him south, by whatever means necessary. He was hoping we'd take the castle at Aberystwyth, and I would find him there. As it turned out, we failed in that endeavor, but we found him anyway."

Llelo was still frowning. "But this had to have been before Tomos's death, right? That's how you were—"

"I told him another man had been murdered, and I needed him to investigate the death. He traded his services for his family's freedom. You have no cause to think he meant any slight to your lord." Maredudd spoke as if coercing Gareth and Gwen into investigating a nonexistent murder was not something to get upset about.

And Llelo didn't, overtly anyway. He gazed at Maredudd through a count of five and then said, "I see."

Under the table, Gareth unobtrusively tapped Llelo's foot with the toe of his boot, telling him he would explain further once they were alone.

Maredudd continued, now as more of a *by the way,* "Your father discovered on his own that Rhodri's death was a ruse, after which I related to him everything I'm telling you. Our brother feared a traitor in his midst. That is all."

"But is it?" Llelo looked directly back at Maredudd. "What I can't stop thinking about is how Rhys should have died in that clearing too."

Maredudd tipped his head. "I am glad I did not lose both my brothers that day. I can't thank you—"

Llelo made a dismissive motion with his hand, similar to the one Maredudd had made earlier. "I appreciate your thanks, but that is not what I mean to bring up. Imagine if all these plots had come to full fruition: Rhys and Cadell would have died in the Coed Rath, and you would have been murdered beside the River Teifi. Who stands to gain from the death of the entire ruling family of Deheubarth?"

"Earl Clare, for one," Rhys said. "We already know this."

"We have more enemies than just him, brother. You know we do." Maredudd rubbed his chin. "We have not always been loved. There are lords out there who would like to see themselves on the throne. If it were empty. If they could take it."

Rhys made a face. "Besides which, the loss of the three of us would not, in fact, be the end of the House of Dinefwr. Not even the ruling house."

Llelo's eyes narrowed. "It wouldn't? How is that?"

"You're speaking of Einion." Gareth found himself easing back in his seat as he put more pieces of this increasingly complex puzzle together.

"Who is that?" Llelo looked bewilderedly at his father.

"Einion is the son of Anarawd. He arrived in this very castle with us today." Gareth tipped his head to Maredudd. "You sent him to lie to me about Rhodri. He was the sentry on duty at the time." To Gareth it was still an outrageous act, but not their concern at this moment. "He was the one who found Rhodri's body in the first place."

Maredudd nodded. "Einion helped Tomos and me carry him from the riverbank. Once I explained what I'd said to you, he was amenable to carrying on with the deception. In fact, he thought it was a lark."

As Maredudd had explained to Gareth as part of his non-apology for deceiving him, most of what he had told Gareth initially hadn't been a lie. He had merely embellished the truth, credibly describing the bare bones of the murder. Einion had given it flesh.

"That isn't even to mention our cousins Maurice and William," Rhys said. "They have claim to Deheubarth through their mother, if all other lines fail." He was speaking of Maurice Fitzgerald and his older brother, William. Both were sons of Gerald of Windsor and his wife, Nest, who was Rhys's aunt through his father.

Maredudd was suddenly looking fierce. "Einion has been with me this whole time. I don't see how he could have been absent long enough to meet with Earl Clare even once."

"What if Clare sent one of his men to meet him?" Llelo was suddenly sitting up straighter, and he explained about the open postern gate at Dinefwr.

"That's more than possible," Maredudd admitted, albeit somewhat grudgingly.

"You are surrounded by enemies," Gareth said softly. "I am sorry."

Rather than looking grim like his brother, Rhys gave a low laugh. "You see now why I asked Llelo to come."

45

Day Three

Gwen

"Left out again, I see," Dai said as he surveyed the hall.

"You are never overlooked, Dai." Gwen glanced into her son's face, concerned to hear him speak that way.

But he grinned at her, his expression bright and mischievous as ever. "You misunderstand, Mam. I am pleased. Let Llelo conspire with the great ones. We have a mystery to solve, don't we? What better way than in a hall full of suspects?" Practically chortling with glee, he held out his hand to Tangwen, who took it, and the pair of them set off down the row of tables. Tangwen was never happier than when she was keeping up with her older brother. Tonight, she could be his introduction to a hall full of strangers.

By contrast, Taran shrank a bit to Gwen's side, uncharacteristically shy. After an exhausting day of travel, the little boy was wary of yet another unfamiliar place with so many strangers. Gwen would stay here long enough to eat and be polite. Then they could retreat. In truth, it would be a relief for her, too.

She and her parents found seats at the end of one of the long tables. Ieuan and Bran were seated a few places farther along. They'd been included amongst Maredudd's men, so were thus accepted by Cadell's too. Besides, they were Welsh. Nobody could tell by looking at them or listening to them that they weren't good men of Deheubarth.

The thought brought Gwen up short. Hadn't Bran spoken with a north Welsh accent when they'd first met him? Somehow, over the last few days, he'd transitioned to one that sounded distinctly from the south. Truth be told, Dai could do the same at will, though (somewhat stubbornly) he was putting on a heavy northern accent tonight. He could switch to French, Gaelic, or Danish at any time too, if he chose. She didn't know if that justified the change in Bran, or if she should suddenly be suspicious of him—though to what end she couldn't say.

Gwen had barely sat down when Huw, Cadell's steward, hurried over, coming from the doorway through which Rhys and Maredudd had taken Gareth and Llelo. He stopped at the end of the table, wiping sweat from his brow with a cloth. "It's warm in here, isn't it? What a crush!" Then he looked them up and down. "But you should not be sitting so close to the door! You are our guests." His tone was affronted, as if they had demeaned Deheubarth rather than the other way around.

Gwen hastened to reassure him. "Do not concern yourself. We are not worried about such things. We have been eating outside for several days and are just happy to have a table to sit at."

"If you say so." Huw mopped his brow again. "It sets a poor precedent, but I can leave it for now."

Even so far from the fire, this was the first time Gwen had been truly warm in two days. The steward, however, was definitely sweating. "Are you well, Lord Huw?"

"I am fine." He turned now to Gwen's father. "Esteemed Bard Meilyr, we are honored by your presence. Is it possible you could play for us tonight?"

"I would be delighted to do so." Meilyr's eyes were brighter than Dai's had been. He loved to perform. Many bards didn't, preferring to write or to teach. Her father was the premier bard of his time because he could do all three.

"And you, madam." Huw turned his attention to Saran. "It is so lovely to see you so well. As a renowned healer, could you look in on King Cadell later? We would all be most grateful."

"I am pleased to be of service in any way you require." Saran was always happy to practice her profession, too.

"Maybe you could visit after dinner, while your husband is playing. Cadell should be able to listen from his room." Huw frowned. "It will mean you can't be in the hall for your husband's performance ..." His voice trailed off, as he thought better of what he was asking.

"If the king can hear from his chamber, then I will be able to hear as well. Besides—" She put a hand on Meilyr's shoulder, "—I have the pleasure of listening to him every day."

"We are blessed to have you both here. We can thank the good Lord for leading Maredudd to you." And then Huw was off again.

Gwen watched him go. "Do you think he is well, Saran? The lines on his face are so much more pronounced than I remember, and I don't like the way he's so flushed."

"He was younger the last time you were in the south. Old age overtakes us all eventually." The voice came from an older man on Gwen's other side. He was about her father's age, with a wool hood pulled down low around his ears, in defiance of the heat in the hall. He had a bushy white beard and was eating his turnips with gusto. She didn't remember him from any of their visits to the south, but he obviously remembered her. "Good in a crisis, always, is our Huw."

"Not this week," Meilyr said, a bit under his breath but still loud enough to hear.

The man shrugged off Meilyr's comment. "If Huw is out of sorts, it's because of the uncertainty around the king's injuries."

"I heard he is improving," Gwen said.

"Is he?" the man said. "To what end?"

"I don't understand what you're implying," Gwen said.

"The ambush, the retreat from Aberystwyth, Tomos's death."

Several of his companions were nodding, their faces pinched with worry.

Gwen was suddenly feeling cautious. "What about them?"

"God has not been smiling on us these last few weeks. The king has even wondered out loud if he is being punished for his sins."

"I can see why he might feel that way, but surely—" Meilyr made to intervene, but then broke off as Llelo appeared through the side door to the receiving room.

Nobody else seemed to have noticed, even the men to whom they'd spoken, who put their noses in their cups. Gwen and her parents, however, watched as Llelo's eyes searched the hall, tension in every line of his body. Instinctively, Gwen knew he was looking for his family, and she raised her hand.

His eyes latched onto hers like she had thrown a rope to a drowning man. He made his way around the perimeter of the hall, politely excusing himself as he jostled the shoulders of the diners. When he arrived at their table, he went first to Saran and bent to whisper in her ear.

She nodded and smoothly rose to her feet. "Fetch my satchel, if you will." Then, as Llelo went off, she leaned in to speak in an undertone only to her family. "We could be looking at another long night. It might be a good idea to start the music now."

46

Day Three

Rhys

Moments earlier ...

Rhys had been laughing to himself, thinking of the strange chain of events that had brought them to this point, sitting in his brother's receiving room with Maredudd, Llelo, and Gareth. Cadell was still asleep, or had been, up until he let out a pained gasp.

Rhys jumped to his feet. "Cadell? Is something the matter?"

"I d-d-don't know." Cadell's right arm came out from under the covers, and he tried to push to a sitting position. He didn't have the strength to do it, however, and though Rhys wanted to help him, he was unable to take his eyes off the right side of his brother's face, which had gone completely slack.

"I-I-I can't see." Cadell next tried to motion towards his face, but his left arm wouldn't move at all.

Llelo was already heading towards the door. "I'll fetch my grandmother."

Where not a half-hour ago, Cadell had been coherent and optimistic about his recovery, now he was struggling even to speak.

Rhys made room for Maredudd, who sat on the edge of the bed to again take Cadell's hand. "I'm here. We are all here. What can we do?"

Either Cadell couldn't understand, or he could no longer speak at all. His right eyelid drooped, along with the right side of his mouth. It was like his body was frozen on one side—the left—and his face on the other—the right.

Maredudd looked up at Gareth, who stood a few feet away, his arms folded across his chest and a grim expression on his face. "What's wrong with him?"

"I would guess he's had an apoplectic fit. It would explain why he's had such headaches. I've seen it before, though, thankfully not often."

By the time they got him lying down again, Saran was there, followed a moment later by Llelo, a satchel swung over his shoulder. Saran went straight to the bed, gave Cadell a once-over and then spoke to Llelo, listing the herbs she wanted him to retrieve for her.

Saran waved a vial containing ginger underneath Cadell's nose. Rhys could smell it from where he stood well back from the bed. Gareth evidently could too, because he nodded, as if Saran's choice of herb was a confirmation of his assessment of what was wrong with Cadell.

"My lord, can you hear me?" Saran had a hand on either side of Cadell's face. "If so, please open your eyes."

"I c-c-can hear you." Cadell was still stuttering. "I am having trouble seeing, and I can't m-m-move my arm."

"I know. No need to worry about that right now. Can you take in a deep breath for me?"

Cadell managed one. It wasn't as deep as Saran would have liked, but it allowed him to settle back more fully into his pillows.

Llelo was still picking through the vials in her satchel, handing one after another to his grandmother. In short order, she had added several herbs to a cup, along with wine, and together they helped Cadell drink it.

He didn't like it, taking two sips and refusing more.

Saran let him stop. "Are you in pain, my lord?"

"N-n-not right now." He seemed to almost laugh. "My head hardly hurts anymore."

Saran looked over at Rhys and Maredudd. "When was his last dose of poppy?"

"I gave him some when we entered the room," Maredudd said. "Within the hour."

Saran glanced back to Cadell whose eyes had closed again. Leaning forward, she said to him, "Give me a moment, my lord. Rest. I'll be right back."

She gestured that Rhys and Maredudd should come with her a few paces more away from the bed. "I'm sorry to say—"

Maredudd cut her off. "Gareth said it's apoplexy."

She didn't take offense at being interrupted. "Yes. That is my assessment too. Did he lose consciousness before I arrived?"

"He was asleep, and then he was gasping, That's when we realized something was wrong." Maredudd appeared to hold his breath as he asked his next question. "Could his fit have been brought on by poison in the drink I gave him?"

Saran put a hand on his arm. "I don't know of any poison which could have the effect we see here. It is true that certain poisons can injure or kill, even when given in small quantities, but they don't paralyze the left side of the body like this."

"Why is his eye like that?" Rhys tried to contain his horror so it didn't carry all the way to Cadell. "He can't move the right side of his mouth."

"That's common in these cases," Saran said. "We will know in the next hours or days if the paralysis is permanent. Was he able to move his left side before?"

"Not well," Rhys said. "But he had been able to stand and walk in a fashion. This all came from the ambush after he fell from a horse. Why-why would this happen now?"

"What did his physicians say about the wound to his head?"

Rhys found himself shrugging. "There was damage. They didn't know how much. They were worried because it was causing him so much pain."

Saran bit her lip. "I can't say for sure, but my guess is the blow to the head caused other injuries inside his skull we can't see. I recommend we send to Richard, Earl of Pembroke, at once for any physicians in his employ who might aid us. Meanwhile, I will meet with whomever you have here. The Augustinians must have a monk among their number who knows healing? Who has been tending him up until now?"

Maredudd was already heading towards the door. "I'll find them."

"Will he get better?" Rhys asked softly, afraid to ask and also afraid not to.

Saran glanced one more time towards the bed. "I don't want to give you false hope. He can still speak, which is a good sign. Beyond that, I can say only that few recover from an attack this severe—or at least not as fully as any of you would wish."

47

Day Four

Llelo

It was was so late by now that Llelo's head was on the table where he was sitting with Rhys and Dai. He was exhausted, while at the same time loath to go to bed. He was afraid he would lie awake, uncomfortable and unable to rest, which would be worse than staying up in the hall. Maredudd wasn't with them because he had spent the rest of his evening drinking himself into a stupor and eventually had been put to bed.

Rhys was drawing circles in puddles of spilled mead on the table, writing something out Llelo couldn't see from where he was.

"I'm sorry, Rhys," he thought to say.

"Thank you. I am too."

Dai had his head in his hands. "I know what Nain said, but I remain worried about treachery. The villain who murdered Tomos is still out there. Could he be trying to finish what the men of Tenby started?"

There were only a handful of people left in the hall. All of the servants had been sent to bed except for one old retainer, who was snoring on a stool by the fire. Even so, since speaking Welsh wasn't going to keep them from being understood, they were keeping their voices low.

Rhys picked up his cup and drained it. "All the other healers agreed with your grandmother's diagnosis. And besides, your father collected the cup and carafe. Nothing seemed amiss with either. We can't even be sure the attack on Tomos was meant for Maredudd. Maybe we are wrong about nearly everything."

"Not everything," Llelo said. "The men of Tenby did ambush us in the Coed Rath."

"True." Rhys saluted Llelo with his now empty cup.

Then Gareth appeared in the doorway from the receiving room and slid onto the bench next to Dai. "We have guesses and suppositions. We are still missing a great deal. We have to be."

"What do you always say, Tad? Secrets are hard to keep." Dai was so tired he was mumbling into his arm.

"And this must be a conspiracy." Llelo was suddenly a bit more awake. "Whether or not the king's current situation is the result of more treachery, we aren't talking about the involvement of only one or two men here. We have the Earl of Hertford, his brother, and who knows how many men of his retinue; the men from Tenby; and a genuine murderer, all still in play."

"My concern is that the killer is *here,*" Gareth said. "Regardless of whether his target was Tomos or Maredudd, or Tomos to get to Maredudd, a Welshman murdered him, not a man from Tenby."

Rhys frowned as he looked over at Gareth. "How can you be so sure of that? The murderer wouldn't have had to come from within Maredudd's company. He could have been following, waiting for his chance."

Dai and Gareth exchanged a glance, which Llelo didn't understand until Dai said, "My apologies, my lord, but we can be sure because we haven't shared everything we know." And then, at their father's nod of encouragement, he continued, "Putting aside the difficulty of staying hidden in territory he didn't know and surviving amongst people who speak only Welsh, he would have been seen."

Llelo frowned. "Not necessarily—"

"He would have." Dai put out a hand to stop Llelo from interrupting and by way of apology, too. "Steffan and Iago followed Maredudd's company after they left Aberystwyth."

Llelo's mouth dropped open in surprise, but Rhys's chin jutted out. "Then they could have—"

"Hywel's men are not to blame for Tomos's murder." Now Gareth interrupted *him*. "They witnessed both Tomos's death *and* Rhodri's. It was they who told us Rhodri died on his own and wasn't murdered."

From Rhys's expression, he wasn't accepting that explanation, so Dai intervened, a little more gently than his father, "They had no reason to lie to us. Until now, nobody but us even knew they were there. If they'd murdered either man, they could have said nothing and been on their way."

Rhys still looked mutinous. "Even if they'd told you they had murdered Tomos, you would have let them go free."

"I would have." Dai looked directly at the prince when he spoke. "My father never saw them. They spoke only to me. But I believe them when they said they didn't do this."

"Then who did?"

Llelo couldn't blame Rhys for feeling combative. He was having trouble accepting this new story, too, and it was his brother and father telling it. "You interviewed practically everyone in Maredudd's company, but the fact that you haven't uncovered the murderer means you must have missed something." Then, at Dai's narrowed eyes, he added, "I'm only pointing out the obvious. The culprit had to have come from Maredudd's men."

"You weren't there, Llelo," Dai said. "Nobody saw anything. Nobody knows anything. Or, if someone does, he must be a very good liar for us not to have found him."

"Then we have to turn the investigation on its head. As with the ambush, which the men of Tenby perpetrated but didn't instigate, maybe we shouldn't be worrying so much for now about *who* could have done it. Maybe we should be thinking instead about anyone else, beyond Earl Clare, who might have *wanted it done*?"

"That would be Einion," Gareth said heavily. "If the other lords of Deheubarth would accept him as king, he has the bloodline to gain the most from these deaths."

"You interviewed him, right?" Rhys was speaking more calmly again.

"He is the one who found Rhodri's body," Gareth said, "and happily spun me a tale—admittedly at Maredudd's request—of how Rhodri had been murdered. He is clearly an excellent liar. But we have witnesses that put him in the encampment at the time of Tomos's death. And, anyway, I find it unlikely that he would have mistaken Tomos for Maredudd, even in the dark."

Dai made a face. "And would he risk himself that way, regardless? It is one thing to take the throne over the dead bodies of your cousins. It is quite another to do the murdering yourself."

"I would ask as well," Llelo said, "how he might have come to have a relationship with the Earl of Hertford and the men from Tenby. Would it be Earl Clare pulling Einion's strings, or the other way around? And that's only if Einion is involved at all, something for which we currently have no evidence."

"Putting aside whether or not he might have the fortitude to murder," Gareth said, "he would not want to taint his claim to the throne in case he ever had to speak to a churchman about it."

"Look at Cadell, fearing his injuries are God's retribution for his sins." Rhys rubbed his chin. "Didn't you say Tomos was murdered in the exact same way my brother told you Rhodri was?"

"Yes." Gareth said. "Einion was the first person I interviewed about it. As I said, he lied with aplomb, albeit at your brother's bidding."

"This fact intrigues me." Rhys dismissed Gareth's concern about Einion's lying with a wave of his hand. In truth, the entire endeavor showed how Maredudd could lie with aplomb too. "Why would the murderer be trying to make you think he'd murdered both men?"

Gareth pursed his lips. "I have wondered about this. His intent had to be to deceive us. To deceive *me*."

"So then I must ask, *why would he think he could?*" Rhys said. "Even more, why would he even consider it? How does taking credit for a nonexistent murder help him?"

At that, Llelo lifted a hand. "Because he had an alibi for the first murder, so nobody would be looking to him for the second."

A pleased expression appeared on Rhys's face, as if they were only proving his point for him, even if Llelo didn't yet see it. "In that case, the only reason the murderer would think to deceive you in this manner about his role in Rhodri's murder would be if *he also thought there had been one.*" He sat back in his seat, waiting for all of them to catch up to him.

Llelo wrinkled his nose. "Wouldn't Einion have told him the truth?"

"Maybe Einion isn't, in fact, involved," Rhys said. "Or, if he is, he made sure he didn't have anything to do with Tomos's actual murder. He might not even know who was sent to do the job. That way, when Maredudd died. assuming that was the murderer's intent, he would know nothing about it."

Gareth's eyes were on his cup of mead, though he wasn't drinking it. "If you're right about all this, that means the murderer joined Maredudd's company *after* we did."

"Or when you did," Llelo said softly.

Gareth surged to his feet. "We brought him with us."

"We have two choices." Dai was suddenly wide awake and on his feet too. "Either it's Ieuan or …"

They spoke at the same time. "It's Bran."

48

Day Four

Gwen

Gwen was awake, as she so often was after the midnight hour, having nursed Angharad back to sleep. If the usual pattern held, she would have a good three hours before the little girl woke again. Now that Taran was older, he slept solidly most nights, his arms and legs akimbo with that delightful abandon of a small child. Even with all the worries of the last few days, he remained oblivious enough to sleep untroubled. Tangwen was sleeping once again with her grandparents in the next wagon over.

So far, Gwen appeared to be the only one affected by the weeping on the other side of the thin canvas that formed the walls of their wagon home. The initial deep sobs had eased, and now the person was crying softly to himself.

Gwen's hesitation at leaving her wagon to comfort whoever this was arose less because she didn't want to interfere in someone else's troubles—never a problem for her, given her profession—but because the crying person was a man.

Nonetheless, after another few moments of dithering, during which time the person let out a dozen more gasping breaths, she slipped out of bed, pulled on her boots, which she'd left at the end of the bed, wrapped a thick wool blanket around her shoulders, and climbed down out of the wagon. Gareth hadn't returned from whatever he'd been doing these last hours. That he had not come to bed yet was the least surprising thing about the evening. There had been times over the years where Gwen had been anxious to learn about and discuss every detail of his findings. This week hadn't been one of those times. The more she knew, the worse she felt. It really could be better not to know.

The wagon was parked within a foot of the stables. The weeping wasn't coming from inside, but from behind the building, between the stables and the wooden palisade that protected the castle. The only light in this area of the bailey came from a single torch above her on the wall-walk. The bright light up there made it even darker down below in the shadows, which was probably why the person had thought it safe to retreat there. Unfortunately for Gwen, or for him, out of sight wasn't out of hearing.

After popping her head into her parents' wagon to ask them to listen for Angharad or Taran in her absence, Gwen peered around the corner of the stables. "Hello? May I be of service?"

Instantly, the weeping ceased, accompanied by that unmistakable hiccup of someone swallowing down tears. Then, the man shifted, allowing the light to momentarily reflect off his white hair.

"Huw." Gwen came around the corner fully. "What troubles you?"

"Nothing! Nothing!" He was himself enough not to raise his voice above a harsh whisper. But, as his breath wafted over Gwen, she caught the distinct sweet tang of mead. Gwen's father had been a drunkard once upon a time, and she had seen every possible mood from him over those years of hardship. Self-hatred and weeping had been standard fare for him by this hour of the night. For a while, that had been every night. She had helped him to bed more times than she could count.

During those years, Meilyr had been lamenting the dual loss of his wife and his position in King Owain's service. Gwen was quite interested to know what had caused Huw's tears. It could just be grief at seeing Cadell laid so low, but if his reasons had any bearing on their investigation, she wanted to know them.

"Let me help you." Without waiting for his assent, Gwen slung his arm over her shoulder, while simultaneously catching him around the waist. "Let's get you somewhere warm. Where do you sleep?"

He didn't demur. "In the great house."

By *great house*, he meant the two-story building on the other side of the stables. The castle keep, looming on its Norman motte, consisted of a single, narrow tower three levels high. The middle floor was reserved for the lord's bedchamber, though Cadell was currently sleeping in his receiving room off the great hall.

As the castle bailey was so large and had been used by significant numbers of people over the years for many different purposes, it contained a great hall, a guest house, barracks, and a *great house,* as Huw had called it, in which residents of the castle could sleep. Like every building but the keep, it was predominantly made of wood, which, though easy to work with, burned easily. Thus, in the battles that accompanied each change in ownership, the structures within the castle had burned down and then been rebuilt.

Maredudd's orders had been to take Hywel's castle at Aberystwyth without resorting to fire, since he didn't have the wherewithal to rebuild it. Caerfyrddin was in the borderlands between Norman and Welsh-controlled territory. It would have been a good candidate to be rebuilt in stone, but that was unlikely to happen on Cadell's watch, either. The Welsh way was to take what they could, whenever they could, and then, when pressed, abandon fortresses such as this. It was a simple matter to take to the hills, with life and limb intact, in order to fight again another day. That Hywel had chosen to defend his castle instead of abandoning it, or burning it to the ground himself so Cadell couldn't have it, had been unusual. But it was also the reason he'd won.

Hywel had chosen to defend the castle because it was the seat of his rule in Ceredigion. Relinquishing it would be similar to King Owain abandoning Aber in Gwynedd, or Dinefwr for Cadell in Deheubarth.

With Huw putting a good portion of his weight on Gwen, the pair staggered towards his quarters. Gently, with what she hoped was disarming sweetness, she said, "What happened to King Cadell is not your fault, Huw. You couldn't have known."

"Cadell is injured beyond repair, and Tomos is dead. How did the world come to this?"

That wasn't the response Gwen had expected. "I am sorry about Tomos. Were the two of you close?"

"I have known him my whole life." Huw let out another sob.

"Tomos died a hundred miles away from the Coed Rath. What does his death have to do with Cadell's injuries?"

"Nothing! Of course, nothing."

Gwen cursed inwardly for being so direct. At the same time, Huw's protest belied the amount of weeping he'd been doing. "I don't think that's true, Huw. If there's a connection, you must tell me."

"How could there be a connection?" Huw's head wagged. "No. This isn't something that we should be talking about. I didn't; I didn't—" And then he collapsed in another storm of weeping.

Gwen would have shushed him, for his sake as well as that of her children's sleep, if the extent of his denials didn't make her think she was getting somewhere at last.

"You didn't ... what, Huw? What didn't you do?"

"I didn't mean for any of this to happen!"

And there it was, the lament of every regretful or accidental villain.

Gwen slowed their pace, not wanting to reach the great house too soon, before Huw had finished his confession. Fortunately, there were few people about at this hour, and the two men, who'd stepped out of the great hall since Gwen had been walking Huw across the bailey, took one look at the pair of them and turned the other way. At dinner in the great hall, the man sitting next to her had said Huw was a good man in a crisis. That might be his experience; so far, it wasn't hers.

Huw's chin was practically on his chest. "It's all my fault. None of this would have happened if I'd said something. I didn't want to believe it, and my feelings were hurt. I have no spine!"

Gwen did a quick canter around her conscience and decided she had no qualms about getting the truth out of a drunken man. "Were you the one who conspired with Earl Clare to murder Cadell, Maredudd, and Rhys?"

"With Earl Clare? You think I would betray my king with a Norman?" Such was Huw's shock at the suggestion that he gaped at her. "I would never!"

That sounded like the truth. "All right. I believe you. Then, what did King Cadell ask of you that you so regret?"

"Nothing! Nobody asked me to do anything!"

Gwen was clearly missing a very basic piece to this puzzle. She turned to face him, her hands on his upper arms. He was hardly more than an inch taller than she was, so she could look him in the eyes. "Tell me what has so upset you, Huw."

Her command finally broke through his reticence. "It was Einion, Anarawd's son. I have always had a soft spot for the boy, even once I knew what he'd become. I should have known better—" Huw broke off, unable to finish the thought.

This was the crucial moment. Gwen could feel it on her skin, as easily as the gusts of wind that had started wafting through the bailey. Though she wasn't a priest, men had confessed plenty to her in her years as a spy and investigator. There was a time to hold back, and a time to press. This was a time to press. "What did Einion do?"

"At Dinefwr, he left the castle by the postern gate in order to meet another man. I was in the latrine just above them and overheard a bit of what they said. I didn't catch everything, but I distinctly heard the name Maurice Fitzgerald. You know who I mean?"

Gwen nodded. "He is a cousin, son of Gerald of Windsor and Nest." That was enough to tell Huw she knew about whom he was talking. Maurice had been in Dinefwr four years ago, too. He and his brother, William, continued to loom large over south Wales. Their father had built Carew Castle, and today both men served Richard de Clare, the Earl of Pembroke. Their mother had been Welsh, but they were Norman, through and through.

Huw's face screwed up like he was going to cry again. "I—" He shook his head. "I knew he was up to something, and I didn't tell anyone what I'd overheard."

"Why not?"

"Until his father's death, Einion was raised to think he would be king. He was too young, though, when his father died, only thirteen, not even of age. Once Cadell took the throne instead of giving way to him, his disposition turned inward. He took to slinking around the castle. Outwardly, he might appear sunny, but I've seen him tell lies when the truth would have been easier or served just as well. The servants know what he is really like, even if most others would not believe it."

"And yet, you still love him. And want to protect him."

Huw hung his head. "He was a boy when Anarawd died. Cadell had no time for him. He gave him to Dafydd, who, let's just say, didn't coddle him."

"I still don't understand why you wouldn't tell Cadell what you'd learned, whether or not you cared for Einion. You had to know he was up to something."

"I was angry. The king had made clear, not just to me but to others of his advisers, that my time as his steward was at an end. He was going to put me aside because I objected one too many times to his activities."

Gwen felt her heart thump extra hard at that, though she tried to keep her tone level. "Activities?"

Huw's chin wrinkled up. This was dangerous territory. Even in his inebriated state, he knew it.

So, she hazarded a guess. "You mean the way he has conspired time and again with Cadwaladr of Gwynedd?"

"You know about that?" Gwen's nod served to convince him he was committed. "And with the Earl of Hertford and the Earl of Chester."

That last name would have had Gwen widening her eyes if it had actually surprised her. She would love to know the specifics of that alliance but now was not the moment to ask.

Huw was still focused on his own issues. "Right before he left for the Coed Rath, Cadell said he'd found—" he made a frustrated motion with both hands, "—irregularities in the accounts. Irregularities! As if I would ever steal from him! It was a lie." His voice abruptly rose in anger. "I have served the House of Dinefwr my entire life, as my father did before me. I have been nothing but loyal."

Gwen believed him about this too. "Do you think now that Einion met someone from Maurice's camp that night? Or from Earl Clare's?"

"I do. They are working together. It seems obvious now, doesn't it?"

"With the death of Cadell and Rhys, Einion would gain—"

"—the throne, of course."

It was cold in the bailey, even without the ice trickling down Gwen's spine at Huw's revelations and their joint conclusions. It was time to get him inside. "Was it your thought that if Einion took the throne, he would keep you on as steward?"

"He would have had to, wouldn't he?" Huw said as Gwen got him moving again. "What does he know about running a kingdom? But I was a fool."

"In what way?" Gwen could think of a great many ways, but she wanted to hear what Huw thought.

"What if he had succeeded? Einion would have taken the throne, yes, but he would have been forever in debt to his Norman masters. He would have been their pawn—and the House of Dinefwr would have been at an end anyway. *All because I feared to lose my position.*"

49

Day Four

Dai

With the realization that Bran had to be the murderer, possibly on Einion's orders, they split up. Gareth and Rhys headed to the great house where Einion would be sleeping. It was something of a risk to roust him, given that they still had no evidence against him. He had supporters, a few anyway, who reckoned he should have been king instead of Cadell after Anarawd's death. But with their new information, they could at least talk to him. Their excuse to bring him to the receiving room would be the discovery of some new threat to Cadell's life.

Meanwhile, Llelo and Dai went to the barracks to find Bran. It was more than a little irksome to have been so easily deceived by him. Iago's scenario must now be the right one: Bran had used the cover of bathing to murder Tomos and then washed off any remains of the deed. The footprints Dai had followed from the scene had simply been those of an innocent bystander who earlier had spent time by the river.

When they arrived in the dormitory, they were confronted with three long rows of men, laid out asleep on pallets.

"There must be nearly fifty people here," Llelo whispered to Dai. "How are we going to find Bran without waking them all?"

Just then, the man closest to the door scrambled to his feet. "Who are—" It was Daron, Rhodri's cousin. He broke off as he recognized Dai. "Can I help you?"

"We are looking for Bran. He came down the road with us."

"I remember. He's at the end." Then Daron's eyes widened as Llelo raised his lantern higher so they could see down the rows better. "Pardon, Father. I didn't recognize you at first."

Father? At hearing Llelo called thus, Dai thought the man was confusing Llelo for Gareth, though, in truth, they looked little alike, other than both being tall with dark hair. Then he realized the man thought Llelo was a priest. It was such a strange way to think about his brother Dai didn't even know how to respond.

Llelo didn't bother to dissuade him of the notion, which wasn't relevant in this moment anyway. "Thank you. We won't trouble you further." And then to Dai, he said, "You should get him. He knows you."

Since Llelo was right, Dai tiptoed the thirty feet down the long aisle to where Bran lay sleeping. Reaching down, he shook him.

Bran's response was to roll over, indicating maybe he, like Maredudd, had drunk more than his share of mead tonight. Eventually Dai shook him hard enough that he opened his eyes, and sat up. "What is it?"

"We need you to come with us."

Bran got to his feet without protest or even a question. Before he could leave, however, he put out a hand to the empty pallet beside him and patted the bundle of blankets. "Where's Ieuan?"

"I don't know." Dai had noted the empty pallet, but hadn't thought anything of it. "Maybe he's in the latrine. Last night, he told my father he wasn't entirely well."

Now Bran did frown. "He didn't say anything about it to me."

Dai made a motion with his head, not happy to be standing in the dark barracks still. "Can you come?"

By way of an answer, Bran gathered up his boots and cloak and set off after Dai. Once at the bottom of the stairs, he stopped to put on his boots. "What's this all about?"

"Prince Rhys sent us to fetch you."

That had Bran hesitating, one boot half on, before shoving in his foot all the way. "Am I for the dungeon? I'm Hywel's man, after all. Though it didn't seem to bother Lord Maredudd."

"Just come," Dai said, feeling both betrayed by Bran and a little guilty for playing on the trust he'd developed in Dai's family.

Bran didn't like it, but he followed them out the door, only to run straight into Gareth and Rhys, who was just reaching for the latch when Dai opened the door.

"I see you found him." Gareth stepped back. "You had better luck than we did."

"You didn't find Einion?" Dai said.

"He wasn't in his bed." Rhys's eyes were on Bran. "Where is he?"

They'd concluded that whoever murdered Tomos had to be an excellent liar, but Bran's surprise at Rhys's question couldn't have looked more genuine. "I-I-I couldn't say, my lord."

Rhys saw it too. Instead of glaring further, he looked at Gareth. "Where could he be?"

"In the latrine with Ieuan?" Bran said tentatively.

"We looked there. It's empty. If Ieuan is supposed to be there, he is not." Gareth motioned that the five of them should move towards the center of the bailey and stopped in what might have been the exact middle.

Bran came more willingly this time, his trust in Gareth greater than in Dai. "Did I do something wrong, my lords?"

"We were thinking you murdered Tomos," Gareth said dryly, "at Einion's behest."

When Gwen had questioned Bran after the discovery of Tomos's body, he had been defensive. This time, his jaw was on the ground. "Einion? Why would I lift a finger for Einion?"

Dai put out a hand to Gareth. "We got it wrong, Tad. It isn't Bran we should have been looking for." A vision of the empty pallet rose up before him. "It's Ieuan."

50

Day Four
Gwen

Gwen had never experienced a middle of the night quite like this one—and hoped never to again. Huw was asleep from the moment his head hit the pillow, after which she made her way back out into the bailey. There, she found the men standing with their heads together. After a hurried sharing of their conclusions, it was hard to know if Einion or Ieuan was the more important target.

"We'll split up again." Rhys was decisive. "If they are still within the castle, we have to find them."

They each ran off in their separate directions. Dai and Llelo, with Bran in tow, went to see if either man was sleeping elsewhere, even some corner of the hall they'd missed. Llelo also said he'd check the postern gate. Rhys and Gareth returned to the great house from which Gwen had just come, thinking Einion might have found another room in which to sleep. Gwen went to the gatehouse.

A guard wrapped in a cloak sat somewhat morosely in front of a brazier. He would be taking turns at this post with another guard on the wall-walk. With the arrival of Maredudd's men, Caerfyrddin had a full complement of soldiers, so there was no shortage of watchers. And this close to Norman territory, with their king disabled, they had a real desire to stay alert.

He stood up at Gwen's approach. "My lady, what are you doing awake at this hour? Is there trouble?"

She had arrived in a swirl of skirts, but not out of breath. All the walking she had been doing with Angharad every day had left her fitter than she had been before her pregnancy. "The prince sent me to warn you not to allow anyone out the gate."

She had decided on her way over that, since these men didn't really know her, and she was still, to all intents and purposes, an unwilling guest at Caerfyrddin, she should start with Rhys's authority. Or Maredudd's, if that was the prince they were thinking of.

"Nobody has come and gone." As expected, the guard straightened. "I just came on duty in the last hour, my lady. It has been quiet."

"You've seen nobody at all tonight?"

"Nobody."

"That isn't entirely true." Steffan stepped out of the darkness of the blacksmith's works, followed by the much larger form of Iago. "Lord Einion and a companion, whom I took to be that boy, Ieuan, rode out since you came on duty."

The guard's eyes widened to hear the northern accent. "Well, yes, but they're not—"

"They were on horseback?" Having accepted the Dragons' presence with a resigned sigh, Gwen returned her attention to the guard. Just as Dai had described when questioning the sentry after Tomos's death, *nobody* meant something different to them than it did to her.

The guard nodded. "And in a hurry."

"We saw them go," Steffan added. "No point in following. They're long gone by now."

Gwen pressed her lips together in a way that made the guard hasten to say, "Was that wrong of us? I had no reason to stop or question them. Lord Einion can come and go as he pleases. He isn't a stranger!" He pointed to Steffan and Iago. "Not like them!"

The guard was already marshaling his defense, as he would. Before coming to Caerfyrddin, Gwen might have been worried for him, but even were Cadell not incapacitated, he had never been so untethered as to punish his underlings for mistakes that weren't their own. That was Cadwaladr. And besides, it was Maredudd or Rhys in charge at the moment.

"You couldn't have known anything was amiss." Gwen tried to reassure him. "You had no reason to stop them."

"Well—" Surprisingly, the guard made a qualifying motion with his head, "Lord Einion often leaves at odd hours. I have wondered about it; I even talked to my captain the last time it happened. He told me Lord Einion was not to be questioned. He is the son of our former king and not my concern."

That sounded to Gwen like Cadell (or Maredudd or Rhys) needed to inquire into the loyalties of their commander here. Or, at the very least, his judgment.

By now, Gwen could see the silhouettes of Gareth and the young men approaching. The sight of the gathering at the gatehouse had them picking up their pace. When they arrived, Rhys recognized Steffan and Iago immediately. They'd been at Wiston Castle, too. In fact, they'd been instrumental in the taking of it.

At the sight of them, instead of being accusing, Rhys began to laugh. "I could ask what you're doing here, but I think I won't."

"My lord." Iago bowed, very gracefully for such a large man. "We are here as ambassadors from Prince Hywel. He offers any support or aid you might require at this trying time for Deheubarth."

It had always been Aron who was the quickest thinking of the Dragons, but Gwen reminded herself that all of them were capable, never more evident than in this moment. There was no possible way that the two men could have ridden to Aberystwyth, spoken to Hywel, and returned in the allotted time as his ambassadors. That didn't mean they couldn't still speak for him.

"I am glad to make you welcome."

Iago not only explained how they'd witnessed Einion and Ieuan's departure, but then gave himself and Steffan away fully. "You should know that we were charged with trailing your brother's company from Aberystwyth. We were up a tree when we witnessed the murder of Tomos. There was nothing we could do to avert it; certainly, we didn't see the murderer clearly enough to identify him. But tonight, in a similar darkness, we both knew Ieuan for the same man.

He is your murderer." If a man was to be tried, two witnesses were all that were required for conviction. Not that Ieuan would ever be tried.

"And because of Huw, we know what he was doing with Einion," Gwen said, "but how did they know to leave tonight?"

"We can perhaps answer that, too. We arrived here some hours before you this evening, so we could judge the lay of the land, so to speak." Steffan cleared his throat without going into details as to why, if they were ambassadors, they hadn't made themselves known at that time. "You arrived after dark and were focused on other things, so perhaps you didn't notice that Einion entered nearly last. Just before he reached the gate, another man came out of the darkness. I couldn't hear well enough to make out the conversation, but I can tell you they spoke in French."

What he didn't explain was how he and Iago had subsequently infiltrated the castle. Maybe it was better not to know.

"So, he's gone, probably to our enemies," Rhys said heavily.

"It's a loss, for certain. We can take comfort in the failure of every one of his schemes," Gareth said.

And then Dai added, a bit more brightly. "Ieuan mistakenly murdered Tomos instead of your brother, and both Cadell and you lived to bear witness to the events in the Coed Rath."

"But whom did Einion meet?" Llelo said. "Nobody could have known to warn him hours ago that we knew the truth about his conspiracy because we didn't know ourselves!"

"Someone knew something." Rhys looked at the guard. "Wake your captain. I want him on alert."

"Should I wake the garrison too?" The guard asked.

"Not yet. I would advise them to sleep while they can." Then he looked around at Gwen's family, every one of whom was swaying on their feet with exhaustion. "As should we."

51

Day Four

Gareth

They slept, praise the Lord, for six blessed hours, before Gwen and Gareth, and maybe the whole castle, were awakened by a shout from the top of the rampart. "It's Earl Clare! Earl Clare has come!"

Gareth couldn't scramble into his attire fast enough, cursing himself for not sleeping fully clothed. He should have known better, especially after hearing about Einion's conversation (in French!) with his contact. If the Earl of Hertford was here, bringing a force against the castle, he could have sent someone to tell Einion and Ieuan to flee before they were blocked in by a siege.

It would be just Gareth's luck to have escaped Aberystwyth, only to be besieged in Caerfyrddin. And with the children and Gwen now too. Pulling on his boots, he found himself praying harder than ever before in his life that there could be some way out of here, that their lives weren't going to end starving to death in a castle with the princes of Deheubarth. At least the castle had a functioning well. They wouldn't be running short of water.

Thankfully, too, the children had slept through the shouting. After a kiss for Gwen, as a reminder of what mattered, Gareth leapt down the steps of their wagon, still adjusting his shirt.

That Earl Gilbert would bring an army this far west and north, given what he'd ordered done in the Coed Rath, was something Gareth had never imagined happening. It just went to show that what a man worried about in the early hours of the morning was never what actually happened. He would have admired the earl's audacity if he hadn't been so terrified of the consequences.

It was a misty but not quite rainy morning, warmer than it had been last night, but not so warm Gareth didn't need his cloak, which he swung around his shoulders. He mounted the steps up to the wall-walk two at a time before pulling up short at the sight of the banners coming towards him.

And then sagged against the rail of the palisade in relief.

Because it wasn't, in fact, Gilbert de Clare, the Earl of Hertford, who was coming towards them, but Gilbert's nephew, Richard de Clare, the Earl of Pembroke. The guard was correct that he was an earl and a Clare. Just not the one they knew to fear.

By now, most of the castle was awake, too, as perhaps would have been the case anyway, given that dawn had come and gone. It was only miscreants such as himself and the princes who'd slept late. In truth, Gareth didn't even know where Llelo and Dai had laid their heads, though probably in Llelo's quarters near Prince Rhys.

Gareth was still on top of the wall when the two pairs of brothers, Rhys and Maredudd, and Llelo and Dai, staggered down the steps of the great house. Maredudd had been drunk last night, so it wasn't any wonder he was a bit groggy at this early hour; the three others just didn't have enough sleep on board. Gareth hurried from the top of the palisade to meet them.

"It's Richard, not Gilbert," Gareth said before either prince could ask about what they faced.

Their relief matched Gareth's, and when the guard on the wall-walk called down to ask, "What do we do, my lord?" Maredudd barked at him, "Open the gate, of course!"

"But—"

"He's the Earl of Pembroke, not the Earl of Hertford. Let him in." Maredudd's tone implied that the guard was an imbecile.

"Yes, my lord."

Slowly the great gates swung wide, revealing Richard, by now some thirty yards away, with a relatively small band of men, some two dozen at most. Seeing he was welcome, he quickened his pace and lifted a hand in greeting as he passed under the gatehouse. Then, in a matter-of-fact style Gareth had come to expect from him, never mind that he also was all of twenty years old, he dismounted and approached the two princes. "I have learned of your brother's injuries. Please know how sorry I am that he is so unwell. I have brought my own physician to see him."

It was what Saran had suggested should happen last night, though Gareth didn't think anyone had yet been sent.

Richard de Clare, the Earl of Pembroke, was one of the most powerful men in Britain. His rule ran from Pembroke, past Caerfyrddin, all the way to Chepstow. He had ridden to Caerfyrddin this morning with less than an army, knowing he could be viewed as an enemy, captured, and held for ransom.

And yet, he had come. Himself.

"Thank you," Maredudd said, a little stiffly. They had let him in because Maredudd knew, even if the guard didn't, that just because the two Earl Clares were related did not mean they were allies. He had to be wondering, however, as they all were, what role this particular Clare had in these events.

Richard would have to be blind not to see the suspicion in their faces. "I was hoping to speak to him about what he plans to do next."

"Next?" Rhys said.

Maredudd wet his lips. "We have not determined our course of action yet."

"Good. There's more for you to know. Is there some place we could speak in private?"

"Of course. This way." Maredudd gestured for Richard to walk with him. "Your men may find food and drink in the hall."

"Thank you." Richard had just fallen in beside Maredudd when he caught sight of Gareth. His step faltered briefly, and then he laughed. "I feared you would act against the garrison at Tenby before you heard my news. Now, I see you already have adequate counsel at your disposal. Perhaps I came for nothing.”

Maredudd motioned for Gareth to walk with them too. “I see introductions are not necessary.”

“We were all at Dinefwr when we took Wiston,” Gareth said. And then to Richard, he added, “A pleasure, my lord. Thank you for your assistance regarding the events of last spring.”

Richard nodded. “I hope the monks are well?”

“I left them well.” Gareth also hoped the monks were well. He just couldn’t promise it. The band of Cadell’s men who’d taken the eastern road from Aberystwyth had not yet arrived in Caerfyrddin, if they were even coming here. They could have followed the mountain road to Dinefwr. They might not even know yet about the events in the Coed Rath.

“The king is in here.” Maredudd thrust open the receiving room door, causing it to rebound off the wall. At the noise, Huw, who had been bending over Cadell, holding his hand, swung around. Gareth was surprised to see the steward awake, given his revelations and mead consumption last night.

As Huw recognized Earl Richard, he bent his head. “My lord. Welcome.”

“I wish I had come under better circumstances,” Richard said. “How is he?”

Cadell himself flapped out his right hand. “I am awake.” His words were still slurred. “So Pembroke has come to gawk at a fallen king, is that it?”

As Richard moved towards the bed, he blanched at the wreckage of Cadell's face. If anything, the right side seemed less mobile than it had been last night. "Not at all, my lord."

Then Cadell's eyes latched upon Gareth's. "You! I want to talk to you."

The others gave way to Gareth, perhaps with some relief. As they moved out of sight towards the table, Gareth settled on the stool placed close to Cadell's bed. "I am here, my lord."

Cadell met Gareth's eyes with the only one of his that was working. "Water."

Obligingly, Gareth got an arm behind Cadell's neck and shoulders in order to lift him up so he could drink.

Once Cadell was settled back down, he said, "I can see in your expression that I'm as good as dead. You don't have to say it; I know it, too. Apoplexy, your mother-in-law says. The others concur."

"That isn't what I was thinking." Gareth made to get up again. "Are you sure—"

Cadell gripped Gareth's hand with surprising strength. "Don't go. I only want you. Those youngsters won't understand, but you will. You've been through the fire and come out the other side. That will not be the case with me."

Gareth settled back down. "I am ready to listen."

Cadell couldn't really nod, but Gareth got a hint of the attempt anyway. "You should know I meant to give Rhys up to Gilbert de Clare as a hostage."

This had been Rhys's first guess, way back in the clearing before Cadell's life, as he knew it, had ended. It would have been Gareth's first guess, too, had he been there.

"Why then order the boy to hide?"

"I didn't trust Clare." Despite his illness, Cadell retained the wherewithal to snort. "They could have him only after everything was agreed."

Rhys had been listening to their conversation, because of course he had. "But why?"

Cadell didn't try to look at him. "Already men are starting to follow you. They respect you." He spoke as if this was a bad thing. "Maredudd will understand, soon enough."

"The only reason I sent for Llelo in the first place was because I sensed you didn't trust me!"

Cadell was too far gone to respond to Rhys's anger with any similar force. "I needed you alive but out of my kingdom. Believe me when I say I never wanted you dead, Rhys."

Llelo came closer now as well. Cadell had wanted to speak only to Gareth, but he was getting everyone else anyway. "That's why that rider circled through the woods. He was looking for Rhys because he knew he should be there. They hoped to kill him too. They even said as much, right before they left."

Cadell's eyes had closed. "Father, forgive me, for I have sinned."

Gareth glanced behind him to Llelo, who looked stricken. Rhys pushed at him a bit, however, telling him to go to the bed, which he did. As Gareth gave way to his son, Llelo took the king's hand. "I am not a priest, my lord, but I can fetch one."

Cadell didn't appear to hear him. "I dealt falsely with my brother, and, like Cain, I am cast into the wilderness. But I will make things right before I go. I surrender my crown to my brother. From this moment, Maredudd is king." His tone was as calm as could be, even if now he seemed to be fading into unconsciousness.

"To this we can all attest." Gareth found his voice, even if his feet were frozen to the floor. That made him no different from anyone else in the room. "Only two witnesses are required."

Maredudd's face was pale. "I don't believe it."

"He said it. I heard it, too," Huw said. "Maredudd is king."

"The end of one era is the beginning of another. I am honored to act as witness to these events, and I will testify to them to any who might ask." Richard met Maredudd's gaze full on. "May your reign be filled with peace and prosperity, King Maredudd. Long live the king."

52

CASTELL AMROTH

Llelo

Four months later ...

They had prepared for this moment all these months, wanting circumstances to be exactly right. In the coming hours, they would take Tenby or die in the attempt. And somehow, God help him, Llelo was beside Rhys again, ready to fight and determined to preserve the prince's life at all costs.

The night was as near to perfect as to make no difference. There was no moon at all and, according to those who knew more about these things than Llelo, the tide was as low as it would be this month, exposing a vast expanse of beach from here to Tenby, seven miles away.

Because of Dai's facility with languages, and thus his ability to pass as a Norman, he'd been one of the spies sent into Tenby town to investigate their defenses and preparedness. Four months was a long time to maintain a high level of vigilance. The Tenby garrison wasn't exactly lax these days, necessarily, but they had eased up on their degree of attentiveness. What's more, their gaze was directed always towards the land, never imagining the Welsh could reach them by coming along the beach.

In truth, they weren't wrong to face inland. The men of Deheubarth *were* marching towards them from the landward side, led by Maredudd. That army, however, was the distraction, the feint. If all went well, those men wouldn't have to do anything more exciting than shoot a few arrows over the walls.

The key to their plan tonight was the fact that Deheubarth still controlled the castle of Amroth and its environs. Tenby was an English town, but not all the Welsh had been evicted from this region of Wales. The little Welsh village (and church) where they'd acquired Cadell's bier after the ambush was still going about their business as they had for a thousand years. Welshmen from near and far had come at the princes' call and were here to march at their side—as were Llelo, Dai, Gareth, Steffan, and Iago.

Four months ago, Llelo had held Cadell's hand as he'd resigned his kingship. When Cadell had woken later in the day, he had seemed at peace with his decision, in some sense more accepting of the new reality than Maredudd.

Contrary to his expectations, though, he continued to live. Eventually, he was moved to a monastery where he could be better looked after. Cadell had pledged, if and when he was well enough, to make the pilgrimage to Rome, and Iestyn had promised to ensure he got there.

Meanwhile, Maredudd and Rhys had focused their attention on a very different agenda, namely, the taking of Tenby. They knew, even before Earl Richard had pointed it out the day of Cadell's resignation, that revenge was best undertaken with a cool head—and when one's enemy was no longer expecting a fight. Time did not matter. Tenby would be there when they were ready.

That first day of Maredudd's kingship, Richard had sworn not to interfere in the attack. He had come to Caerfyrddin solely to beg for the lives of the townsfolk. In addition, after Rhys and Maredudd had their revenge on the garrison, he asked that they turn the town over to his own commander (and their first cousin), William.

As it turned out, Richard had come to Caerfyrddin in the first place because, only the day before, William's brother, Maurice Fitzgerald, had confessed his role in the plot to assassinate the three brothers. Once Maurice had heard Cadell had survived and could name his attackers, he had wanted to preempt Richard learning of the scheme from someone else. William had never been one of the conspirators.

Richard had guessed correctly that Maredudd had no interest in even attempting to control a town populated by English families. Nor did he have a desire to murder women and children.

As to Einion, they learned in the intervening months that he had fled to the court of Gilbert de Clare, along with the murderer, Ieuan. Even as Maredudd's cousin, Einion would not be welcomed back into Deheubarth under any circumstances. Or so Maredudd said now. Llelo knew from long experience in Gwynedd that a king's cousin—or brother—might be welcomed back, no matter how heinous his crimes, if circumstances changed sufficiently to warrant it.

Earlier that evening in Amroth's great hall, Meilyr had sung of past victories to build the men's courage. One song in particular, *A Song to Tenby,* had struck at Llelo's heart. Meilyr credited Taliesin himself with the writing of it. Hundreds of years in the past, before the coming of the Normans, Wales had been plagued by Saxons. The song spoke of an alliance between Gwynedd and the men of the south where they'd worked together to repel an attack by their mutual enemy.

He hoped Meilyr's audience heard the song in the same way he did, as a sign of a hopeful future.

A fair fort stands upon the sea shore.
Within its hall, all men find what they desire.
As the men of Gwynedd
bring spears to join our bows,
none can match our resolve.

A fair fort abounds in song.
Atop the crag we sheltered.
Hair was red with blood, harps lamented.
The freedoms we seek are already ours.
Above, a sea bird calls.
It takes to the skies and is soon out of sight
beyond the mountain.

A fair fort stands on a high rock.
Its hall is warm, its men brave.
The waves lash; the spray explodes;
the lord of the hall rises
to defend us from all who would make our home their own.
What was lost shall be ours once more.

Almost before Llelo was ready, Rhys was standing in his stirrups. "We go!" He raised his sword above his head. "And may God have mercy upon their souls, for *we* will have *none*!"

Historical Note

Researching events in medieval Wales can be similar to putting together a puzzle. A tidbit of information is available over here; more can be found over there; and a bit more someplace else. Aspects of this time period involve guesswork—hopefully intelligent guesswork!—but guesswork nonetheless. This is because many original sources were destroyed in the Norman conquest, the Reformation, or simply lost to time.

Thus, knowledge has been passed down through generations in scraps or by word of mouth. In addition, specific events can be related differently depending on whether they were written by a Welsh person or an English person.

For example, regarding the events of *The Shattered King*, the Wikipedia entry on King Cadell merely states: "When out hunting, he was attacked by a Norman force from Tenby, who left him assuming him to be dead." The only references the article cites are from a book by John Edward Lloyd, written in 1911, in which he cites a reference from 1849.

The next tidbit comes from a general article on twelfth century Wales, stating that Cadell was hunting in the Coed Rath. No citations are given but, after more digging, I found a description of these events in an 1888 book called *The History of Little England Beyond Wales* by Edward Laws. He writes,

> Cadell was hunting in the Coedrath [sic], which lay between Saundersfoot and Pendine, when he was set on by certain Flemings from the neighboring town of Tenby, who grievously wounded him. His brothers Maredudd and Rhys quickly avenged the wrong by taking Tenby and putting its defenders to death ... Cadell was so injured that he went abroad and does not appear again in Welsh history.

The last statement isn't entirely true, but we can leave what does happen to him, as well as to Earl Gilbert and Einion, for another time. Edward Laws also dates this event to 1150, and implies that Maredudd dies at this time too, neither of which is accurate either.

However, he adds in the footnotes a version of the story from a translation of the *Brut y Tywysogion* (The Chronicle of the Kings), which presents these events from a Welsh point of view:

> While Cadell ap Gruffydd was hunting in Dyfed, some of the English of Gower set an ambush to kill him ... they assaulted him; but he being a brave and powerful man, maintained his post and killed some of his foes, and put the rest to flight. But he received a severe wound of which he languished a long time. And when his brothers Maredudd and Rhys saw that, they ... took the castle of Tinbych (Tenby) by surprise, and

slew the garrison, for those who had lain in ambush to kill their brother Cadell had flown to that town.

Another version of the *Brut* says instead that Rhys's force attacked Tenby at night, broke the gate and, after they took the castle, "delivered it into the hands of William, son of Gerald." This is the same William referenced in *The Shattered King* who was the castellan of Pembroke and served Richard, the Earl of Pembroke. He was also Rhys's cousin.

Finally, a private English website talking about Amroth Castle says, "It [the castle] was in Welsh hands again by 1151 when Lord Rhys, Prince of Powys [sic] led his army silently across the sands in the dead of night to launch a surprise attack on the town of Tenby, who were expecting an overland assault." This tale never mentions the ambush of Cadell as the reason Rhys was attacking the town of Tenby. It also repeats the story told by Edward Laws about putting Tenby's defenders to death, with the further elaboration, "Tenby town was razed to the ground and every man, woman and child put to the sword."

Whatever the truth of these events, the job of a novelist—my job—is to write in such a way that history is put into the context of medieval Wales *and* makes sense. Beginning, of course, with why Cadell was hunting in the Coed Rath in the first place.

ABOUT THE AUTHOR

With over two million books sold to date, Sarah Woodbury is the author of more than fifty novels, all set in medieval Wales. Although an anthropologist by training, and then a full-time homeschooling mom for twenty years, she began writing fiction when the stories in her head overflowed and demanded that she let them out. While her ancestry is Welsh, she only visited Wales for the first time at university. She has been in love with the country, language, and people ever since. She even convinced her husband to give all four of their children Welsh names.

She splits her time between her home in Oregon and in Wales.

Thank you for continuing this journey into the Middle Ages with me! Please don't worry that this is the last *Gareth & Gwen Medieval Mystery*. There will be more! If you'd like to know as soon as the preorder for the next book is available, feel free to subscribe to my newsletter at
www.sarahwoodbury.com